The
SILENT
FILM STAR
MURDERS

Copyright © 2025 Melodie Campbell
This edition copyright © 2025 Cormorant Books Inc.
This is a first edition.

No part of this publication may be reproduced, stored in a retrieval system or transmitted, in any form or by any means, without the prior written consent of the publisher or a licence from The Canadian Copyright Licensing Agency (Access Copyright). For an Access Copyright licence, visit www.accesscopyright.ca or call toll free 1.800.893.5777.

 Canadian Heritage / Patrimoine canadien       Canada Council for the Arts / Conseil des arts du Canada

 ONTARIO CREATES | ONTARIO CRÉATIF   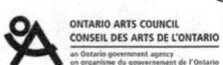 ONTARIO ARTS COUNCIL / CONSEIL DES ARTS DE L'ONTARIO / an Ontario government agency / un organisme du gouvernement de l'Ontario   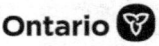 Ontario

We acknowledge financial support for our publishing activities: the Government of Canada, through the Canada Book Fund and The Canada Council for the Arts; the Government of Ontario, through the Ontario Arts Council, Ontario Creates, and the Ontario Book Publishing Tax Credit.

LIBRARY AND ARCHIVES CANADA CATALOGUING IN PUBLICATION

Title: The silent film star murders / Melodie Campbell.
Names: Campbell, Melodie, 1955- author.
Description: Series statement: The merry widow murders ; 2
Identifiers: Canadiana (print) 20240460561 | Canadiana (ebook) 2024046057X | ISBN 9781770867833 (softcover) | ISBN 9781770867840 (EPUB)
Subjects: LCGFT: Detective and mystery fiction. | LCGFT: Novels.
Classification: LCC PS8605.A54745 S55 2025 | DDC C813/.6—dc23

United States Library of Congress Control Number: 2024944653

Cover art and design: Nick Craine
Interior text design: Marijke Friesen
Manufactured by Friesens in Altona, Manitoba in January, 2025.

Printed using paper from a responsible and sustainable resource, including a mix of virgin fibres and recycled materials.

Printed and bound in Canada.

CORMORANT BOOKS INC.
260 ISHPADINAA (SPADINA) AVENUE, SUITE 502,
TKARONTO (TORONTO), ON M5T 2E4
SUITE 110, 7068 PORTAL WAY, FERNDALE, WA 98248, USA
www.cormorantbooks.com

For Don Graves,
dear departed friend who inspired this series.

CHAPTER 1

DAY ONE AT SEA

"WHO IS THAT?" said my maid, Elf, in a voice barely above a cannon blast.

I peered over the railing of the *Victoriana* ocean liner, with a perfect view of the gangplank. Quite a crowd had gathered on the pier below, at the port of Southampton. I could see the flash of camera bulbs as an entourage reached the ramp.

"Your eyes are better than mine," I reminded her. Nevertheless, I strained mine to take in the elegant figure waving to the adoring crowd.

Yes, female. I could see silver furs draped across her shoulders, a little overdone for this warm time of year. Her hair was very dark, cut fashionably short in a bob.

"Turn around," I muttered under my breath.

Like magic, the woman did. I heard Elf gasp.

"Renata Harwood!" Elf blurted. "Saw her in last month's *Motion Picture* magazine!"

"Ah, the one who played Salome, right?" And apparently caused quite a sensation, with her shockingly erotic dance and barely there costume. I hadn't seen the film, but you couldn't have missed that firestorm unless you had spent the last year in Antarctica. Every newspaper in the Empire had picked up the motion picture studio promotional photo of her in the Salome costume, which undoubtedly helped their circulation numbers.

Her outfit today was just as becoming, but rather less revealing. Even so, one usually didn't see evening wear being worn in the daytime like this. Of course, film stars lived a different kind of life from the rest of us, I reminded myself: always on stage. The flame-red ensemble had a dropped waist and a low, draped neckline with large faux diamond clips at each shoulder. At least, I assumed they were faux. Startling red lipstick matched the dress and set off her jet-black hair. Looked like Lanvin but could have been Patou. I could see we shared that at least: a penchant for beautiful clothes.

"Who's that man with 'er, holding 'er arm?" Elf had pitched herself up on her toes to see better. Still, she barely came up to my chin.

"Where?"

She pointed. The small party had travelled farther up the gangplank and would soon arrive on the deck where we stood.

"The one who looks like a coffee plantation owner from East Africa? Or perhaps a retired military man from the same continent." *Yes, I would bet my life on it. Either that, or he enjoyed playing the part.* The thin, well-trimmed mustache was particularly telling. His belted tweed jacket and khaki trousers were not standard travel wear for the average British gentleman.

"He an actor, ya think?" said Elf.

I smiled. "You've echoed my very thoughts." I watched as he held Renata Harwood's elbow most possessively.

"And that girl beside her — the plain-Jane one in the drab frock. Who's she?" said Elf.

I peered at the young woman wearing eyeglasses. They gave her a studious rather than glamorous appearance. Her ensemble was slightly out of date and simple compared to the shimmering Renata-bird beside her. "Secretary, maybe? All these celebrities have someone to handle the boring parts of the job, I've heard."

Others had joined us at the railing, such that Elf had to lean over to see around them.

"Wait," she said. Her whole body quivered in excitement as her feet left the ground precariously. I grabbed the back of her frock, just in case she overbalanced. "Luce! You see what I see?"

I returned my gaze to the party climbing the gangway. Renata led the threesome, and she suddenly stopped and beamed a brilliant smile. The sort of smile that savvy women saved for handsome men. Both gloved hands reached forward to grasp those of the well-dressed tall, dark man who had come partway down the ramp to meet them. I saw her lean in for a kiss and gasped.

"Tony?" I exclaimed. I couldn't believe my eyes.

"Lord Poncy-face!" said Elf.

"Don't call him that," I said automatically.

"Okay, Lord Toothless," she muttered.

I rolled my eyes. Tony's father was a viscount, but as a third son he didn't stand to inherit. Elf didn't have much use for him. She much favoured the somewhat dangerous man I tarried with now. But then, she would, as all three of us had come from similar pasts that were unaristocratic, to say the least.

Flash went the camera. People crowded against the railing now, calling and waving at Renata, trying to get her attention.

She looked our way and gave us that millionaire smile made so famous by the silver screen. She added a short wave, which caused her to detach one hand from Tony.

No mistaking him. It was my former beau Tony standing with Renata, and it was pretty clear this wasn't the first time they'd met. He was shaking hands with the film star's gentleman escort now.

I was spinning with questions. As far as I knew, Tony was supposed to be in Essex. And I knew Tony pretty well. We'd spent an awful lot of time together when he accompanied us two months ago on a similar crossing on the *Victoriana*, back from New York. I knew intimately of the past that haunted him from the killing fields of France. My own beloved late husband had shared the same history. And I knew Tony's tragic present as well as any close friend would, or so I'd thought. He'd picked up the habit of temporarily killing memories from Ypres and the Somme with hard spirits and gambling. Those devastating habits had come between us and a fledgling romantic relationship.

"Figured he'd be in a sanitorium drying out," said Elf.

"He was," I said wryly. That had been the plan, after his return home to England two months ago; even he had agreed to it. I knew his family had been eager to get him out of sight and out of mind, and I knew the name of the exclusive facility in which he had been placed. Most patients spend the better part of six months there, from what I'd been told. How could he be on this ship so soon?

"Maybe he heard about you and Danger Man?" said Elf. "That why he signed up for this swim across the pond without telling you?"

I looked over with a start. Could he have found out about myself and Graham West? But how? Would that explain his sudden, unexpected appearance on this ship? Or did it have more to do with the beautiful actress clinging to his arm?

"Cor blimey. You know the best thing, Luce? If Lord Poncy-face knows Renata Harwood, we'll get to meet her for sure!"

Elf must have been reading my mind. This was exciting. Because right now, all I could think of was how had Tony come to know Renata Harwood?

We were to find out momentarily. No sooner had I voiced those words in my mind than Elf bolted away from me. Along the deck she ran, passing ladies and gents alike at breakneck speed. What the heck was she doing?

I followed her as best I could, squeezing behind the people at the railing, and was just close enough behind her to see it all happen. Anyone would have thought it was an accident, but I knew better. Elf steered toward one of the cameramen — who happened to be crouched down, leg extended — and caught the back of his foot lightly with her own, careening to the floor in a splat. Right in front of Tony, Renata, and her entourage as they boarded the ship.

"Ooomph!" Elf moaned from the deck. Renata gasped.

Tony dropped Renata's arm to help Elf up, as she knew he would do. He recognized Elf as my maid and companion, of course. Tony had been a regular visitor to our country pile since before Johnny and I were married. He'd been Johnny's best man at our wedding, and was a pallbearer at his funeral, nearly five years ago.

Elf leaned on him and attempted to pull herself up. It wasn't far to go. Elf's chin barely cleared a kitchen counter.

I heard Tony ask after her condition. But before she could answer, his head swung around to survey the crowd, and his eyes settled on me. His face broke into a smile.

He let go of Elf and held out his arm to me. Elf plunked down on her butt, cursing as we talked over her.

"Lucy, by all that's wonderful!" He drew me forward. "Let me introduce you to Renata Harwood. Renata, this is Lady Revelstoke, a very old and dear friend of mine."

"Not so much of the old," I said, smiling. "How do you do, Miss Harwood. It is indeed an honour."

Renata, for her part, was quick to give me the once-over. I could see her eyes take in my appearance with the precision of a croupier. They started with my chic little cloche hat and moved down to examine the striking drop waist black and white dress with the pleated skirt. Each black pleat opened to white underneath when one walked.

"Chanel?" she said, referring to my ensemble.

"Patou," I replied.

She nodded and gave me a thousand-watt smile.

"Any friend of Tony's is a friend of mine," she said. "We must dine together tonight. Meg, will you make arrangements?" She gestured to the mousy-looking woman beside her. It was clearly an order rather than a question.

"Oh, do forgive me," said Tony. "I'm forgetting my manners. Lady Revelstoke, I'd like you to meet Meg Harwood, Renata's sister, and Roy Armitage, Renata's husband."

Fascinating how every introduction was made in reference to Renata. Her sister ... her husband. Every planet certainly circled around a sun, and this one had a strong gravitational pull. I wondered, particularly, how her husband felt about that.

We all voiced how-do-you-dos. I could feel Roy's eyes on me, in a way that was definitely uncomfortable. Funny how some men can look at you with frank appreciation and it feels good. Whereas others ...

Close up, this man did indeed look like he had just stepped off a coffee plantation, with his tanned face, rugged looks, and substantial build. But I was willing to bet he had been brought up in Bermondsey or Wapping. That accent was a bit too perfect, and something behind his eyes bothered me.

After forcing a smile at him, I turned to address little sister Meg.

"Is this your first crossing?" I ventured.

Renata answered before her sister had a chance. "We're both virgins on the water, aren't we, darling?" Her laugh was a tinkling sound. "*Virgin*. Imagine. It's been a long time since I could call myself that, unlike dear Meg here."

"Steady on, darling," said Roy Armitage. "Meg has yet to be married, is all. That will come in time, won't it, Sparrow?"

Sparrow? I could hear Meg take in air, and clearly felt her embarrassment. She didn't seem inclined to speak.

I turned my head to look at her. I could see where the unfortunate nickname might have come from. The common house sparrow is a small bird, cute in a way but drab in colour. Meg was a similar height to Renata but a tepid version of her. For one thing, her hair was a dull brown, pulled back in a roll, and she wore no discernable makeup. It struck me, seeing the sisters side by side, that it was like viewing two versions of the same drawing — one in black and white, and the other in colour. Renata was the full colour version, Meg, the shades of grey. Meg had similar dark eyes, but the overall effect was mousy, like her hair. The high-necked brown day dress she wore did nothing to dispel this image.

Renata, on the other hand, had striking blue-black hair and shone like a newly minted shilling. She was resplendent, and she knew it.

"Darling, here's the captain," said Renata. She turned her attention from me to the handsome officer who had come to stand in front of her. I chuckled.

"Not the captain," I said, moving forward before Tony could step in. "Miss Harwood, may I introduce Mr. West, the ship's purser. Mr. West, I am sure you will be delighted to meet Miss Renata Harwood."

He did indeed look delighted. I'd razz him about that later when we were alone.

Graham West had the sort of honey-blond good looks I associate with medieval Saxon warriors. He stood over six feet tall, as did Tony, but unlike Tony, this man was broad across the shoulders and solid through the chest. The officer's uniform looked dazzling on him, but I happened to know he looked even better without it on.

Renata grabbed the arm of the officer — *my* officer, I liked to think — and allowed herself to be escorted into the grand hall. The sister and husband followed in her wake, along with the posse of photographers.

Tony hung back, as did I. I was truly amused. Tony, less so.

"Who's the sailor?" he said.

I covered a snort. "Mr. West is a senior officer, the purser. You've met him before, Tony. He sat at our table during the last voyage. Which reminds me ..." I paused to find the right words. "What exactly are you doing on this ship? Aren't you supposed to be at some lofty country retreat, taking a cure?"

He shoved his hands in his pockets and winced. "Didn't like

it. Damned uncomfortable sort of place — you have no idea, Lucy. No fun at all, and the grub! Had better in the trenches, we did."

It was sobering, his casual mention of the trenches. "The Lost Generation," a famous author called us, and wasn't that the truth. I had my own nightmares after nursing so many wounded soldiers.

My husband, Johnny, had succumbed to TB a few years after being gassed. Tony's affliction was longer term — I'd call it a life sentence — shell shock haunted him constantly and caused him to take refuge in drink and gambling.

Hence the expensive retreat, funded by the family. "So, you did a bunk."

He perked up. "Went over the top in the middle of the night. Grand adventure. Took a few chaps out with me, just like in France." He grinned. "Capital lads. Hid them in the mill house. Nanny's looking after them until I get back."

"Oh, Tony." I let out a huge sigh. It was as I expected. Tony wasn't going to recover. He had no interest in changing, no matter how much his family pleaded with him. The drinking and gambling would continue as long as those war memories of death and destruction from the front continued to haunt him.

I'd been wise not to fall for him. It had been a close call. I'd known Tony all my married life, and he was a strong arm to lean on when Johnny died. We'd both been punched in the stomach by that. Lately, he had spoken of a decent interval having passed, and I admit the idea of marrying again had crossed my mind.

But not now. Not yet. After more than four years of being in charge of my own destiny, I wasn't about to hand over all my freedom and assets to a husband. As long as I remained a widow,

I could control my own future, not to mention my fortune and that of my young son.

"So, what brings you out on this voyage? Are you travelling with Miss Harwood?" I asked.

"No, I had no idea she'd be on this trip," Tony said. "The pater was on the rampage. Had me promise to leave England's green and pleasant land in return for a continuation of the allowance. Thought I might try the Wild West this time, instead of New York. And" — he winked at me — "I heard you were booked for another crossing. Tickled me pink to surprise you."

"Well, surprise you did. Did you have any trouble booking?"

"Not at all," said Tony. "Even managed to get the same cabin as before."

Which was better than I had done. But I couldn't resist asking, "Where did you meet our silver screen star?"

"Old friends," said Tony. "Nipped backstage with an old schoolmate during the war a few times when she was playing Salome in the West End. Back in the days when she did stage, before film. Not even sure she remembered me today, to be honest. I had to remind her of Monty. That did the trick. Of course, she was keener on Monty than she was on me. First son and all, destined to inherit the boodle. We were inseparable for a while. Officers in the same company. Poor bloke bought it at the Somme."

We both automatically lapsed into silence, remembering the dead. *Funny how that doesn't leave you.*

"Quite a sensation, our girl, Renata," Tony continued. "Had no idea she would be on this ship. The mousy sister's all grown up. Never met Armitage before. Seems a bounder, if you ask me."

Funny that Tony used the same word I had to describe Meg. She would still have been at school during the war years.

I wondered if the relationship between Tony and Renata had involved a little more than "nipping backstage." If it had — and I was by no means certain — this had no doubt taken place long before her latest marriage. Roy Armitage didn't look like the type to tolerate any hanky-panky.

"Feel an urge to see cowboy country, my darling?" Tony said. "Just why are *you* on this crossing so soon after the last, by the way?"

"Business in New York," I said, as casually as possible. "Shareholders meeting. I inherited a lot of responsibility when Johnny died."

"Too tiresome, that." He reached around me with his arm. "What you need is a nice strong man to take the weight off your shoulders."

Oh fiddlesticks. With Graham West already in my bed, and Tony Anderson vying to stake a claim, this was going to be one deuce of an awkward trip.

CHAPTER 2

WE SPLIT UP, Elf and I returning to the rail to watch the ship push off to sea, and Tony removing himself to follow Renata and company.

I never get tired of the excitement when a ship leaves dock. The exhilaration of the crew is palpable. There's a frisson of excitement when anchors get lifted, the propellers start churning, and the smokestacks roar to life. The noise of the ship's siren is almost deafening. You can see crew running to and fro, manning the huge lines that hold the boat to shore until they are finally let free.

Every passenger aboard seemed to be at the rail, waving to the crowd of people on shore. I've often wondered how the ship doesn't list to one side with the weight of the bodies gathered there.

"Ready to scram?" said Elf. She tugged on my sleeve.

I reluctantly turned away from the rail.

I wouldn't see Gray until the early hours of the morning, when it was safe for him to travel the first-class corridors unseen. Yes, we were both consenting adults, but it might ruin his reputation as purser to be found cavorting with a passenger, particularly if they found out I owned the very ship we were travelling on.

My own reputation? I had stopped worrying about that after Johnny died. When you lose the love of your life, little else matters to you.

I thought about Johnny on the walk back to our cabin. We had met on a similar transatlantic crossing, just before the war. I was eighteen — just old enough to leave my questionable family behind and strike out on my own, thanks to my dead mother's jewellery. God bless her for leaving me that small fortune. I was able to escape the scrutiny of my criminally employed uncles and start a new life with the proceeds, just like she'd planned.

I'd met both Elf and Johnny on the same voyage. Life had been both joyous and unfathomably sad since then, but oh, I had lived it. I had lived my own life instead of taking the path prepared for me by my family.

Some would find it unusual, perhaps, how much I valued the ability to make decisions for myself. To be able to establish a moral code of my own, without male relatives dictating what I should think. And particularly, to make decisions about where I wanted to live, and whom I wanted to live with.

Johnny's tragic death had left me with a wonderful son, Charlie, now at boarding school, and a slew of investments, including this shipping line. I was determined to do right by him and guard my son's legacy well without the help of any man.

And if that made me a brazen new woman of questionable virtue, so be it.

WE WERE BACK in the cabin two hours later. Elf had unpacked all my clothes, after slapping my hand away when I tried to help. I've often thought Elf would make a better prison warden than a maid. Of course, it wasn't surprising that image sprang to mind as she had spent time in the nick ...

"Time to dress for dinner," I said, lazily paging through the fashions in *Vogue* magazine.

"First night. You dressing informal, as usual?" Elf said.

"No, I don't think so, this time," I said thoughtfully. In first class, it was tradition for the first night of a voyage to be less formal than the rest as people might be weary from travelling. Quite often, reaching port involved a long rail trip and numerous transfers. And if you didn't travel with a maid eager to unpack your trunks, you might still be living out of a suitcase. Hence the practice of not requiring formal attire on Day One.

But I was acutely aware that Renata Haywood expected me to sit at her table, and I was willing to bet our silver screen star was not about to dress down. She had very dark hair, so I was also willing to bet she would wear red tonight. I wanted to stay in her good books, so this meant I had better not choose the scarlet silk. But at the same time, whatever I wore had to be worthy. With Tony at the table as well, I felt the need to make a special effort to appear at my most fashionable.

"Let's go all out tonight, Elf. The sapphire blue with the sequins. Bring out the jewellery too."

I saw a small smile cross Elf's face. "You gonna outdo the doxy?"

"Elf!" I scolded. "Such language. And we don't know she's that way in real life." True, her on-film persona was somewhat risqué. Not to mention her reputation for going through husbands. Divorce had been legal since the middle of the last century, but no question, the Matrimonial Causes Act of 1923 had made it easier to obtain one. Adultery by either husband or wife was now a sole ground for divorce, and a wife no longer had to prove additional faults against the husband.

When married, I'd never had cause to even think about using the law, but as a woman, I was well aware we had come a long way in the past few years. And I was grateful for it.

I slipped into the sapphire-blue dress and dutifully sat in front of the mirror as Elf fussed around me. Lots of eye makeup. Elf is a whiz at that. My hair is easy enough to arrange. I look like a cross between Theda Bara and Louise Brooks, with a shoulder-length, chestnut bob.

Elf is like a sergeant major when she gets me ready. Today, for some reason, she appeared to be in a particularly grumpy mood.

"Wish I was allowed to come," she muttered, sliding the brush carefully through my hair.

Oh dear. I hadn't stopped to consider Elf's attachment to the silver screen and her love of all celebrity gossip. There were so many times when the class system on board ship or at home didn't seem fair.

"I'll report back on everything she says and does," I said. "And maybe I'll have an opportunity to invite her back to our suite for tea or cocktails."

Her hand stopped mid-brush, and I heard a gasp. "Oh, would you, Luce? That would be simply swanky." She finished with a long sigh.

I left the cabin with a smile on my face.

THE FIRST-CLASS DINING room was located on the saloon deck. The days of art nouveau for ship decor, with its elaborate scrolls of nature motifs, were over. The *Victoriana* may have been named after a past era, but the interior design of this ship firmly followed the modern style of art deco, clean and geometric, and I loved it. The first time I had entered this room, several months ago now, it pretty well took my breath away. Even now, crossing the Atlantic for the second time on this ship, I remained impressed.

My heart soared, just like the ceiling, which rose three decks high. Fluted columns led the way in, and gorgeous art deco light standards joined several lovely chandeliers in providing illumination. Light danced off the lacquered wooden floors and walls. Original paintings between the portholes reflected a jaunty nautical theme.

I loved the delightful table arrangements of cut flowers and crystal, set upon immaculate white tablecloths. Each piece of pristine white china bore the ship's monogram. Everything seemed to shimmer.

I arrived by myself, which was unusual for me and not the cultural norm. On our last sail across the pond, Tony had accompanied me to the table most nights. I had rather expected he would come to my cabin with that in mind. No doubt, this time he was under the spell of our screen celebrity, and I didn't begrudge him that. My affections were now firmly with Graham West, who wore ship's uniform and wore it very well.

I stopped in the double doorway to the dining room and waited as three men in staff uniforms rushed forward. Oh, there is a certain joy in being a beautifully dressed woman in an environment where most of the other patrons are mainly older and male.

"Lady Revelstoke!" said the grey-haired head steward, an acquaintance of mine from the previous crossing. "You look beautiful tonight. Please let me escort you."

"Hello, Roberts. How nice to see you." I took his arm. "How are your two young grandsons?"

Roberts beamed. "Scallywags, m'lady. Pure scallywags, I'm embarrassed to say. Scrappers and into everything." I could see he was quite proud of this.

"Take after their dear grandpapa?"

Roberts laughed delightedly. Funny how men who are not rogues themselves like to be thought so. Oddly enough, it doesn't go both ways with women. Certainly, I had gone to great lengths to cover my notorious childhood.

I felt eyes from all around the room follow me as Roberts led me to the table to which I had been assigned. Two men stood up as we came near. Roberts pulled out a chair for me, and then left with a short bow when I was seated.

I smiled at my male dinner companions. "Please sit. How nice — I'm delighted to see you again."

The taller man — Captain Miller — gave me a warm smile as he sat. "My pleasure indeed, Lady Revelstoke. You bring light to this entire room."

This was my first time travelling with Captain Miller, and I found him to be a charming man with thick grey hair that spoke to his age and experience. While this was a new ship for him, he was a veteran of the Transatlantic crossing.

His companion, a man known to just about everyone in England, remained standing. "We meet again, Lady Revelstoke. Please … call me Lord Harry," he said with a wink. "It is indeed an honour to share this table with such a beautiful woman."

Aha! He didn't want to be pointed out to all and sundry as part of the Royal Family. Mere aristocracy was enough. I'd play along and smiled back.

"And how is your dear grandmother?" I asked.

"Bringing hell upon the servants at the castle," he said. "And the pater." He laughed in that queer, high voice that seemed to affect this generation of lesser royals.

As he sat, I contemplated the several empty chairs at our table. Our screen star would be last to the gate, I presumed. She would wait until there was a full audience in attendance.

And I was right. No sooner had I considered that thought than the whole room became hushed.

Renata Harwood knew how to make an entrance. She was indeed a vision in crimson satin, cut daringly off the shoulders, with small straps. The drop waist featured waves of chiffon frills, set on the bias. A diadem of diamonds circled her head. One would have taken her for royalty.

Flanked by her colonial husband on one side, and a handsome young officer on the other, she almost glided into the dining room. Her head went this way and that, smiling at the excited faces eager to make her acquaintance. What stories they would tell when they got back home!

I looked for her sister, presumably lost in her wake, but … no other woman accompanied them. That was curious.

Both of my dinner companions were already on their feet. The trio stopped just before our table. Renata struck a theatrical pose behind the chair next to Lord Harry — that's the best way I can think to describe it — while waiting for someone to help her sit. I could smell her heavy perfume from across the table.

I saw the young officer awkwardly move to the side as he allowed — good Lord! I'd already forgotten his name. It wouldn't be Mr. Harwood — that was Renata's stage name from an earlier marriage. How embarrassing it must be for him, with people like me going blank.

The husband (I made a note to pay attention to his name next time he was addressed) deposited his charge in her chair and then beamed across the table at me.

"Lady Revelstoke! I can't tell you what a pleasure it will be having two beautiful women at our table."

"Sit, Roy," ordered Renata, with an edge to her voice. "You're hovering over me."

I returned her husband's smile, as the men plunked down into their chairs. But it hadn't got past me that he had mentioned only two beautiful women.

"Is your sister not joining us tonight, Miss Harwood?" I turned to face Renata.

"Migraine," she said quickly, as if the subject in itself was distasteful.

Her husband added, "Poor Meg gets them. She'll dine in our suite, if she feels up to it."

Renata waved a manicured hand through the air dismissively and smiled as she set the full extent of her gaze upon me. "Call me Renata. Is that another Patou?"

"Schiaparelli," I responded, smiling back at her. "And my name is Lucy." We seemed to be engaged in an uneasy smiling contest.

This close, I could see that some of her beauty was due to artifice. She had the kind of face that took well to makeup, and indeed her signature look depended on it. She had even features, pleasant rather than exceptional, but the kohl surrounding her dark eyes made them look huge. Her mouth had been shaped into an unnatural red bow. I had to admit, the contrast between her white face and almost-black hair would look stunning on camera.

But looks aren't everything. There is such a thing as charm. I was uncomfortable with Renata's quick dismissal of her sister. It made her less beautiful in my eyes.

Tony rushed over at this point and claimed the empty chair next to me. "My apologies, everyone. Lay down for a quick kip and lost track of time." He smiled at Renata and nodded to the men.

Stewards descended upon us then, and great trays of food started to arrive. Dinner was a lush affair, starting with antipasto, seafood, and then a generous serving of beef tenderloin. We were at a table capable of seating eight, with only six chairs occupied. Meg would have made seven, and I wondered who else might be missing. It wasn't unusual for weary travellers to prefer to be served in their cabins on the first night. Our missing companions would show up tomorrow, no doubt.

Meanwhile, I had my ear cocked to the conversation across the table. Lord Harry might be royalty, but Renata was the one holding court.

"Of course, I had to break my contract with Elstree to take this role in Hollywood," she declared with a sweep of her hand.

"What is Elstree?" whispered Captain Miller into my right ear.

"A fairly new motion picture studio in Borehamwood," I replied, also in a low voice. "I hear they are planning to do talkies." I had indeed heard this from an expert. Elf.

"Whatever will be next?" Captain Miller shook his head.

The band had started to play, which made conversation difficult with anyone except those right beside you. I like that while I'm eating. Too wearying, trying to make witty repartee while yelling across a table and forking meat into your mouth. One thing at a time, and this delicious dinner was worth my entire concentration.

The band stopped for a break. Dancing would commence later, for those who wished to stay. Coffee had been served and conversation was dying around the dining tables. It was as if the whole room was waiting for something momentous to happen.

The table of men beside us pushed back their chairs, the first in the room to do so. I watched with amusement as Renata rose abruptly, signalling to the rest of us that it was time to make an exit. Why amusement? She waited for me to join her. No doubt she wished for the maximum audience and was willing to temporarily share the spotlight with me to get it.

It worked. The men at the next table stayed standing as they waited for Renata to walk past them. She smiled her appreciation and, before you knew it, we had an impressive entourage. Movie Star, Captain, and Royal ... who wouldn't be looking? Tony and I, although appearing upper class, were small potatoes in this delicious smorgasbord.

"It's nice to have another sophisticated woman at our table," she said, clutching my arm. "Tomorrow, we must sit together so that we may talk. Men can be so boring."

I had to smile at that. Was that the reason she went through so many of them?

"I'd be delighted," I said. "Will you be here at breakfast?"

"Oh no," she said, pausing to smile and strike a pose for a table of young men. "I always have breakfast in my suite. And I never eat lunch. Must do what is necessary to keep this girlish figure. The camera can be cruel," she confided.

She had managed to stay slender for her age, which suited these current fashions that favoured the flat-chested. I, on the other hand, had no hope of appearing girlish.

"Then I will look forward to seeing you at dinner," I said.

Renata walked with me to the doors, the men and all eyes in the room trailing behind us. Again, I had to admire her savvy. No doubt she'd learned this lesson working with her female co-stars and understudies. In any case, I was duly impressed by her cunning. She was a lot more intelligent than the movie magazines gave her credit for.

As we glided through the doors, she released my arm. "Tony," she said, "are you joining us at the tables?"

Uh oh, I thought. Gambling was one of Tony's weaknesses, and I knew this invitation would be too much for him to resist. I cursed to myself, wondering if there was anything I could do to prevent another repeat of the last voyage. I may not love Tony in the romantic way he had hoped, but I still care about him. He is a dear friend.

I became aware of a disturbance behind us. Before I could turn, Roy Armitage's voice rose above the others. "How dare you!"

I felt Renata stiffen beside me. She spun around first, and I was right behind her. A young man, good-looking in a hefty sort of way, had grasped Roy's arm.

"For God sake's man, can't you leave her alone?"

"I just want to talk to her," the younger man pleaded. "Where is she?"

Roy firmly removed the other man's hand from his jacket sleeve. "She has a migraine. She's in our suite and you are not to disturb her, you hear me? Don't you realize she came on this trip to get away from you?"

I felt Renata back away from the conflict to the shadows behind me.

"I don't believe you," said the frantic young man. "She wouldn't do that. I just need to talk to her."

"Get back to second class," Roy said with a pompous sneer. "You shouldn't even be here. Steward!" he called out loudly.

Oh no! He was going to make a scene. Surely there was a more discreet way to handle this.

I heard Renata's quick intake of breath. It was then that I saw the full measure of our screen star's acting skills. I watched in fascination as she threw an arm up to her forehead and swooned in a picture-perfect portrayal of feminine helplessness. Moving picture, that is.

"Oh, Roy," said Renata, pretending to be overcome. "Get me out of here. Please!"

Roy left the young man and rushed to Renata. "Come dear. Everyone, please stay back." He steadied her with an arm around her back and whisked her down the hallway. The other man cussed in frustration and took off in another direction.

I watched along with everyone else, in bewilderment. I didn't notice Tony sidle up along beside me until he spoke.

"Well, well," he said. "That was as good an act as I've ever seen her do on stage."

"What was that all about, Tony?"

I turned to him. He tipped his head in the direction behind him and shoved his hands into his trouser pockets. "Seems our plain-Jane Meg has got an admirer, and that the not-so-illustrious film star and her colonial husband don't think much of the poor bloke."

I tried to raise an eyebrow. The shine had come off the star. Seems Tony wasn't as enamoured of our Renata as I had thought. *Good.* "Do you know who he is?"

"Not a bean of an idea. But I'll find out." A small smile spread across his face. Like most of his class, Tony took keen enjoyment in the art of gossip. Of course, on a ship there is very little else to do.

The crowd behind us dispersed. We stood back against the wall to allow people to pass, and then Tony walked me to my cabin. As we walked, I was still thinking about the scene that had just taken place. Renata had seemed awfully determined to prevent the drama from escalating. I wondered why. Was it simply that the attention wasn't on her? True, she did very effectively switch the focus of the crowd from Roy and the young man back to her, with that swoon.

I wondered what it must be like to crave the applause and approval of an audience all the time. I said this to Tony.

"Not your style. It must seem foreign to you," he replied.

"It does," I replied. He smiled, knowing the distance I go to avoid any undue attention. As far as I knew, Tony didn't have an inkling of the reason why. I guess he just took me for a well-bred upper-class woman who avoided the limelight so as not to appear vulgar. Truly, that was the least of my concerns.

The truth was that I had a young son who had inherited his father's title. Charlie was bright and lively, and the apple of my eye. He was currently away at school and doing well. The last thing he needed was for word of my background to leak out to his friends and their families. He would be a social pariah, through no fault of his own.

I kept my privacy well. Even Tony didn't know about my criminal family back in Canada. He may have wondered about my choice of maid, but knowing Tony, he would put it down to some altruistic virtue on my behalf to help an unfortunate woman escape the streets.

And to be honest, that was partly true. But the entire story of how Elf and I came to know each other was far more dramatic than that.

Tony interrupted my thoughts. "Are you in the Victoriana Suite?"

I shook my head. "This floor, just a way down."

We walked along the panelled corridors with their beautiful sconces. Ship's lighting had greatly improved in the years since the voyage I took when leaving my homeland over a decade ago. What a relief it was to be in modern times, where a woman could cross the ocean with just her maid and not be seen as shocking or an item of pity. The Great War had been a terrible thing, but I relished the freedom we women had now, in part because of it.

"This is mine," I said, as we reached the cabin I had been assigned. The *Victoriana*'s grand suite had been engaged well in advance by our screen star, so I had settled for a regular first-class cabin. It was grand enough for Elf and me.

Tony pushed open the cabin door. Elf stood there with her arms crossed.

"What took you so long?" she barked.

Tony backed away from me. "Leaving you to the House Matron. Really, you've got to talk to that girl, Lucy. See you tomorrow at lunch."

I held back a laugh. Tony was right. Most people would not understand the relationship I had with Elf, which defies rational description. Suffice it to say that I sometimes find our roles reversed, meaning it was hard to tell who was the mistress and who was the servant.

But Elf had been my loyal companion for many years, and calling her fiercely protective of me doesn't begin to cover it. What she can do with a knife would scare the pants off any red-blooded male of any age.

I SPENT THE next several minutes describing the occupants of the dinner table to Elf. Her wide brown eyes positively gleamed. I'll never know why it is that some people fawn over actors and actresses. Is it that we need escape from real life so badly, and they provide the escape? But really, they are only the window dressing. Surely, we should be worshipping the writers who create the stories that give us escape even more.

But no doubt, they aren't as glamorous.

I finished up my colourful account and waited for her to comment.

"Jiminy. This other bloke got a name?" Elf was keen to get the whole story. I smiled, knowing she would be eager to share it with her steward friends. *Love of gossip isn't restricted to the British upper classes*, I mused.

"I didn't hear it. Tony said he'd find out. But it was obvious they all knew each other." And fairly well. I was willing to bet the young man had recently been Meg's lover, from the strength of his reaction.

Which reminded me. "Elf, have you got a place to sleep tonight?"

She grinned. "Bunking with Polly." Polly was a spunky female steward working for the first-class cabins. We'd met her on the last crossing.

I smiled back. "You're a lifesaver."

She cocked her head. "See if Danger Man can get us some oranges. I like oranges." With that, she gathered up her small carpet bag and headed for the door.

Elf had taken to calling Graham West "Danger Man" on our last voyage two months ago. I'm not sure exactly why. It could be because he was the one man who knew of my past, having come from the same crime syndicate as me before we each turned honest. So, he was a danger to me, or rather my privacy. But we had known each other as kids, and I trusted him from the start. You instinctively trust the people who had your back when you were young.

Or perhaps Elf called him that because he was a different kind of danger to me. Gray had found his way into my heart and bed, after all.

Or perhaps she had christened him that because he has the appearance of one who could be dangerous. Gray looked incredibly handsome in his uniform, but at six-foot-two and broad-shouldered, he was not a fellow to be trifled with.

I didn't have to wait long. About ten minutes after Elf left the room, the cabin door swung open. A large silhouette of a man filled the doorway.

"Are you alone?" he asked.

"Are you? No film star on your arm?" I teased.

Gray chuckled. "No room for anyone but you, beautiful. I know what I want."

I welcomed him into my arms.

CHAPTER 3

DAY TWO AT SEA

GRAY LEFT AT dawn, with an order to find oranges. I fell into a sound sleep and didn't budge until Elf slammed into the room at eight.

"Wake up, Luce. I got news!"

I groaned and rolled over. That wasn't enough for Elf, so she came over to the bed and bounced up onto it.

"Hey, listen. This is good." She punched me in the side.

I opened one eye and waved a hand so she would stop.

"Polly has the inside scoop, see? Renata Harwood doesn't travel with a maid. She uses that soggy sister of hers instead. Treats her like a servant." Elf's voice held disgust. I was pretty sure it was directed toward the sister who allowed herself to be treated like a maid. God knows, Elf didn't.

"So?" I managed to utter.

"So, Polly does for both of them. She's their steward. And guess what she found out?"

"Can't even," I muttered.

"Renata dyes her hair!" Elf said triumphantly. "Last night, Polly found all the fixings hidden deep down in the rubbish bin."

I sighed and made an effort to sit up. "So? A lot of women dye their hair."

"Poof." Elf waved that away. "Lotsa actresses bleach their hair to go blond. Don't know any who go darker."

"Older women use dark dye," I said. "To keep their natural colour and look younger. Are you saying she's older than she looks?" I had to smile at Elf's enthusiasm. Long ago, I'd learned to tolerate her penchant for celebrity gossip. It was almost a commodity among the servants.

Elf shrugged. "Could be. Wonder how old she really is?"

I threw off the covers and put my feet to the floor. "Some women start to go grey in their thirties." Which made me realize how lucky I've been to date. "Whatever, it certainly makes for a lovely contrast on the screen. Her fair colouring and that extremely dark hair."

Elf nodded. "Looks a treat, she does. Polly got a photo of her last night. Signed, even." She sounded envious. I'd have to see what I could do about getting Elf a photo of her own.

I reached for my cream velvet dressing gown on the chair. "So, Renata could be older than she claims. Hence the hair dye. Any other news?"

Elf wiggled her feet off the end of the bed. "Polly says Renata and her hubby are regular lovebirds. Always touching and kissing. Seem to be crazy about each other."

I tied the dressing gown around my waist. "That surprises me, I admit. I don't find Roy Armitage particularly attractive. But each to his own."

"A lid for every pot," said Elf, who had earthy wisdom to spare. "Per 'aps she goes for the rugged bushwhacker type."

Still, it surprised me that a sophisticated woman like Renata

Harwood would be over the moon about him. For some uncomfortable reason, he reminded me of a saying we used to have back home in Canada: Big hat, no cattle.

"Any other news before I head out to breakfast?"

Elf pushed off the bed and set down on her feet. "Nope, but seeing Polly for lunch after she does for them. Should have more then."

"I live in eager anticipation," I said mendaciously, and headed into the loo.

BREAKFAST IN THE dining room was a quiet affair. Most of our table was missing. Renata, of course, had said she wouldn't be there. But neither was her sister, Meg, nor Tony, nor our Royal personage. The captain, of course, would be on the bridge.

When I reached my chair from the night before, I wasn't surprised that Roy Armitage shot to his feet and said, "Sit by me, Lady Revelstoke. Seems we are the only brave hearts willing to leave their beds on this fine morning."

I smiled and gladly took the chair he held out.

"Will Meg be joining us?" I asked.

"I don't think so," said Roy. His heavy eyebrows came together as he frowned. "In fact, I don't mind telling you, I'm worried about her. She hasn't been herself lately."

"I'm sorry to hear that," I said. Odd, his confiding that. Most British people aren't that familiar, unless well-acquainted.

He grunted. "She's kept to her room ever since we went down to dinner last night. I know migraines can be wicked, especially, Renata says, at certain times ..." His voice trailed off in what I took to be mild embarrassment.

"I'm sure she'll join us when she feels up to it," I said, perusing the menu. "These meals are such an event, aren't they? I almost feel like we are making history on these voyages, don't you?"

"An interesting way of looking at it," said Roy. "Certainly, there have been incredible changes to maritime travel since the war."

"Oh, did you serve in the Navy?" I asked innocently.

"No, no." The big man squirmed in his chair. "I was in Africa. Don't like to talk about it."

"Of course," I replied, with sympathy. "My husband was in France. He didn't talk about it either."

And so ended that conversation. It surprised me that Roy didn't mention his regiment, or at least explain the theatre of war he had participated in. Most men were quick to tell you the country or specific battles, even if they were scant on details.

I also considered that Africa was a convenient continent to mention if you wanted to keep your wartime years in shadow. It would be difficult to check up on his past.

But it did fit with my earlier impression of Roy Armitage dressing the part of a colonial plantation owner. Certainly today, he looked the part and played it well. Most men in first class didn't wear tweed jackets to breakfast.

Also, most men these days didn't wear their hair as long and shaggy as he did. An affectation? Or a throwback to colonial days in Africa?

And most disturbing, why had I thought *played the part well*?

A middle-aged steward arrived to take our meal choices and interrupted my unsettling train of thought.

"Delightful to see you again, Lady Revelstoke!" His fatherly smile beamed.

"And you too, Roberts. I'll have the omelet with fruit instead of potatoes, please, and coffee rather than tea."

Roberts winked at me. He always remembered.

"Not tea?" said Roy Armitage to me after giving his order for a full English breakfast. We were a British ship, after all.

"I prefer coffee for breakfast."

"Ah. An afternoon tea drinker. Sugar? Lemon? How do you like it?"

"Left in the pot," I said.

He stared at me a moment, and then threw back his head and laughed.

"So, no cream tea for you in the afternoon."

"Now, wait just a darn minute," I said. I pointed a finger at the table. "Leave my share of the scones with Devon cream and jam right there, and I'll do you proud. I have a wicked sweet tooth."

He continued to smile. "Then we will get on famously."

Oddly enough, I was beginning to like the man. He had a certain intelligence and charm I hadn't expected.

"I've always felt sorry for those women on the *Titanic* who passed on dessert," I said wistfully.

He looked at me again as if to check that I was serious, and then shook his head, chuckling.

It was always hard for me to turn down dessert. But with Renata so slender, I was going to have to make sure I didn't gain an ounce this voyage. It would be my personal challenge.

Our breakfasts arrived, and we spent the next few minutes in companionable silence. This suited me fine. I don't need any interruptions to my noshing.

I was so intent on devouring my eggs and fruit that I didn't see the man before he was upon us.

"Where is she, Armitage? Where have you put her?" I looked up to see the hefty young man from last night leaning over the table from the other side. He was red-faced and brimming with pent-up energy.

Roy threw his serviette on the table and rose slowly to his feet. "Steady on, George. Just what are you talking about?"

"Meg! She's not there. She hasn't been there all night. What have you done with her?"

I gaped at him and turned to watch Roy's reaction.

He clenched both fists. "What are you talking about? She had a migraine last night. She didn't leave her room."

"You bloody liar. Check with your steward. I did. She hasn't been there all night. Her bed wasn't even slept in. Where are you hiding her?"

Roy stared at the man with his mouth open. "Hiding her? Don't be ridiculous. How would I do that?"

"Put her in another cabin. In second class, or on another deck. I don't know! But she's not there, and Renata says she doesn't know where she is. Says she hasn't seen her since before dinner last night."

The room was eerily still. We had the full attention of the entire dining room now. Roy seemed to be frozen in place.

The other fellow was leaning on the table with both hands. "Lord knows, you've done a lot of dirty things to keep her from me, Armitage. But I never thought you would stoop to this."

"Renata hasn't seen her …?" Roy's voice trailed off. His face blanched. Before anyone could do anything, he sprang to life and left the table with a heavy gait. We all watched as he fled through the double doors.

You could have heard a pin drop in that room. We were all left speechless. The young man opposite me stared after Roy, mumbled something grim, and then took off after him.

Gradually, chatter started up at the other tables. Roberts materialized at my side.

"Are you all right, m'lady?"

"Yes, thank you," I said, looking up at his kindly face. "That was quite a scene. I don't know quite what to make of it."

"There will certainly be talk in the servants' quarters today." He shrugged and reached for Roy's half-eaten breakfast plate. "Makes for a change."

I smiled up at him. Sometimes I thought the staff on the *Victoriana* regarded those of us in first class as a peculiar breed of performing wildlife. Which might not be far from the truth.

I BARELY GOT through the cabin door before Elf was upon me.

"You'll never guess!" she blurted.

"Meg Harwood is missing," I said, throwing my wrap on the chair. "Her bed hasn't been slept in and she hasn't been seen since before dinner last night."

Elf stood open-mouthed. "Not fair," she said finally.

I smiled. "Roy Armitage was at breakfast. We had quite a scene in the dining room." I described it to her, including Roy's hasty exit from the room in front of a full audience.

"Blimey," said Elf. "That's better than Polly's story."

I laughed. "I figured that's who you heard this from. What did Polly have to say?"

"Same stuff. Polly went in this morning to do beds and found Meg's had never been slept in. Film star quite miffed because of it.

Thinks little sister found a man and hoofed it. Everyone's talking about it in the steward's lounge."

"You mean, she's bunked up with a lover?" I was startled. Surely, she wouldn't have found someone that soon on this ship. Unless he'd planned this in advance and followed her onboard, like the man called George. But honestly, having *two* suitors surprise her on the voyage? That defied imagination. Now, if this were Renata, maybe I could believe it. She had a massive following, a shocking reputation, and a series of unhappy men behind her. But little Meg? The gal Roy Armitage called Sparrow?

"I don't think that's likely," I said. "For one thing, there hasn't been time for her to meet anyone. She wasn't at dinner last night."

Elf took that into consideration with a slow nod of her head. "Where do *you* think she is?"

I sat down on the bed and kicked off my shoes.

"It could be as this George says. She could be in hiding. Maybe from her young man, as Roy suggests, or from Roy and Renata themselves. The purser might know if she wangled another cabin on another deck."

Elf grinned. "And he'll tell you if she did, even if he was sworn to secrecy."

I nodded agreement.

"We gotta tell the purser," she insisted.

"Elf, we're getting ahead of ourselves here. So far, we only know she's missing."

"But you always say they have to work quickly if someone goes missing on a ship. *The ocean isn't forgiving*, you always say."

Drat. She had me at my own words.

I wanted to think about this more. "Surely her sister would

have seen or heard her leave their suite. Unless Meg snuck out of their cabin very late when everyone was asleep ..."

"Let's see what Danger Man has to say." Elf slid off the bed, all charged with energy. Before I could stop her, she had pulled open the cabin door.

"Wait!" I yelled to the empty room.

CHAPTER 4

WE STOOD IN front of the purser's door, which was shut.

"Elf, we can't go running off to Gray every time we have a whim," I scolded.

She knocked on the door. Three sharp raps. "Bollocks," she said.

"Enter," came a deep voice from within the room.

Elf flung the door open. I heard it bang against the side wall.

Gray looked up from his desk. I saw his expression change from mild panic (looking at Elf) to relief (seeing me behind her).

"You hear about the missing sister?" Elf blurted.

Gray turned over the paper he was working on and pointed to a chair. "Close the door," he ordered. I did as told because Elf had already plunked down into the chair. Honestly, who was the maid around here?

"Old news, Elf. Someone already beat you to it," said Gray.

Elf harrumphed.

Gray rose from behind his desk and pulled another chair over for me.

"Was the other person a rather hefty young man who claims to be her lover?" I asked.

"He said *intended*." Gray's eyes twinkled at me as we both sat down.

I blushed. Well! I guess calling a man your lover was still a little brazen to say out loud. He would remind me of that in bed tonight.

"What do you know?" said Gray.

Elf and I both started talking at once. As usual, she won out. I backed off, ready to fill in anything missing.

"Polly — you know, what's-their-steward — says Meg's bed hasn't been slept in. Clothes still in her closet. Where's she been all night?" Elf leaned forward. "High and mighty film star thinks she's been sharing spit with a man in his cubby. Boyfriend thinks the star's husband has her socked away in another cabin. An' maybe she's gone overboard —"

"Hold on a second," said Gray. "What do you mean, gone overboard? Is there any sort of evidence?"

"Elf exaggerates." I glared at her. "I heard Meg might be depressed. That is all. But no, there's no evidence of anything."

Gray leaned back in his captain's chair. Boy, that uniform looked good on him. Something about the gold buttons that ran down his chest …

I shook myself free.

"You know as much as me," said Gray. "George Eversleigh thinks the Harwoods are keeping Meg hidden away because they assume she will elope with him. Didn't seem likely to me." He ran a hand through thick, honey-gold hair. "He wanted me to check all the empty first-class cabins on board for her. I said there aren't any. We're fully booked. Then he suggested" — he winked at me — "and I do say *suggested* in the nicest possible way — that Roy Armitage most likely booked a cabin in second class under a different name just to hide her away, and I should look for her there. I asked him what name I should check under." He raised both palms in the air. "That's when things got testy."

Elf grinned. "He got you busting into all the cabins in second class?"

"Not bloody likely," said Gray, smiling back. "I told him, if he could give me the name he suspects an additional cabin might be booked under, I would make discreet enquiries. Or if he could give me the name of a man she might be — ahem — rooming with, I would make even more discreet enquiries."

"And that's when things got testy!" I said, chuckling.

Gray linked the fingers of his hands together. "Nothing I couldn't handle."

We exchanged gazes. Frankly, I couldn't think of anything Gray couldn't handle. But I got back to business. Facing reality was a strong point of mine.

"You really can't do anything until Renata asks you to," I said. "As next of kin."

"Thank you for understanding," said Gray, unlinking his hands. "This could very well be a case of a young lady being seduced by an older, attractive man. I can hardly institute a ship-wide search for her without causing a scandal. Can you imagine the outrage from her family? Until there's a request from next of kin, I can't do much. Until then, I'll keep my eyes and ears open. You do that too."

I nodded, rose, and dragged Elf up by the arm. She seemed reluctant to go.

"What is it, Elf?"

"That Mr. Mason," she said. "He around?"

"Good thinking!" I said. "He could definitely help." Mr. Mason was a retired police detective who had been hired to act as security on our last voyage. He had proven to be a terrifically smart older gentleman, as well as a secret ally in our last adventure.

"Not on this trip, sadly," said Gray. "Last minute appendix operation. We've had to do without."

"Oh, that is a shame. I hope he recovers well." I really liked the man. "I should send something to him, Gray. A fruit basket or something. And please make sure the shipping line pays for any hospital costs."

"Already done," said Gray. "I'll see about the fruit basket."

A knock at the door ended that discussion.

"Enter," said Gray. A silver-haired man in uniform smiled at us as we walked past him out the door.

I waited until the door had fully shut before saying what had been on my mind.

"At least we know the full name of Meg's young man."

"George Eversleigh!" said Elf.

IT OCCURRED TO me that most of ship life revolved around meals. Breakfast, luncheon, tea, and dinner in the dining room ... although tea was often taken in one's room, or among friends in one of the ship's numerous lounges. Passengers filled the time in between meals with ablutions, dressing, walking the corridors, perhaps picking up a book in the library. The men had more options, of course, and could gamble or smoke in the rooms designed specifically for those purposes.

A woman would change her attire for each of these meals with her clothes becoming increasingly more formal as the day went on. Times were changing though, and often I wore the same outfit for breakfast and lunch. Many women breakfasted in their rooms, of course, and were spared at least one wardrobe change.

Between meals, I usually chose to spend time in my cabin or the library, reading. Mystery fiction had become my guilty secret. I was totally enthralled with the fiction of Dorothy Sayers, and more recently Agatha Christie, whom I had met and now called a friend. But today I was restless. Elf was driving me mad with her incessant chatter about the missing sister. I knew she was planning to meet up with Polly in the next while, so I decided to do some sleuthing of my own.

Well, not really sleuthing. More like getting to know the lay of the land. I knew, for instance, that Renata Harwood was in the Victoriana Suite. I knew that because I had wanted it for this voyage — it's the most exclusive room on the ship — but it had already been assigned by the time I was able to make my late booking.

To be honest, the main reason I was crossing the ocean this time was to be with Gray. It wasn't the only reason — I had business papers to sign in New York, and it was quicker for me to go there to sign them rather than have them shipped to me in England and then shipped back. But the lure of being with Gray every night for the crossing there and back was too much to resist. We had started our romance only months ago, and since then, I'd only been able to see him for a few nights every two weeks between voyages. I wasn't going to let a long while go by without seeing him merely because he had to report to work on the *Victoriana*. Especially since I owned the ship.

And because I owned the ship, I knew perfectly well where the Victoriana Suite was located. So, that was where I headed. Luckily, I had a valid reason for seeking Renata out.

Renata's suite was one floor up from my deck. I took the grand staircase, as always marvelling at the gorgeous natural light that streamed in through the enormous iron and glass dome above. At night, when only the moon and stars remained in the sky, it was left to beautiful sconces and candelabra to illuminate the ornate oak panelling.

I nodded to couples on their way down and walked the generous corridor to the rear of the ship. When I was most of the way down, Roy Armitage came out of the door and turned to face me.

"Well, hello, pretty lady! Are you on this floor?" His smile beamed.

"No, actually. This is convenient, meeting you. I'm looking for Renata. Is she …?" I waved a hand at the suite.

He took my arm and turned me around to retrace my steps up the corridor.

"You missed her. She's in the salon, I believe. Making herself beautiful for the fancy dress dinner tonight. Do you know where that is?"

I nodded. He meant the hair salon, not the first-class dining saloon.

"Try catching her there. And who will you be going as, my dear?"

"It just so happens that's what I want to talk to her about," I confided. "Wanted to make sure I wasn't treading on any toes." I was curious to see if he would get my meaning.

He did. Roy chuckled and used his right hand to pat the hand that was tucked into his arm. "Smart girl, you. Never mess with a diva. I'm sure whatever you wear will be absolutely charming."

I took a chance and asked, "Any news of Meg?"

He shook his head and patted my hand, sadly, I thought. I didn't ask more as we were almost at the grand staircase.

We split up there. Roy headed for the men's smoking lounge, and I continued down the steps, way down to the service level that housed the beauty salon, men's barber, and small shops.

The shops were new on the Empire line. I'd heard that one of the French ships had recently installed a cinema, and it was on my list to discuss with shareholders when I reached New York. What a delight that would be, going to the cinema on board ship!

The beauty salon was directly in front of me, and I could see it was bustling. Salons were also a new service on ocean liners. In previous years, many women in first class travelled with a maid. Since the war, maids were in short supply, hairstyles were much simpler, and many women — particularly married ones who had husbands to help them do up frocks — travelled without help. Thus, the blessed convenience of having beauty salons on board.

I paused at the open doorway, peeking around the glittering, well-lit room for a glimpse of our silver screen star. Light from sconces and chandeliers danced off the many gilt mirrors. Ah! There she was, in a chair toward the back of the salon, having the final touches put to her coiffure. I entered, waved at the young receptionist, whom I knew, and carried on to the far end. I felt several pairs of eyes watching me as I approached Renata.

She saw me coming and beamed. Her makeup was perfect, just a little more than was deemed proper for daytime. I smiled at Renata, and also at the stylist serving her. "Hello Esther," I said cheerfully. Esther gasped with excitement and dropped to a curtsey, which always made me want to giggle. "I'm not royalty, Esther. You don't have to do that."

She did it again.

I pointed to the chair next to Renata, and she reached out her hand for me to take.

"Lady Revelstoke! I'm delighted to see you. Have you tried the services here? Simply divine."

"It's Lucy, remember. I'm so glad you like the salon. It's a fairly new service, and one, frankly, that my American shareholders were a little skeptical about. All men, of course. But I can tell you, it's been a wonderful success." I let go of her hand and parked my bottom in the empty chair next to her.

Her dark eyes opened wide. "Your shareholders? You mean for the salon? Or — wait ... do you mean you own this ship?"

I had to smile inwardly. Renata was much sharper than people gave her credit for, I thought for a second time.

"The ship and the line. My late husband left me the business. He had great faith in me," I said with some pride.

"And it seems that faith was not misplaced." She looked at me with new eyes.

Now this was interesting. What had prompted me to divulge this information to Renata? Usually, I kept my association with the *Victoriana* and the Empire line private. Perhaps I sensed a kindred spirit in her, another woman who had made her way in a man's world.

"I came looking for you for a reason," I said. "Actually two. Fancy dress is tonight, and as we are sitting at the same table ..."

"You wanted to make sure we didn't choose the same costume," Renata said triumphantly. "How clever of you."

I returned her smile and told her what I planned to appear as.

"We are safe." She laughed. "I shall keep mine a secret until tonight."

"Fair enough," I said. And then I sucked in a breath before slipping in my main reason for this conversation. "Should I worry about what Meg will be wearing? Will she be joining us tonight?"

Her face turned to a frown. "I sincerely don't know. She seems to be leading a life of her own these days. I've hardly seen her since we boarded."

Well, that was an interesting way to put it. Renata seemed more annoyed than worried. Or perhaps I was wrong because she leaned forward to say, "To be frank, I'm quite concerned about her. She seems to have taken up with some man or other. And the little minx has walked off with my best evening bag!"

So, that was the story she was going with. As she described the evening bag in detail, I couldn't help but wonder what concerned her more: the plight of her sister or the loss of the purse.

I fixed my attention on her. "It's such a worry," I murmured. "Would this be the man who approached your husband after dinner last night?"

"What a disagreeable scene," said Renata, waving a manicured hand through the air. "But I'm not even sure it is him. I fear it is someone even more unsuitable, Lady Revelstoke." She feigned mortification. "Frankly, I'm very worried."

I say *feigned* because I had to smother a laugh. When I thought of the many unsuitable men Renata Harwood had been seen associating with, all of whom were recorded in the English tabloids …

"Your concern for your sister is laudable," I said, soothingly. "We both know what men can be."

She seemed pleased to be regarded as a woman of the world; it was certainly a part she played to perfection. I had already pegged Renata as the sort who loved a title. Her adoption of Tony and the way she'd fussed over our minor royalty last night made that fact clear. Yet for all her acquired well-bred demeanour, I was willing to bet our Renata had clawed her way up from the East End.

"And the second thing?"

"I beg your pardon?" I said, coming out of my reverie.

Renata smiled. "You said there were two things."

"Oh! Thank you for reminding me. It's my maid, Elf. She's friends with your steward, Polly. I happen to know that you gave Polly a signed photo last night, and …" My voice trailed off.

"You'd like one for your maid too."

As I said before, Renata was quick.

"Hand me that bag over there." She pointed and I retrieved. "I should have one or two in here." She reached in, frowned, and came out with a 5" by 7" glossy photo. "I can sign it if you like."

"Would you? She'd be thrilled. The receptionist will have a pen and ink."

We walked together to the front of the salon. I nodded here and there to the guests and staff with whom I was acquainted, knowing that whispered chatter would follow me out the door and set the salon on fire for some time after. The combination of a notorious actress chumming with a peeress of the realm was bound to create delicious gossip. That didn't bother me. There wasn't a lot to do on a cruise ship, so the more lurid excitement I could generate for passengers, the more fun for everyone. And that was always good for business.

As I have said, Johnny had a lot of faith in my business sense.

Millie, the receptionist, leapt up from her chair when she saw what Renata had in mind.

"What's her name again?" Renata asked.

"Elf, short for Elfreda," I said.

Renata filled the pen at the desk and scribbled swiftly. "How's this?"

I read over her shoulder:

For Elfreda —

May you reach your dreams,
Renata Harwood

"You are too kind," I effused. "She'll be delighted!"

She straightened up and handed me the photo. I held it carefully, almost reverently, as if it were ancient parchment. "Thank you so very much. I'll leave you now, to finish up here. A nap is in order for me. I want to be fresh for tonight — the fancy dress is really a lot of fun."

"Looking forward to it," said Renata. She gave me a million-dollar smile.

I returned it, waved, and turned to make my way out of the salon.

CHAPTER 5

ONCE AGAIN, ELF pounced on me when I got back to the cabin.

"Guess what?" she blurted.

"Whatever it is, I'm going to top it." I handed her the photo of Renata.

"Oh!" she screamed. "Oh! How did you …?"

"Found her in the hair salon. Begged on your behalf."

"Yer the best!" screeched Elf. "Wait 'til Maisie sees this!" Maisie was the upstairs maid at our London townhouse. She and Elf were crazy about the pictures and saw every film at the cinema together. Sometimes more than once.

It felt good to see Elf so excited.

"So, what about what?" I threw my wrap on the chair and prepared to be informed.

"What?" said Elf, not lifting her eyes.

"You said 'Guess what' when I came in."

"Oh!" She put the photo down on the chest of drawers. "Polly says Meg never changed! Left the cabin in the very clothes she came on board in. Not only that, but none of her toiletries was missing." Elf looked triumphant.

"Now, that is interesting," I admitted. A woman might stay overnight with a man, but surely, she would take essentials with her. Or at least come back for them in the morning.

This wasn't adding up. "Elf, think this through with me." I sat down on the bed. "Meg meets a man. Maybe a new one, but more likely someone she already knows. Perhaps they made plans to meet on board, because honestly, there hasn't been much time to meet anyone new yet. Things get carried away — or maybe she wanted to defy her sister. Who knows? She sneaks off with this man to his cabin. Has a tryst. Maybe stays overnight. That will really get the sister riled up. Suddenly, the scandal and attention are on Meg and not Renata! That will never do. Oh, I have a low view of human nature, don't I?"

Elf just grinned.

"But stay with me here. Wouldn't Meg come back to her own cabin in the morning? Wouldn't she at least go back for her things?"

"You mean face gunk and stuff," said Elf.

"Not only that, but new underwear, lingerie, good clothes. Unless she had planned to stay hidden in his cabin all day and night for the rest of the trip, she'd want her clothes."

"And even if she hid out by herself in another cabin, she'd want her toothbrush and bathroom stuff." Elf nodded along. "Why didn't she take her things?"

"Or why didn't she send a steward back to get them for her?"

We sat in silence for several seconds. I felt a chill run down my arms.

"What does that point to?" I asked.

Elf is sharp. "That she ain't alive anymore."

WE SAT QUIETLY for a moment as the chill washed over us.

I remembered a conversation from earlier in the day. "Roy hinted that Meg had been unhappy lately, and a little unstable."

Elf joined me on the bed. Her feet dangled off the end, not even close to the floor. "You think she did herself in?"

"It's something that can't be overlooked. But then, why haven't they found a note? Usually, people who commit suicide leave a note to make others feel guilty. Not to mention ..."

"No body," said Elf, getting quite excited. "There should be a dead body somewhere. People who do themselves in don't go to lengths to hide it, ever. I know that because of this bloke from Bermondsey who seemed like a good sort but turned out to be a rozzer —"

I held out my hand. "Stop! I don't need to hear the sordid details." Elf's amorous adventures were legendary, and usually quite bawdy to recount.

"If she went overboard ... it could be an accident," Elf posed. "Gone to the edge, looked over, and phwump. Bob's your uncle. No coming back from that."

"Possible," I said. "But before dinner? In broad daylight, with passengers milling about? Surely someone would have seen something. No, if she went overboard, it would have to have been at night."

"She stayed in the cabin until night and then fell in or threw herself in the drink?" asked Elf.

It was an explanation, but it left me uneasy. With no note left behind, I didn't buy it.

"There's a third possibility," I said slowly.

"Yup," said Elf. "She had a little help goin' for that swim."

I WAS LATE to lunch. A few people were already exiting as I entered the dining room, and only Tony sat at our table. He shot up from his chair as I came forward.

"Just got here myself. You heard about Meg?" He pulled out the chair beside him and waved me into it.

"Being missing?" I said as he sat. It was unlikely he had more information on that than I did. He didn't have an 'Elf,' after all.

"Armitage is beside himself, poor man. Renata must be a wreck."

I didn't bother to tell him that Renata had been having a grand time in the beauty salon preparing for her big entrance tonight. Let the poor boy keep his illusions.

Our steward came by with Tony's drink order and menus. This was always a delightful process for me. To choose between the smoked salmon plate and steak frites was a tremendous dilemma, one worthy of my full attention. In the end, I chose the less caloric salmon dish, remembering the costume I had to wear tonight.

"Just coffee to drink, thank you." I handed the menu back to the steward. No dessert for me until after the fancy dress!

Tony gave his order, after which I turned my attention on him. "Meg's champion from dinner last night has already reported her missing to the purser," I said. "But they don't know quite what to do about it."

"Oh! About him. Fellow by the name of Eversleigh," said Tony. His eyes trailed the scoop neckline of my fashionable day dress.

"George Eversleigh," I added.

Tony sat staring with his mouth open. "How did you …?"

"Never underestimate the power of the female grapevine where a good-looking man is concerned," I replied, enigmatically.

"Did you find out anything about him? I only have a name."

Tony harrumphed. "Seems to be a decent sort. Public school and all that, but no money to speak of. Second son of a second son of a cousin to one of the Horse Guards, or some such. Father in trade, most likely."

"I wonder why Roy reacted so strongly last night. Doesn't sound like such a terrible match to me," I mused.

"That's because you're not a snob, my dear." Tony took a swig from his whisky glass. "Renata will be hoping for money or a title in that match. This fellow has neither. Remember, I know something about the way that diva thinks, to my regret."

Interesting, but I knew enough not to ask for details. I had to wonder if Tony hadn't made the grade. His older brother would inherit the title and estate, but Tony himself had nothing but an allowance that could be cut off at any time. Perhaps not a glittering prospect, especially with his penchant for gambling.

"At least George Eversleigh seems decent. Does he work?" I asked.

"I'll do my best to find out," said Tony. "You're really interested in poor Meg's situation, aren't you?"

To be honest, I was. Women might have gained the vote, but property was a totally different thing. Without money of their own, women were dependent on the generosity of their relatives. Renata didn't seem very generous toward Meg.

In that way, it was similar to Tony's position. He had an allowance but wouldn't inherit much. In well off families, young ladies might be willed a dowry, but never the estate. Money meant freedom. And who knew if Meg's family had any money at all?

I turned to him. "I note that you call her 'poor' Meg. Is she poor, in the monetary sense?"

"Completely dependent on big sis and the new hubby, as far as I know."

That was bad. It explained why she had no freedom and was expected to be at her sister's beck and call.

"Do you know anything about the family? Do they have money?" I asked.

He shook his head. "None to speak of. Renata never talked about them. I think that's why she is so driven to succeed."

It made sense. I'd have to ask Elf if she knew more celebrity gossip about Renata's background. "And the new hubby? Is he dependent?"

Tony looked shocked. "Now, that I don't know." He seemed uncomfortable, playing with his glass with one hand. "Doesn't act like he is."

I didn't have to wonder what that meant. Obviously, Roy Armitage had been busy in the card room. Which meant Tony had also been busy at the tables, and that made me sad.

Tony had professed to love me. But that wasn't enough to strengthen his resolve to quit gambling. Anyone who thinks love can change a person is in for a rude awakening, sadly.

I wondered about Roy Armitage. He seemed a lot older than Renata. I said so to Tony.

"Fifteen years there at least, I wouldn't doubt. Can't gather what she sees in him, frankly," he said. He finished the end of the whisky.

I had to smile. "Me neither. I'm always puzzled when men marry women a great deal younger than themselves. I understand that it feeds their ego, but I don't understand why it does. Women don't feel the same way in reverse. At least, I don't."

Tony seemed surprised. "Really? I thought for sure you

wouldn't mind a bunch of twenty-year-old bucks following you around like lost puppies."

I checked a shiver. "Not in the least. Talk about inviting problems. Young men don't interest me much, to be honest. They have no life experience yet." I toyed with my water glass. "You and I, we've been through the war, Tony. How could they possibly relate to our experiences and sorrows? No, I have no interest in younger men falling in love with me. Or in lust, if you want to put it that way. Why would I?"

Tony stared at me. He harrumphed, then gave a small chuckle. "Sorry to break it to you, Lucy, but almost any man of any age would find you extremely attractive. I can tell you this, though. For men, it's all about ego. Men want to believe that every woman in the world finds them attractive, no matter how old they are. Foolish though it may seem."

I sighed. "Men and women. Women and men. Sometimes I find it hard to believe we're the same species."

"Ain't it the truth," said Tony. He signaled a steward to refill his glass.

Our luncheon plates arrived, and I spent the next few minutes in quiet contemplation of all the marvellous food put in front of me. Both Elf and I share a similar trait: We can find pleasure in simple things, like a good meal. So many times, I have been grateful for this humble blessing.

I looked up from my plate to see Lord Harry sitting across from me. When did he arrive there? I acknowledged him with a cheery nod.

I was just finishing up when Roberts arrived at my side with a message.

"M'lady, the captain would like to see you in the officers' lounge as soon as it is convenient."

"Of course," I said, removing the napkin from my lap. "I'll go now." I reached for my wrap and handbag and said my goodbyes to the men.

The officers' lounge was on the same deck as the bridge, close by to it. A good choice for our meeting as it was relatively private but respectable. A lady simply couldn't visit a man's cabin — not even the captain's — without tongues wagging. And the bridge itself was a busy place with many ears.

I knew my way, having been there on the last voyage. I always think of it as being like a London gentlemen's club. Brown was the overwhelming colour. Lots of wood panelling, generous wainscotting, with paintings of naval warships from the past century on the walls. A portrait of the King graced the short wall between two portholes. Large comfortable club chairs sat around small wooden tables, with ashtrays on every surface. It was definitely a place where men would feel comfortable, and women … well, I may have been the only woman ever to enter this place.

Still, I liked it. There was an odour of pipe tobacco about the place, which reminded me of Johnny.

Captain Miller was seated in one of the club chairs with a plate of sandwiches in front of him. He shot to his feet when I entered the room.

"Lady Revelstoke! Have you eaten yet?" He came round to pull out the chair opposite him, and I allowed him to seat me. Such a delightful, old-world gentleman to women like me, and yet I knew he could be a demanding and formidable sea captain with the men. The respect he commanded was well-earned.

"Yes, thank you. Please go ahead yourself." I waved a hand at the plate.

He sat down and smiled. "That can wait. I've just received a bit of news I wanted to share. Not good news, I'm afraid."

I put my hands together on my lap and waited.

"We've had word of a tropical storm heading up the coast of the United States. It's veering out to sea, and that could be a problem for us."

"Oh dear," I said. My eyes scanned his face.

Usually, I saw the captain in pleasant social situations, where he could be incredibly charming. This serious side to him was something new to me, and yet ... there are some men who just radiate confidence. He was one of those rare personages. I could see why the crew were in awe of him.

"It is hurricane season, after all." He leaned back in the chair. "We can't outrun it, unfortunately. I'm suggesting we attempt to stay north of it and slow the ship down if necessary."

"This will cause a delay," I said.

He nodded at my comment. "Astute of you. The better part of a day. Maybe less. But my first priority is the safety of the passengers on this ship."

"Of course," I said, relieved. "That must be our priority — safety above all else." Memory of the *Titanic* was never far from mind to those of us making an Atlantic crossing. I had to stop myself from shivering.

His faced relaxed, and it seemed that he looked fondly at me. "I wanted to let you know immediately because of your connection with the shipping line. I'll keep you informed if anything changes."

"Thank you." I smiled warmly. It was kind of him to do so. We both understood that Captain Miller had full responsibility for the ship, and my permission was not sought or necessary. But I could reassure shareholders in New York that appropriate precautions had been taken, and I, as a member of the board, had been consulted. Delays cost money, after all. Not only that, but I would be a good ambassador for explaining the delay to fellow passengers.

I rose and so did he.

"Will we see you at dinner tonight?" I asked.

He shook his head. "I expect the situation will take my full attention. Perhaps Mr. West can take my chair. I'll speak to him."

I felt my heart leap. "I won't keep you then." We said our goodbyes quickly.

Heavy weather. That's what was going through my mind as I left the officers' lounge and found myself on the promenade deck, looking out to sea. Going north was not a sad thing for me. I didn't mind the delay, as being on the sea was something I loved. Truly, I treasured every day of it. Still, one had to wonder how this absolutely gorgeous, sapphire-blue ocean in front of me could turn into something hellish and black with massive waves that roared thunder. And yet it could — I'd seen it, experienced it.

"Lady Revelstoke! Hello again." The singsong voice came from behind me. I turned from the railing to find Renata Hayward gazing at me.

"Hello," I said cheerily, moving over to make room at the rail. "Taking a spin around the deck for the air?"

"Exactly that," she said, joining me. "It really is refreshing, especially after the fumes in the hair salon. Luckily, it's not too windy right now."

I smiled. To go from the hair salon to the exposed deck was taking a risk. Wind was the enemy of newly coiffed hair.

"Miss Harwood?" The voice was young and female. We both turned to find two well-dressed teenage girls staring eagerly at Renata. They looked to be sisters, possibly two years apart. Obviously star-struck. I had to smile. They hardly gave me a glance.

"Hello," Renata said, smiling at them.

The older one stepped forward. Correction: The slim brunette positively leapt forward, holding a magazine in one hand and a fountain pen in the other.

"Could you …? I mean, would you …?" She held the magazine out to Renata. I could see the title now: *Motion Picture Magazine*.

"Would you like me to autograph it?" Renata said. She reached for the magazine. "I'd be happy to."

"*Thank* you!" said the grateful young lady. Her younger sister stood speechless in awe. They stepped back a little, in respect, before turning to each other with excited chatter.

Renata came back to the rail. It pleased me to see that she had given her signature with grace.

"People must stop you all the time," I said. "The curse of being so famous."

Oddly enough, she seemed to preen at that. "I don't mind."

Funny how people are different. I would hate to be hounded by fans.

"Look at that young girl. Isn't she gorgeous?" Renata said as the two sisters walked away. "Like a gazelle."

I looked after the older sister and could see what Renata meant. She was slim in the way that teen girls are before they get hips.

"I'm sure we both looked like that in our salad days," I remarked.

"Oh, I never eat salad," Renata said, apparently not getting the reference. "I know it's good for slimming, but it doesn't agree with me."

I smiled at her curious response. Yet I certainly understood the problem. It doesn't pay for a celebrity so much in the public eye to have to cope with tummy noises and possible unpleasant odours. Best to be careful and eat safe foods.

"I should head back to the suite before Roy sends out a search party," she said cheerfully.

We separated soon after that. But something about her salad remark stayed with me. It niggled.

AFTER A LONG, luxurious bath, it was time to let Elf pounce on me.

"Time to get dolled up for the fancy dress," she ordered, with pointed finger. "Sit."

I let Elf fuss around me in her usual way. We both took pleasure in this ritual, although I could have done with fewer orders to remain still. *Perhaps this is what sisters are like*, I mused.

"So, who's your favourite film star?" Elf asked me.

"Golly. That's hard to choose." I gave it some thought. "Probably Mary Pickford. We grew up with her, in a way. Remember *Pollyanna*? And she was terrific in *My Best Girl*."

"'America's Sweetheart'," Elf quoted.

"Which is really quite an ironic title because she is actually Canadian, like me."

Elf snorted at that. "No wonder she's your favourite."

"I also loved Greta Garbo in *Flesh and the Devil*. I think she's going to become a big star."

"As big as Theda Bara?" Elf pish-toshed. "Nobody can beat

her *Cleopatra*. Damn shame she's retiring. Stay *still*," she ordered.

"I also like Clara Bow. I read somewhere that she can cry on demand."

Elf was wielding an eyeliner pencil, so I needed to stop talking, or I'd be the one crying.

"Loved her in *Mantrap*. Wasn't she just the best?" Elf continued yacking about other films she had seen recently with the female staff from our London townhome, while I tried to keep from moving. We continued on this way for a minute or two, while she worked away on my face.

"And of course, the *men*!" Elf sighed dramatically. "Who can forget Rudolf Valentino in *The Sheik*?"

"I prefer Douglas Fairbanks, actually." I said, rather muffled. Gosh, it's hard not to move your face when you talk.

"*The Mark of Zorro, Robin Hood, The Thief of Bagdad* ..." Elf stopped applying eyeshadow and sighed. "There's something right sexy about a good sword fight."

Well, we agreed on that! The romance of it ... and it wasn't just women who felt that way. Growing up, all my brothers had yearned for a long facial scar so people would think they had won it in a duel.

"Done," said Elf, leaning back. "And a bloody good job, if I do say so myself. You can put on your own lipstick." She handed it to me. "Blood red, for the fancy dress."

I did as told and then sat back to observe the result. It was hard not to gasp. The reflection in the mirror was a stunning sight. Once again, I had to ask, was that really me? Could cosmetics make such an enormous difference?

The woman in the mirror had arched brows, enormous smoky eyes, plus full red lips that seemed to promise forbidden passions.

"Just stunning, Elf. You always make me look good, but this is, well, remarkable. I'm not sure anyone will recognize me."

"Hah," she uttered triumphantly. "You're a good-looking woman naturally, and you've got a good face for makeup. I can make you look as innocent as Pickford, or the opposite — a siren, like today." She surveyed me and harrumphed, obviously pleased with herself.

"Now, we gotta get you into that costume."

I spent the next several minutes being ordered around.

CHAPTER 6

GRAHAM WEST WAS to take the place of the captain tonight at our dinner table. I had arranged to meet him there, not knowing whether Tony would insist on escorting me, as had been his custom in the past. However, it appeared Tony had made other plans. No doubt before-dinner drinks and cards had claimed him.

I didn't mind. Tony still didn't know about my relationship with Gray, and I preferred it that way.

Gray saw me arrive at the doors of the dining room and signalled for me to wait for him. I watched him cross the floor, magnificent in his dress uniform, and saw other eyes follow him. Even more turned our way when I took his arm to be escorted to the table.

"Glad you chose to be Cleopatra again. I will never get tired of that costume you are wearing," he said. "Never, ever."

I had to smile. Fancy dress night was a particular favourite of mine on board ship. Such fun, to pretend to be someone else for a short while. To dress the part, to look the part, and throw caution to the wind. To escape being seen as the "poor young widow" for a short while, and instead shock polite society by embracing the role of a glamorous Egyptian queen and temptress. Pure bliss.

I'd worn this costume once before, on our earlier crossing. My take on Cleopatra was perfectly decent, even modest by some standards. Yet there was a sensual simplicity to this one-shouldered gown of yore. I couldn't wear much underneath it due to that bare shoulder, which may have been the attraction. I've always thought that leaving a little to the imagination was more powerful than outright nudity.

I was also determined not to be as provocative as our film star. She wouldn't appreciate that sort of competition from a tablemate. Leave the notoriety to her, I decided, and we'd all be friends.

While my frock was simple, I upped the glamour with period jewellery, just as Cleopatra must have done. The diadem on my head had appeared on the cover of *American Vogue* magazine just a few months ago. I had purchased it in New York, last trip. It was my first big splurge since Johnny died, and the only piece of jewellery I had ever bought myself. Egyptian culture was all the rage since Howard Carter and Lord Carnarvon had discovered the tomb of Tutankhamun back in 1922.

Bangles circled my wrists, as in the practice of ancient Egyptian women. A simple diamond and sapphire brooch in the shape of a leopard appeared to hold the back and front of the linen gown together at the shoulder. It was a beautiful costume, I thought, but not scandalous by any means.

While walking to our table, I took a quick look around the room to see the usual collection of Marie Antoinettes and military heroes. Nobody ever dressed as a serf or serving maid, I was quick to note.

Gray was on the job, so did not wear a costume. However, I was delighted to see that Lord Harry did! While still in evening wear, Lord Harry had donned a short black cape, a tall top hat, and a narrow black mask. He grinned at me mischievously.

"Oh, let me guess!" I said, clapping my hands. "Raffles?"

"Got it in one, Lady Revelstoke!" He giggled infectiously. "'The Gentleman Thief.' Always wanted to play the part at our costume dos, but Grandmama would have none of it."

"I can imagine that," I said with a smile. "I found out recently that the author of the Raffles books was the brother-in-law of the man who wrote Sherlock Holmes, Arthur Conan Doyle."

"Fancy that," said Lord Harry. "Must run in the family."

Like crowns, I thought to myself.

We had just sat down when Renata and her husband appeared at the double doors. No Meg again, but that wasn't a surprise.

The dining room hushed. Renata stepped forward, spoke briefly to Roberts, the head steward, and then beamed at the faces drinking in her appearance. And it was truly like that, as if everyone in the room was star-struck to incapacitation.

Because here was the Salome of the silver screen, in the flesh. It must have been the very same costume she wore in the film, and it fit her like a second skin. A movie coming alive for the shipboard audience, and a dream come true for many.

As she got closer to us, that notorious costume revealed itself. The top consisted of two large teardrops suspended from her shoulders, covering her breasts and not much else. The point of each teardrop was connected to a thin piece of fabric that circled her neck, and beyond that, I could not figure out how they stayed in place. The skirt was a marvel of transparent chiffon layers, with a hip-hugging gold taffeta girdle (*girdle* in the medieval sense) that rose to a point at her waist in front. Layered over that, from mid-thigh to mid-thigh, perhaps two dozen rows of beads hung down nearly to her knees, a spectacular apron that swayed provocatively as she moved. Thick bracelets circled both her ankles.

Truly my description could not do it justice. Shocking, exotic, sensuous, notorious — it was all that, plus spectacularly beautiful.

She looked this way and that, smiling like a pro, obviously delighted by the reaction. Yes, some elderly matrons twisted their faces in disgust, but for the most part, Renata's audience on the ship was enthralled. Chatter picked up as she passed each table in turn.

As they reached our table, Lord Harry shot up from his chair. "Right ho," he said. "Those are damned spiffy glad rags, don'tcha know."

Renata beamed at him and walked to the far side of the table so that she faced the entrance. *More people to see her in that position*, I mused. She waved an arm at a specific chair, and we all watched as a small contest took place between Harry and her husband, with Roy winning the honour to pull it out. She sat with a feline grace and put her arms on the table in such a way that I wondered if it was so her jewellery might be admired.

And what a collection it was! Bracelets running up her arms to her elbows. Rings on at least three fingers of each hand. I was dazzled by the brilliance of gold and gemstones. *Could it all be real?* I remembered my late mother saying to me once, "Take note, Lucy. Don't skimp. If some of your jewellery is real, then everyone expects all of it will be."

I wasn't the only one at the table mesmerized. Graham was unusually silent, I noticed with amusement. In fact, it was I who spoke first. "Renata, you look splendid. Is that the actual costume from the film?"

The delight on her face was something to behold. "Yes. I've been dying to wear it again. This seemed the perfect opportunity."

"Indeed," I said, charmed by her unexpected girlish enthusiasm.

"Perfect for tonight. I'm not sure they would fully appreciate it at Simpson's or the Ritz."

"No indeed." Her laugh was a throaty chortle. Harry joined in with his characteristic giggle.

Roy Armitage had also embraced the spirit of tonight, in a way that made me smile. Dressed in high boots, a brown tweed suit with jacket belted at the waist, and a safari helmet on his head, he looked for all the world like the African colonial planter he wanted people to think he was. Or was I being unkind?

Tony raced over, grabbing the empty chair next to me. "My apologies, folks. Hard to leave the cards. Had a winning streak there for a while." He looked around the table, eyes wide. "Oh bother! I forgot it was fancy dress."

"You naughty boy. Cards trump our company, I fear, Lady Revelstoke," Renata quipped, and she laughed again, this time more openly. *How strange*, I thought. This was starting to be fun. I had thought being at Renata's table was going to be a chore, but truly, she was far more natural and entertaining than I had imagined.

The laughter stopped suddenly. I heard a collective gasp around the room, and then Harry mumbled, "Who's that?"

We all turned. There in the doorway was a gorgeous woman, standing alone. Young, dazzling, and very sure of herself. She stared directly at us and headed right over.

Even I gasped as she approached. She was wearing the identical costume to Renata. Identical, down to the very headdress and sandals.

"Good God, it's Stella Burke!" blurted Roy Armitage. Renata appeared frozen in place.

"Who is Stella Burke?" Gray whispered to me.

"Another actress," I whispered back, but that didn't begin to cover it. Stella had been the understudy to Renata in the stage version of *Salome* before Renata turned to film. In fact, I knew from Elf that Roy Armitage and Stella Burke had once been linked together, and that it was through Stella that Roy had met Renata. Hoo boy, this was not going to be a pretty reunion.

All four men at the table leapt to their feet. Stella gave them a passing glance but turned her full attention on her rival.

"Renata, darling! Isn't this fun, being on the same ship? And I see you've saved a place for me. How sweet of you." The smile on her face was almost predatory.

Renata didn't bother to respond and instead launched into the social armour of introductions.

It's at times like this that I most admire the English; their obsession with etiquette to smooth over social occasions has its uses. Renata held her own as she introduced Stella around, as gracious a hostess as I have ever seen. You would have to be very savvy to see the fury that seethed under the cosmetics on her exquisitely madeup face. Or wait — was that fear?

I wondered. *What would she have to fear from this younger woman?* Her career had taken a stellar leap, with that move to Hollywood. I had to wonder ... could her fear be more personal? Maybe Renata wasn't so sure of her husband after all.

There was a chair next to Tony and an empty seat on the other side of Gray. I saw with amusement that Stella chose that one. It wasn't so much that Gray was the most handsome man at the table. She hardly gave him a glance. No, this was a calculated decision on her part to put herself directly opposite Renata.

My Lord, what a contrast they made. I was reminded of a negative from a camera. Renata in a Salome costume with her sleek black hair, and Stella in the very same skimpy costume with a honey-blond bob. Stella was younger by about a decade, but under all that makeup, it was hard to tell. Worse than that ... while Renata had a figure that suited today's streamlined clothes, Stella had a body that would look fabulous out of them. Good Lord, she made me look flat-chested, and that's a feat, Gray would say. I was reminded of torpedoes ...

"Hello, everyone," she announced, looking around the table. "Sorry I missed last night. Took me a while to get my sea legs." She turned to look directly at Roy. "Hello, darling! It's been simply ages. And how have you been keeping? Poor dear. Haven't you been well? You look dreadful."

Gray choked beside me. I was beginning to appreciate that he sat between me and the viper next to him.

Roy gave her a death stare. "What are you doing here, Stella?"

"At this table? But you have room. Don't you want me here?" She gave him a coquettish look that I could just manage to see from my position on Gray's right.

"On this boat," Roy said through gritted teeth.

"Well naturally, darling. It's the only way to travel to New York. I've been requested to play the part of Salome on Broadway. Didn't you hear?"

There was a gasp from Renata. *Good gracious*. I watched as the blood drained from her face.

"You? Broadway?" Roy nearly choked as he said it.

"You didn't know? Where have you been? In Africa?" Her voice trilled.

I was pretty sure nobody at that table could have known this bombshell of news. Elf hadn't mentioned it to me, and I know she would have. So, if Elf — who was up to date on all show business news — hadn't heard, then it was far from common knowledge. And it was something Stella had taken great delight in springing on us.

Stella spared a glance to her rival. "Well, I'm sure Renata will be thrilled for me. After all, you were my idol, Renata dear. I learned so much as your understudy, all those *years* ago."

All those years ago? It couldn't have been more than five years ago! And she stressed *years* with an inflection that couldn't be mistaken for anything but unkind. Renata remained silent, and I admired her for that. Good thing they were seated at a distance across from each other, instead of within reach. If I were Renata, I probably would have launched myself across the table and gone for her throat.

"After my *Salome* performance in the West End, agents were all over me. 'Never seen anything like it,' they said." She looked over at Renata to see if this hit home. Renata was admirably stoic. I could now see she was deserving of her reputation as a great actress.

Roberts arrived to take orders, and we settled into another drama. Because of course, Roberts started with me, clearly showing that I held status in his eyes. We might think servants are blind and deaf, but I've found men like Roberts hear everything and show their admiration or disdain in subtle but firm ways. And Roberts had certainly heard the nasty comments uttered by Stella.

From me, he moved to Renata, which was a daring violation of the pecking order. I had to smile. Roberts was making a point by ignoring the usual order of things (Harry and Tony, as aristocracy, should have come before commoners) and it was also clear that the message hit home. Renata was being treated like royalty. Stella was not. Renata recovered her serene composure. Stella seemed to be having a hard time controlling a snarl.

Tony moved in to smooth things over.

"New York is a fabulous place. I'll be staying for a week or two. Are you travelling alone? If this is your first time, perhaps I can show you some of the sights."

Oh, Tony! I had to smile. Talk about a stealthy manoeuvre. Stella's face lit up like the lights on Broadway. She went from wildcat to purring kitten with one slick sentence.

She was indeed travelling alone. I didn't envy Tony having to follow through with it, but I supposed he wouldn't mind. Most men wouldn't mind Stella Burke on their arm for a short while. At least until the claws came out.

The whole table seemed to relax as Tony launched into all the sights there were to see, all the nightclubs he could take her to, with Stella oooh-ing and ah-ing in enthusiasm.

I turned to Gray. "Such a shame you can't spend a week in New York to squire Stella around."

He chuckled low. "I'd rather do ten rounds with a Bengal tiger."

I grinned in response. Good to know he had her number.

Tony called for more drinks. I placed a hand over my glass to signal the steward my intentions to pass on more alcohol.

Our salad plates arrived, heaped with oily greens, avocado, and shrimp with freshly made mayonnaise. I launched into mine with a passion only surpassed by my passion for dessert.

"Oh, this is lovely," said Stella, eyeing her plate. "Will you be having only this for your dinner, Renata? I understand older women have to watch their weight."

Renata looked up with a stony face. She rose from her chair gracefully, picked up her plate, and turned. "Roberts, will you send the rest of my dinner to my suite, please?"

With that, she walked to the other side of the table and

dumped her plate of salad on Stella's head!

"You filthy cow!" yelled Stella.

I watched in astonishment as oily lettuce leaves fell to her bare shoulders. A pool of shrimp and mayonnaise slid down her hair. A few crustaceans landed in her cleavage and held firm there.

A hush fell over the room. Renata discarded her plate on the table next to us, with a hundred shocked diners looking on. A few started to clap. She strutted to the double doors of the dining room, head held high. Low-class cuss words pertaining to her carnal habits and parentage escaped Stella and followed Renata out. Even I learned a few new ones that day.

Harry and Gray leapt up to help Stella clean herself off with their napkins. I noticed Tony observing the actress with a frown. Gay and irreverent as he might seem, Tony held decorum in great regard. Women cussing like gutter wenches did not go down well with him.

Only Roy seemed happy with the whole scene. In fact, I would say he was gleeful. "I think this calls for more drinks," he said, snapping his fingers for the bar staff.

That was too much for Stella. She gave a dramatic sob and grasped onto Harry for help to stand. Mayonnaise clung to her skimpy top. Avocado pieces slid to the floor, and there was a cherry tomato lodged in her right earring. Harry and Gray accompanied her out of the room, flanking her on either side so she was partially hidden from view. Stella may have loved an audience, but no woman wants to be seen in such a state.

I wondered what to do. Tony, Roy, and I remained at the table. I looked at Tony for guidance. He shrugged and said, "We sure are getting our money's worth of entertainment at this table." Then he looked down and poked his fork into a shrimp on his plate.

At a loss for words, I did the same.

CHAPTER 7

ROBERTS HAS EXEMPLARY manners. He cleared the abandoned place settings as unobtrusively as possible, and silently replaced them. I could see he was itching to remove Stella's chair for cleaning but controlled himself. That would be done later, when all the diners had departed. He satisfied himself with putting a fresh linen cloth over the seat cushion.

Tony continued to drink hard. It made me sad, but I had to remind myself that I wasn't his keeper.

I was halfway through the salad course before noticing another shadow.

"Excuse me," said a male voice new to me. "I do believe we've met before. It's Anderson, isn't it?"

Tony looked up from his plate, stared, and leapt to his feet. "Leggy! Good Lord, it's Leggy Leggatt! By all that's wonderful!" I followed his eyes to the other man, as he thrust out a hand. "What brings you here?"

The new man took his hand and smiled easily. "I believe they've assigned me to this table."

Tony whacked him on the shoulder. "I mean where have you been hiding, old boy. Heard you were down in Ireland.

Didn't see you get on the ship. Afflicted with the ol' sea fever, were you?"

He nodded but didn't explain. "May I join you?"

"Yes, yes," said Tony. He pointed to the chair next to him.

I stared down the table at the newcomer. He had a pleasant visage, but the kind of face that would blend into a crowd. As a matter of fact, the same could be said of his entire appearance. Medium-brown hair, average features, a bit above average height. Good build, as far as I could tell. No fancy dress costume for this man. His evening clothes were well-cut but designed not to stand out. Quite a contrast to our Roy.

Tony made introductions all around. His voice was a bit sloppy with drink, but it didn't take long with only the three of us left at the table.

"You've come at a peculiar time," said Roy. "We lost two of the ladies in a pitched battle."

I choked on lettuce, which started a coughing fit. The distinguished newcomer looked over at me. "You didn't partake, Lady Revelstoke? Or shall I say, Cleopatra?"

Tony snorted out loud. Damnation, the new man was testing me.

I recovered myself and smiled. "I never let anything come between me and a good meal, Mr. Leggatt."

That got a smile, at least.

It got more from Roy. "Well returned, Lady Revelstoke! Point to you."

I gave him a cheery grin.

"Lovely costume, my lady," said Mr. Leggatt. His eyes showed respectful appreciation.

"Thank you," I said, raising my glass to him. "I have much admiration for the great Egyptian queen and hope she would approve of me as well."

He raised an eyebrow. "You intrigue me. Explain."

Putting me on the spot, was he? This was fun. "Our Ptolemy queen was extremely well-educated. I have endeavoured to follow her lead."

"Interesting. And do you also know five languages?" he said.

"Only four," I replied in a sad tone. "English, French, Italian, and a soupçon of Latin. Unless you consider music to be a language unto itself."

"Most certainly." He smiled warmly at me. "T'is that of love."

I laughed, delighted. Tony looked up, eyes a little unfocussed. "What does he mean?" said Roy.

Mr. Leggatt chuckled. Our eyes met across the table.

"It has been said that music is the language of love," I explained to everyone, playfully. "That would make it five languages I have mastered." Ha! The double entendre was rather delicious. I had no idea if the others would ken to it. Tony appeared dazed.

"Do you play an instrument, my lady?"

Another test. I was in good form today, luckily. "With enthusiasm, Mr. Leggatt. Although being a widow, I am rather out of practice."

"Don't see what the deuce that has to do with it," Roy puzzled. "I know you have to wear black for a time, but aren't widows allowed to play music?"

"Only on Sundays." Mr. Leggatt was all innocence.

"Well, fancy that," said Roy, raising his glass for a swig.

I decided it was the perfect time to have another coughing fit.

What a pleasant surprise this had been. Simon Leggatt looked harmless enough, but I could see it was all a disguise. The man was exceedingly quick; I would have to be on my guard.

Our next course arrived, and I spent the next ten minutes busying myself with doing the chef proud.

Our new tablemate was engaged in conversation with Roy, and I was curious to learn more about him. I took the opportunity, turning to Tony. "Tell me about your friend."

"Leggy?" He pulled himself out of his stupor. "Full name Simon Leggatt. Decent bloke. Cousin of the Viscount of Shropshire and Shrewsbury, with an estate in the back of beyond. Knew him at Eton. Was a year ahead of me, and a damned fine cricketer." He turned from looking at our newcomer to face me. "Don't know what he was doing in Ireland. But Shropshire is border country with Wales, so maybe Leggy has interests there."

I wondered if my Johnny had known him. He had boarded at Eton too, and Lord knows, public school ties were strong and seemed to exist forever. Or plague one forever, depending on your personal experience there. But Tony was still talking, and I should be paying attention to him instead of running off with my own thoughts.

"Did some sort of derring-do in the war, behind the lines. Works for Ol' Stiffy now."

Ol' Stiffy?? Who was that?

"— attached to some new department, very hush hush."

"And he's going to Washington, I believe?" I pushed hair behind my ears.

Tony nodded. "No doubt attached to the embassy. Nothing to keep him at home. Doesn't inherit a title, and his wife and child died in the flu epidemic, poor fellow."

Poor fellow, indeed. Would the sorrow of the last decade ever end?

"JOIN ME FOR a brandy in the smoking lounge?" Roy said to Tony, after coffee was served. "My treat. You too, Leggatt."

"Jolly good of you," said Tony, enthusiastically.

"Nonsense, old chap. I'm sure Renata won't mind being left alone for an hour or two."

I wasn't so sure about that. Men rarely knew what women liked. So often, husbands assumed it would be exactly what *they* wanted. I was reminded of a wonderful quote from the novel *Sense and Sensibility*. How did Jane Austen put it, exactly? *One half of the world cannot understand the pleasures of the other.*

In a way, I was pleased. Anything that kept Tony away from the gambling tables was good in my opinion, even if temporary.

For a moment, it appeared Roy was embarrassed. Since our shimmering bird had already flown the coop, I was the only one left out of the invitation.

I pushed back from the table to stand up. "Well, chaps, it's been a long day. I'm ready to retire, so will leave you men to it." I reached around for my wrap, but realized I'd forgotten to bring one.

Roy rose from the table and came to pull out my chair. Tony threw back the end of the drink he was consuming and stood up. I felt rather than saw Simon Leggatt appear at my side. Interesting man. I was curious to know more about him.

No fawning audience for us, I was relieved to see. Frankly, I would hate to be gawked at like film stars seem to enjoy. We joined the other first-class passengers leaving the dining room at the same time and took turns exiting through the double doors.

THERE IS SOMETHING soothing about watching water at night. Hearing the lap of waves against the side of the ship. I found my way to the rail and stood there, in deep thought.

Was there anything I *could* do next, even? Meg was missing. That was the full extent of the mystery. Others seemed to think she was in hiding somewhere, probably with a man. I didn't hold that view, but it wasn't my place to force the authorities to investigate further. That was up to her relatives.

I felt helpless and a trifle despondent. Poor Meg. I feared the worst for her and longed to be able to do something.

That thought left me with an uncomfortable feeling about my own motivation. Did I actually want bad things to happen, just so I could investigate them? Was I really that shallow, or so desperate for occupation?

Yes, I enjoyed the intellectual challenge of solving a mystery. I had been able to exercise that skill on our previous voyage across the Atlantic and had even taken risks with my own life in order to unmask a murderer. That had been satisfying and thrilling, in a way that had me craving more adventures. But in no way did I want to benefit from the misfortune of others.

Why was I so quick to leap into investigations that did not benefit me personally, and even put me at risk?

Deep down, I think it was a desire for order that I craved. Too many years during the war and immediately after were chaotic and frantic, with no clear path forward. Maybe that was what I sought to do, in some small way. Bring order to chaos. I hoped so.

The rolling sea looked almost black at this time of night, and kept me mesmerized. Right now, the breeze was warm and humid; in an odd way, it seemed to welcome me. Hard to imagine that we faced heavy weather in the next day or two.

Only the brightest stars shone tonight through the light cloud cover, and the moon was a mere crescent. When the night is dark, and the waves are mild, I love to be on deck. By myself. I stared over the railing. There's something about the solid wake created by the ship that comforts me. It speaks of strength and endurance. Alone, I can think upon the past without having to apologize.

Yes, that word. *Apologize.* Here's the surprise about being a widow. People are very kind for the first three months. Truly, their hearts are in the right place. They want to make you feel better. But eventually, somewhere between months three and six, I found even close friends get tired of hearing about your loved one. They want you to move on, get past it. They coax you to do what you aren't ready to do, all very well-meaning. But you can barely put one foot in front of the other, let alone go any distance. And worse, you feel guilty for not meeting their expectations.

So, you make the monumental effort to hide your grief, and save it for times like this, when you are alone.

Four years had passed since Johnny died. Time had helped. I had to admit things were getting better. I no longer wanted to pitch myself over the railing. People seemed to enjoy my company again. When home, I could have eaten out every night, so forthcoming were the invitations.

The clouds had thickened to cover the moon and stars now, such that I couldn't see the waves anymore. Still, I could hear them as they churned on and on, like a briny lullaby. Life was better this year than last. But was it as good as before? Could it ever be? The TB that killed Johnny also took the last of my innocence. The war had shattered the first of that, and now, simply put, I didn't trust the future.

But I could trust that the sea would go on. The great ships would steam across it into the next millennia, as they had done for decades and centuries before. The night sky would continue to harbour diamonds behind clouds, even after my life was over. Some things, I concluded, you could count on.

And there were things to be grateful for. Graham West, my childhood friend, was back in my life and heart. I might not trust the future, but I'd trust him to the ends of the earth.

The breeze had turned cooler now, the chill starting to reach my bones. The sea would be cold, I remembered.

"There you are," said a familiar voice behind me. "Silly goose. Forgot your wrap." I felt Elf reach up to spread the shawl across my shoulders. It was such a sweet gesture. I expected she hadn't bothered with a wrap of her own. Dear Elf — another person I was grateful for.

We stood side by side in silence for a few moments.

"Do you think Meg is out there?" I asked in a voice hardly my own.

"We'll talk it through in the morning." Elf gave my arm a tug. "It's awful late. Come to bed, Luce."

CHAPTER 8

DAY THREE AT SEA

I AWOKE EARLY the next morning. Dawn coloured the sky a pretty orange-pink. Elf was still sound asleep, so I dressed quietly in casual clothes and left the cabin.

It may sound childish, but I like to greet the sea at morning and night when I can. Early morning is my very favourite time of day on deck as I usually have it to myself.

Not today, however. To my surprise, Stella was standing at the railing looking out to sea, blond hair blowing in the wind. Her face was in such a frown that I nearly turned away, hoping she hadn't seen me.

No such luck. She turned at the waist, recognized me, and signalled with her hand. "Oh, it's you. Come join me. I needed to feel the wind. I'm in such a mood. What do they call it when you're deep in dark thoughts — pen, pen something?"

"Pensive?" I offered, joining her at the rail.

"That's it," she said. Her grey-blue eyes held mine, and I saw depths there I hadn't quite imagined before. Stella might not be scholarly, but I would bet the house she was shrewd.

"What do you think of our diva?" she asked me.

"Renata?" I was taken by surprise. I might have expected such a question from an American, but usually the Brits are not so direct. More importantly, I had no idea what to answer. "I haven't known her for long. Just a day."

"Lucky you," she said. She turned her gaze back to the sea. "I've known her since the Armistice, practically. Not long after, anyway. I finally got a break in the West End as her understudy. You can't imagine how excited I was! Working with the great Renata Harwood. Studying how she did it, basking in the reflected glory. Oh, I'd worked hard for the chance to get there, you'd better believe that. Did some things maybe I wouldn't confess to now, but you know how it is for a woman. You've got to take your chances when they come."

She paused, looking over at me.

"Women have the vote now," I said, smoothly. "I'm hoping it will change things for us."

I guess Stella took that statement for acceptance, or at least an indication that I didn't condemn her implied questionable behaviour. For she continued confiding in me.

"At first she was friendly, kind even, to the young gal who worshiped her." She barked a laugh. "Oh yes, I worshipped her, in those old days when she was still married to that baronet. All grand-lady-of-the-manor, benevolent to her court of admirers. I wasn't a threat to her in any way, as she saw it. But I found she could be bloody mean."

I tried to look as sympathetic as possible. This was new information, fresh from the horse's mouth, so to speak.

"It sounds like you used to be friends. What changed?" I was eager to keep the conversation going.

"Quite simply, Roy came into my life, and that changed

everything." Both hands gripped the railing fiercely. "Roy was different. He wasn't a boy, slavering all over me. He was a man who had seen the world, and that was ever so attractive to me. He would take charge, which was so different from the others. Roy could make you feel like you were the most precious thing on earth, and he was determined to protect you. No, *privileged* to protect you."

"I know that feeling," I said. "It can be the most seductive thing in the world." Johnny had made me feel that way. And now, Gray ...

"Yes!" she said eagerly. "You do understand! I thought you might. Well, Renata felt it too, and she wanted it. Wanted *him*. And set out to get him. Which was easy, because Renata usually got what she wanted, and expected to get it. I might have had a fighting chance because Roy really did care about me, I'd swear to it. Except Renata had the one thing I didn't."

"Let me guess." I decided to be brave. "Money?"

She grimaced. "You said it, sister." We both gazed out to sea. "The spoils of two previous marriages. I can understand it, of course. I came from nothing myself. Just didn't expect a man to be likewise motivated." There was a bitter edge to her voice.

"'It's just as easy to fall in love with a rich man as a poor one,' my gran used to say. Or woman."

"Isn't that the truth," Stella said. "Roy puts on a big act about being the colonial plantation owner, but I happen to know he's not quite what he seems. There's no money there. Or at least no money now. I'm not sure there ever was."

Now that was an interesting new tidbit of information. Did Roy's family actually own a plantation? Did they lose it? Or was he from quite a different background? Regardless, the man appeared to be putting on an act that was perilously close to mendacious.

"He can be so charming," Stella said wistfully.

"Most con men are," I muttered to myself. I'm not sure she heard me.

"Renata fell for his charm, all right. I knew in a minute she was going to steal him from me, and that I'd be helpless to do anything about it. All's fair, and all that."

All's fair in love and war. I finished the quote in my head.

Stella shrugged. I got the feeling she wasn't too cut up about it anymore. No question, she understood the type of man Roy was.

"And now she's going to Hollywood."

I detected some green in her voice.

"Which is really quite a turn. Renata, as a Hollywood ingenue? At her age? She's hardly Mary Pickford!"

I hadn't thought about that. Stella had a point.

"Of course, I can see her taking over Pola Negri roles." She laughed rather harshly at that. "She might pull off a *Good and Naughty*, or *Hotel Imperial*."

Pola Negri was a Hollywood film actress of Polish descent, and some repute, bordering on scandalous. As much as I was made uncomfortable by Stella's rather lurid pronouncement, I could see sense in it. Renata had a similar sultry look, and a singular success with *Salome*. There was speculation that — with sound coming — Pola's accent would not transfer to the new Hollywood movies.

"I wonder if she's happy." Stella turned around to face the ship and leaned back against the railing. "I don't think so."

This time, I didn't know what to say.

"I mean, something is wrong. I can't put my finger on it, but something is just wrong with her."

"What do you mean, wrong?" I asked.

"Not right. I don't know how to put it exactly. But she used to spar with me endlessly. Used to give it back with gusto and play the scene. She adored it, I would swear. We both did. The salad trick was in character, but what about all the rest?"

"I'm not quite sure what you mean."

Stella sighed in frustration. "I'm not sure what I mean, either. Just something is different. At dinner last night ... I kept waiting for her to throw a lovely tantrum, scream and yell. Something we could both get our chops into — but she just sat there, all quiet."

I nearly smiled. The shrimp salad departure wasn't dramatic enough, apparently.

"Perhaps she's mellowed," I suggested. "She's older. You're older. Maybe she's actually content with her life, and that's changed her."

"Something's changed her, that's for sure," Stella grumbled. She pushed back from the railing. "Ignore me. I'm not sure I can express what I'm feeling. But it occurs to me ..."

"Yes?"

She paused, with a final look back. "This might not make any sense to you, and I may be crazy, but it feels like we're all in a giant stage play. And I don't know my part."

WE PARTED, AND I hurried back to the cabin. Ideas had been swimming around in my head for a while, and I wanted to share them.

Elf was sitting up in bed now, rubbing her eyes.

"Hey, I've got this plan," I said, closing the door behind me. Elf looked over, with a familiar frown that spoke of scepticism. "Don't look like that," I scolded. "I think you'll like this one."

"Better than the hedgehog and bedpan incident? Or the vicar and the kumquat jam?"

I breathed in deep. "Okay, so there've been a few mishaps. How was I to know the dog hadn't been neutered? But we did find that ruby necklace Lady Mary thought was stolen. And Sir Archibald will be forever grateful."

"Silly bugger, giving his fancy lady the family jewels," Elf muttered. "In more ways than one," she added with a snicker.

I sat down on the edge of the bed. "Here's what I'm thinking." And I told her.

"Could work," she admitted.

"You're in?"

"Like a bull on a cow," she said without guile.

Two off-colour references in three sentences. Could be a record. I was going to have to do something about her metaphors.

"If I get the numbers, you can get us keys?"

"Piece of cake," she said. "I got connections. Leave it to me."

I grabbed a banana from the fruit basket for breakfast and waited. When Elf says she can do something, I know it will be done. Some way or other, perhaps best not to ask how. Especially since she went into the water closet and came out a few minutes later wearing war paint. My late husband would say it wasn't an improvement.

She waved at the door. "See you after lunch."

Meanwhile, I set about my mission. Graham West had told me he would be in a meeting with the other senior officers at noon. Timing would be tight, but with any luck, that might leave the coast clear.

I spent a little time getting ready. It wasn't often I had the stateroom to myself, and to be honest, I enjoyed the occasional solitude.

I'd rushed my ablutions this morning, eager to greet the sea air. Now, I took a little more time. I'd go from there to the dining room directly after, for lunch, so this required a judicious use of cosmetics. Elf wasn't here to help me, so I struggled with eyeliner and mascara, only poking myself in the eye once. Red lipstick today. It was definitely a red lipstick day.

The closet beckoned enticingly. Usually, Elf ruled the wardrobe. It was fun to choose my own ensemble without any input. Blue was the colour for today. Blue, the colour of the morning sea. I changed from my earlier day dress into something a little more flattering.

I went to my lingerie drawer and took from it a small velvet case. I grabbed a large brocade bag to take with me, stuffed a silk wrap into it along with the case, and said a little prayer that his office would be empty.

Yes, this was not exactly on the level. I shouldn't be breaking into the purser's office. And while it was stretching things a bit to say I owned the office — I did own the whole ship, after all — I tried to console myself that I was acting in the public good.

I left the cabin and joined other first-class passengers making their way toward the common rooms. I tried to look in a hurry, to avoid being waylaid by others looking for conversation.

As I turned to enter the quiet corridor in question, Gray was just closing the office door behind him.

Rats! Too late to turn around. He saw me and burst into a smile.

"You caught me on the way to a meeting," he said, moving forward.

"Oh dear," I responded, stopping a few feet from him. We had agreed not to make our relationship public, so I didn't lean in for a desired hug.

"Anything important?" Keys dangled from one hand, his naval hat from the other.

My Lord, he looked good. I took in a gulp of air. *In for a penny, in for a pound,* I said to myself.

"I just wondered if you've given any more thought to checking those empty cabins for our ... missing passenger," I said softly.

Something in his expression changed. "Ah. The cabins. I'm not sure ...." I saw his eyes cloud for a moment and then clear, as if he had made a decision. "I should check the ledger on my desk, but I don't have time now. Perhaps later." He looked off down the corridor.

"Perhaps later," I said in return.

"Must run," he said. "You look beautiful today, by the way." And with a quick smile, he strode off still holding the keys.

And without locking the office door.

Wonderful man, I thought to myself. I wouldn't need the lock picks after all. Gray was sharp, and once again, had proved himself to be on my side.

He turned the corner. I watched him until he was out of sight, then looked both ways to ensure privacy before opening the office door and scooting inside.

I made a point of locking the door before turning around.

For a brief, blissful moment, I was captured by the very male smell of the place — sweet pipe tobacco and that particular scent I associated with him ... hard to describe but something akin to fresh hay and musk. Funny, how odours are captured in our memories.

I shook myself free and embarked on my task.

Gray's office was quite modern in that clean, nautical way. Filing cabinets framed either side of a large wooden desk, with just enough room to walk around on either side. A large ship's clock and barometer shared space with a picture of the King on the far wall.

I focussed my efforts on the desk.

Gray was neat, but not obsessive. His in-tray was full to overflowing, but the surface of the desk contained just a pen set and a few bound ledgers. I didn't have to search far to find the one I was after.

All pursers need to know which party is in which cabin, and where their trunks are stored. I flipped through pages to ensure this register was the one I wanted. Yes, everything was in order of cabin number, with the surname of the occupants opposite. To be honest, I found myself admiring the neat, detailed work that went into ensuring that all entries — there were thousands — were easily read. This painstaking work had to be done over again for every crossing, I marvelled. And it had to be right.

I had been smart to bring the large brocade bag. In went the ledger, hidden from view. With any luck, I'd have it back to Gray before he even noticed it was gone. Or before anyone else noticed, more importantly.

I was to meet Elf after our midday meal, and checking the clock on the wall, it seemed best I should go straight to the dining room without making any stops on the way.

I wandered down to lunch, a tad preoccupied, and didn't notice Tony when he came up beside me. I gasped when he took my arm.

"I've been waiting for you," he said. We continued down the corridor, smiling and nodding to people who passed us.

"That sounds promising," I replied with a smile. Good lord! Elf's lewd inferences must be washing off on me.

Tony perked right up. "Wanted to explain about the Renata Harwood thing. Long time ago, really, when I was a green lad back from the front on leave. Needed escape from the squalor in the trenches ... you know how it was. She was young then ... lively, fun. Pretty thing. Not the overly madeup woman you see today. She's changed a lot." *And not for the good* were the unspoken words I heard.

"We all change in a decade," I said smoothly.

"Too right. Why do women use so much makeup? Hadn't seen her in years until yesterday. Anyhoo, wouldn't want you to think it was important. High spirits and all that, really. It was just a bit of fun."

I'm sure Renata would be pleased to hear she had been placed in the "just a bit of fun" category. Every woman likes that.

"You obviously parted on good terms," I said archly.

"Oh yes," he said, obviously thinking this had gone well. "By the time Monty bought it, she had moved on to serious money and security."

I didn't need to ask what that meant.

As we walked through the double doors to the dining room, I mused at the ignorance of men who saw themselves as sophisticated. Did they really think talking about another woman as "just a bit of fun" would make them seem more desirable in our eyes?

Poor Tony. He really was in earnest. I knew his motive was to assure me that his heart wasn't currently taken by another. But what a laughable way to go about it. Men and women really must think differently on the whole matter of love and lust, I decided. Why on earth would Tony think "just a bit of fun" without attachment would be more acceptable to me than a true love affair?

I shook my head silently as he escorted me over to our table.

It was lunchtime, not dinner, but the dining room looked just as opulent as ever. Chandeliers still sparkled, the china was as delicate, and crystal glasses gleamed under the reflected light. Tonight, we would have the added glory of women wearing their finest frocks and jewels. But even now, the magnificence took your breath away.

I understood the motivation, of course. Train travel may have been around since the middle of the last century, but these immense ocean-going liners were still a thing of awe and seen as something of an engineering marvel. As such, instead of emulating train travel, they strived to recreate the pomp and luxury of the grand hotels in London and Europe.

The Empire line was no exception. One difference from the others: Your dining experience here was courtesy of some of the best chefs in Europe. This was not by chance. What can I say? Food is important to me.

My companions today were limited to men. Lord Harry, Simon Leggatt, Tony, and Roy made our table, with Stella nowhere to be seen.

"Renata doesn't eat lunch," Roy said to explain her absence.

"I only had a banana for breakfast, so I can eat hers as well as mine," I replied.

Someone guffawed.

"What is it with you women and breakfast? Aren't you hungry?"

Tony answered for me. "It's a peculiar custom of the British upper classes. Married women are expected to have a bit of a lie in, particularly at country house parties."

I explained further. "He means they breakfast in their bedrooms. Unmarried women are expected to show up in the dining room, for some reason. I suppose so they don't appear lazy to possible suitors. I don't know who started it. There doesn't seem to be an expected norm for widows, thank goodness."

"Which means you could have a tray in your bedroom *and* join us for a full English here!" Lord Harry could be jovial when he wanted to.

I grinned at him. "That would suit my appetite just fine."

Our food arrived, and we all got busy.

CHAPTER 9

"WONDER WHERE STELLA got to?" Tony looked over his shoulder at the tables behind us. "Not like her to miss a meal."

"Or a chance to appear before her adoring public," muttered Roy. "I'm not sure she was actually assigned to this table."

He was right, of course. We'd had an empty chair last night due to Meg's absence. I expect Stella had simply taken advantage of that.

"Are you ready to depart?" Roy looked at me, but his next sentence addressed the others. "Might take a moment in the smoking room, myself."

I rose with a smile. My tummy was full, and I was happy. No need for tobacco or other vices. Once again, I marvelled at how having Elf in my life contributed to my contentment. She had the ability to appreciate simple things more than anyone I knew. A full meal … a soft bed at night. Thanks to her, I'd learned to take pleasure from small things.

The other men pushed to their feet, and we trailed out the double doors in a loose line.

No need to speculate where Stella had disappeared to anymore. She was standing in the passageway with a small throng about her. So busy was she, signing autographs, that she didn't see us at first, and then some sixth sense must have alerted her, for her head tipped up. She called out "Roy!" her face alight.

She waved a hand, and the crowd seemed to part for her like she was Moses at the Red Sea. The smile on her face beamed as she rushed toward us. I'm saying *us*, but she hardly noticed me.

"You harlot!"

The voice came from behind us. In shocked silence, everyone in the passageway seemed to turn at once.

A middle-aged woman stood there, dowdy in her brown suit, with greying hair. Her face was twisted into a scowl and hate drilled from her eyes.

"I beg your pardon?" said Roy.

The woman raised an arm and pointed directly at Stella. "*She* is a harlot from hell. Seduces good men and then discards them like broken toys. Destroyed my poor Ethan, she did. Made him a slave to her, then tore up his heart. Nothing but a dirty whore, you are! Burn in hell, you will!" Her voice shook with fury.

The woman stepped forward and Simon grabbed her arm before she could strike Stella. I saw Stella stumble back and almost lose her footing. Her eyes looked horrified. No, not horrified — terrified.

"It wasn't my fault," she uttered, in a high-pitched whine. "I didn't know he would do himself in. How could I?"

"Fought for his country, he did. Survived the war to be destroyed by you! The devil's spawn! Curse you to hell!"

The collective hush in the corridor turned quickly to gasps. Never had I seen so many faces turn from adoration to outright rejection.

Simon was having to use all his strength to hold the older woman back. The hate that streamed from her mouth was almost too much to hear.

"Tony, help me take Stella away from here," Roy ordered through gritted teeth.

Goodness, I'd forgotten about Tony. He had been standing behind me, quietly observing the scene. No doubt he was thinking the same thing I was. *So many mothers had lost sons in the war that to lose one in this way was unthinkable. Simply because of the ego and callousness of a wanton woman.*

At Roy's command, Tony stepped forward and silently took Stella's other arm. Together, they guided her around behind me and down the corridor as fast as possible. The older woman struggled to escape Simon's grasp, hurling abuse until Stella was out of sight. Then she broke, bursting into tears. What Simon did then was surprising. He held her against his chest, a kind and soothing gesture. She sobbed there for some minutes as the crowd dispersed. The drama had been titillating, but now people seemed almost embarrassed to have witnessed this complete breakdown of a common woman.

"Let's have some tea," I said to Simon. "That's what we need. Hot tea with plenty of sugar." I nodded to Simon to lead the lady into the library lounge, where I knew we could find a quiet table with chairs.

I rushed ahead of them, searching. Away behind a potted tree, I found such a place. I waved Simon over, where he gently deposited our guest in the chair facing the wall. That was thoughtful of him. She wouldn't have to face others peering in the doorway.

"Mr. Leggatt, can you see to tea?" I signalled for him to seek out a steward.

Simon nodded and left us alone, which was my plan. It gave me a chance to talk woman to woman. I faced her with sympathetic eyes, while she looked up at me in misery.

"My husband was gassed in the war and died of it," I told her. "I know what it's like to lose someone you love dearly. Tell me about your son. I have a young son of my own."

She had found her handkerchief in her sleeve and used it. Then she looked up at me with weary light grey eyes. I could see she appreciated my asking. One thing I do know is, we need to talk about those we lose.

"You're very kind," she said. She blew her nose once more, then took a couple of deep breaths. "Ethan was always a good boy. Quiet but hard-working and strong-armed. Helped his dad in the business until he went to war. That changed him; oh, how it changed him."

I nodded sympathetically. *It changed all of us*, I wanted to say. She looked down at the handkerchief bunched in her hand. I thought perhaps she was struggling to find a dry spot, so I reached into my small reticule and handed her one of my own. She nodded gratefully.

"Didn't want no part of town life after that. Dorset wasn't good enough for him. Fascinated with the nightlife in London, he was. Got a job in a department store there, worked his way up to floor manager, and spent every cent he made going to theatres and nightspots. Started hanging about with the wrong people," she sniffed.

"And that's where he met Stella," I said. It was a common enough story. Young men from good families craving escape from the memories of war. Getting entangled with good-time girls on the lookout for an easier life.

I could see both sides. Even though times were changing, there wasn't much that women could do to better their positions except through men. A young woman might look upon a decent young man with prospects as someone who could provide for her either as his wife or, for a shorter time, his mistress.

The trouble came when she switched her attentions to someone with even better prospects. And that is what I expect had happened here. Our Stella went after a bigger fish.

Poor naive Ethan. It wasn't fair to trifle with the hearts of war veterans who had given so much ...

Simon arrived with tea and biscuits. I was surprised to see that he had waited and brought the tray himself. Now there was an observant man. He had thought to give us a few minutes by ourselves, and then eliminated the need for Ethan's mother to face a steward with her tears.

Yes, I thought of her as Ethan's mother. For I knew that you are still a mother in your own mind and heart, even if your child has passed. Once a mother, always a mother.

I could relate; I felt that way about being a wife.

"I just don't know how to go on. Ethan was our only son. You lost your husband young," she said, looking up. "How do you go on after that?"

I sat still a moment. Then I reached deep inside for the truth. "I think — for the first while — it's like walking through a stage play. You put one unsteady foot in front of the other just to get through every activity of every day. It was like that for me, the first year. In truth, it felt like I had been shot into space and was spinning out there, all by myself."

She stared at me, finally nodding.

I moved on. "Then, I think for women, you have to find something to care about. Someone who needs you. I had my son. You have your husband. Someone who would be devastated if you ceased to exist. That keeps you going until the worst of the grief passes. It never goes away entirely, of course."

I looked over to Simon who had been quiet while pouring out tea.

"It helps to know we're not alone. Mr. Leggatt lost his wife and child to the flu."

"Good heavens!" said Ethan's mother.

"How did *you* manage to get through it, Simon?" Oh dear — this was the first time I had addressed him using his first name. I wondered if he would notice. This was also too personal a question for people of our short acquaintance to ask, but somehow, I didn't think he would mind.

He thought for a moment, and then responded simply. "As you said. One foot in front of the other. And then, finding a purpose. I threw myself into service of King and country."

There were a few quiet moments as we sipped tea together. Finally, I said, "Life is hard, isn't it? Even if you have enough to eat and a roof over your head, life is hard." And I suppose it's all about perspective. If you've known what it's like to go without enough food or a place to sleep, like my dear Elf experienced ... well, your viewpoint on hardship might be different.

I once knew a titled lady who said she'd rather starve than do without flowers on her table. Elf had sniffed, and told me, *there was a woman who had never been hungry.*

Simon added, "We could go through life without loving people. But what a barren life it would be."

"Sometimes I think it would be easier than losing them," said Ethan's mother.

I reached for her hand and held it.

CONVERSATION HAD PETERED out as we all contemplated the ones we had loved and lost. Sometimes shared grief can help, even if the grief is for different people. Just knowing that another is going through something similar can be comforting. They understand, where others don't.

After we finished tea, Simon offered to walk Ethan's mother back to her cabin in second class. She seemed to regain her composure, and I put it down to Simon. He had a rare gift for spreading calm.

I let them leave first and sat in quiet reflection for a few moments. So much had happened. There was a lot to think about, but the day was getting on. Time to return to the cabin for my rendezvous with Elf. We had a job to do.

AS PROMISED, ELF was waiting for me in the cabin when I returned from lunch. Her wry smile told me we were in business.

"Got the goods," she said.

"Well done, Elf! For how long?"

She wrinkled her nose. "An hour, give or take. You got the numbers?"

I nodded.

"Well, ain't we a pair of Mata Haris." She followed with what passed as a snigger. I could feel myself blush. No question how she had acquired her ill-gotten gains.

"Better make haste," I said. "Oh, just a minute. Got an idea." I gazed around the room. "Have you seen my sketchbook?"

"In here." She leapt to attention and opened the small trunk we had kept in the cabin. "One pencil enough?"

I nodded and held open the brocade bag I had been carrying. "Put them in here, and let's scram." Good Lord, I was picking up Elf's slang.

We were on our way to the second-class deck, as the ledger had indicated there were no vacant cabins in first.

"The first unoccupied cabin on this list is two forty-five," I said to Elf.

"Uh, nope," she responded.

Her response made me slow my pace.

"What do you mean, no?" I turned and gave her the full eye treatment.

She fiddled with her hands. "Don't need to go there. I already checked that one out."

"Eellllllffff?" I drew out all three letters.

She shrugged. "It's kind of a meeting place for me an' —"

"Okay! No need to elaborate." I threw up my hands and resumed full speed. Good grief. How embarrassing. Good thing she was with me on this immediate quest, because otherwise I might have walked in on Elf and her steward friend's love nest.

She walked quietly beside me, like the picture of virtue. Rather clever of the two of them to seek out an empty cabin, I had to admit. *Wonder if it was her idea?* His keys would open it, not that they needed keys. Elf was proficient with most entry systems, given enough time.

But time is of the essence when you're breaking into somewhere in broad daylight as we were today. I was grateful she had managed to lift the keys.

"This should work," I said, taking the stairs down. "I've devised a cover story. You're my maid —"

"I *am* your maid," she interrupted.

"Shush! You're my maid, and your snoring is driving me crazy, so I'm checking out vacant second-class cabins to move you to so I can get some sleep at night."

"Good one," she said. "Even I'd buy that. Do I really snore?"
"Why don't you ask your steward friend?" I said wickedly.
She just harrumphed.
One up for me.

CHAPTER 10

FIRST CABIN

CABIN NUMBER 288 was further down the corridor, on the other side of the hall. I let Elf work the lock as I stood guard. Like magic, she had us inside before anyone who happened upon us would question what we were doing.

Elf scampered in first. I closed the door firmly behind me and stood still for a look around.

There wasn't much elbow room. I'd been used to the spaciousness of first class and was a little chagrined to realize I hadn't even checked out how the other passengers lived. The decor was attractive. Brown and cream soft furnishings and linens graced the room. The walls were attractively panelled in wood, but the whole effect was not nearly as extravagant as the first-class cabins.

"Looks just like two forty-five," said Elf, nonchalantly. "'Cept the bed's made."

I gave her a stern look.

The bed was indeed made up. Nothing sat on the top of the single set of drawers. There were no shoes on the floor, and no sign of occupation. I pulled open the wardrobe door.

"Holy Toledo!" said Elf.

I was a bit shocked by her reference. Elf had never been to Toledo. But I understood her excitement. This was a closet with no clothes. Instead, bottles and bottles of booze littered the floor of the wardrobe. Gin, rum, whisky, vodka, even wine and champagne — all manner of bottles in all stages of fullness.

"Somebody's hiding a stash," I said.

"Probably one of the staff," said Elf. "Sneaking bottles from the bars."

"More likely the dining room," I countered. "Bottles get opened at tables and not necessarily finished. I wonder if it's one person or the whole dining staff?"

"One person," Elf said confidently. "Else I'd have heard about it."

This time I rolled my eyes. Probably, I should be upset about that. It was my ship after all, and this was a form of theft. Still, I had to marvel at the ingenuity.

"Let's go. Meg can't be here. No one's living in this cabin," I said, turning toward the door.

"Wouldn't mind giving it a try," she said, still poking around the wardrobe. "You could book this one for me —"

"ELF!" I grabbed her arm and steered her around, then out the door in front of me.

Only one older man was coming down the corridor. He looked like clergy, so I gave him a big smile as we passed him.

"Ladies," he said.

I expect he was hard of hearing. Because it was patently obvious that a funny sound of glass on glass travelled down the hall with Elf. Silently, I cursed myself for a fool. I should have expected it.

"Elf, you're clanging." That maid uniform had deep pockets.

"Sorry," she said.

No doubt, there were at least two fewer mickey bottles left in the cabin.

SECOND CABIN

THE SECOND CABIN, 334, was on the same level, across the main hall. As we made our way toward it, two elderly women nodded to us as they passed in the corridor and I could hear one exclaim to her friend about my frock, in a voice that suggested some deafness.

This intrepid adventure into housebreaking (cabinbreaking?) was a risk, of course. Passengers on this deck might be curious as to why they hadn't seen me in this corridor before. But we had our cover story, if necessary.

"Here it is," I announced to Elf when we'd reached the cabin.

I played watchman as she flipped through keys. In just a few seconds, she had the door unlocked. Elf pushed it open and stalked in, booze bottles clanging in her pockets. I moved in after her, closing the door behind me.

At first glance, this cabin seemed similar in size and design to the other — even to the same colour scheme. It had one porthole, unlike my more spacious suite with two. But something was sorely amiss. I hardly had time to turn around before my nose curled in revulsion.

"What's that smell?" I said aloud.

"ACK!" she whooped. "AAA aaaa aaa aaa ..."

What? Elf was acting very peculiar. She seemed to be jumping up and down, unable to speak real words. I watched her, my mouth open, as she leapt on a chair and pointed.

I followed the disjointed arm movements to the bed. Upon the bedspread sat three or four wicker baskets. A large square one lay sideways on the bed, lid unlatched and open. It appeared to be empty.

Something hissed from beside the bed.

"SNAKE!" she yelled. "RUN!"

I might have seen the spectral image of a biblical serpent on the floor, or it could have been my imagination. But when Elf says "Run!" I generally find it's a good idea to do exactly that.

I lost no time and was out the door first. There was a pause, a curse, and then Elf pounded out after me.

THIRD CABIN

WE WERE STILL moving fast when we got to the centre corridor. People were milling about, so I pulled Elf over to the staircase and pointed down. Not so many people hanging about in the darker, lower corridors, I reasoned.

"Slow down. Need to catch my breath," said Elf as we reached the bottom of the staircase. She leaned against the wall.

I stayed a few moments, then ventured out into the corridor and looked around. The halls seemed narrower here as well. I chided myself for not knowing more about the differences between shipboard class decors and amenities.

Elf came up to me.

"Did you close the door?" I asked her.

She nodded. "You know that snake followed you out. I had to wait for it."

I looked quickly behind me. Nothing, thank the Lord. "Did you see where it went?"

She shook her head.

"Oh dear. I'll have to tell Gray about that."

"Hate snakes. Nasty creepy crawlies." Elf actually shivered.

"They can hide anywhere. Only thing good about them is they eat rats. Did you see all the baskets on the bed? It wasn't the only critter there."

"Hopefully it was the only one that got out," I said. "You got a better look at it than I did. Any idea what kind it was?"

"A big green one?" she said helpfully.

I just moaned. What was it doing there? "Is it someone's pet?" I asked. "And what was in the other baskets?"

"Don't know. Don't wanna know," she said firmly.

Darn. No hope for it, I would have to tell Gray about this, for sure. Right after we searched the next cabin. So much for trying to keep our detecting a secret, or at least claiming it was harmless. I'd have to prepare for a lecture.

"What's next on the list?"

I took a look at the paper in my hands. "One twenty-eight," I said. "On this deck, I'm betting."

"Good. I don't wanna go back to the snake deck."

Oh lovely. We had a name for it now. Made me wonder what we were going to find on this lower deck. Elephants?

We passed one elderly couple leaving their cabin, nodded to them, and waited until they turned the corner. I guess we made a curious sight — one extremely well-dressed passenger walking with a maid in second class. Usually, second-class passengers didn't travel with maids. But we had a reasonable excuse if needed.

FOURTH CABIN

THE FOURTH CABIN, 128, was down a deck and way at the end of a long corridor, Perfect, if you were trying to hide from people. I had a good feeling about this one.

When I determined the coast was clear, Elf moved ahead of me to open the cabin door. As usual, she bolted in front of me without waiting. I have never been sure of her motivation for this. Most maids wait for their mistress to enter a room first. It could be that Elf was exhibiting some sort of instinct to protect me by meeting monsters — and snakes — head on before they could reach me. Or it could be that she had no maidly instincts or proclivities whatsoever, which seemed more likely, alas.

"Blimey," she said. "Think we hit pay dirt."

I pushed her slightly to slip through the entrance and pulled the door closed behind me.

It was a second-class cabin very much like the others, with the same wood panelling. It was empty of snakes, I was relieved to see. The double bed had been made up neatly and sported an identical brown and gold brocade bedspread to the ones in the first two cabins, but a colourful woven shawl had been carelessly tossed across it. I looked further around the room. A hook on the far wall next to the water closet door carried a woman's dressing gown in pearl satin. Bingo! My breath caught in my throat.

"Check the wardrobe," I urged. I sat on the bed and fingered the shawl. Wonderfully soft with a little bit of sheen ... probably a silk blend. Obviously expensive and probably treasured.

Elf swung open the mirrored door to reveal a single long evening gown in slate grey — not particularly glamorous but suitable for many occasions. Just the sort of thing I could imagine the sister of our film star wearing. Good quality, but no chance of upstaging the diva.

"Oh wow," I said. "Someone has been using this room. Meg and her lover?"

"Only a woman," said Elf, sounding disappointed. "No man's duds."

I got up to view and finger the gown. Shot silk, with underarm wrinkles that proved it had been worn at least once since steaming. "That would fit with the scenario," I explained. "Does your steward friend keep anything in the cabin you abscond to?"

She just grunted. Of course he didn't. He'd want to cover his tracks. Just like this one.

I walked back to the bed and sat down.

Elf closed the wardrobe doors with more care than usual. "Loverboy has his own cabin to cover his tracks."

I nearly laughed! She took the words right out of my mouth.

"Probably a married man, travelling alone." I stood up to take a gander at the water closet. No man's shaving case. The towels looked unused.

"This is his love nest." Elf nodded. "But where are they now?"

"Good question. Maybe at lunch? A private dining room?"

"In second class?" Elf was sceptical.

"Hmm … don't know." It didn't seem likely. "Maybe in his cabin. In any case, we shouldn't wait around here to see. I would hate to be caught."

"So, you're thinking …" She went to the bed and picked up the shawl.

"Exactly. It's pretty distinctive. Really rather beautiful, don't you think? We'll talk to Renata — or maybe Roy first, as he's not likely to throw a scene — and see if he recognizes this as Meg's." That would put my mind at ease.

Elf handed me the wrap, then turned around to grasp the door handle. "Let's vamoose."

Really, all these American movies she adored were beginning to corrupt her English.

"We'll try to find Roy. But first we should get those keys back to your steward friend. Are they in your pocket?"

She patted the side of her maid's costume. It really was a good costume. Maybe one day she'd even aspire to being one. A maid, that is.

My mind was racing. Roy first, or steward first? *No.* "Oh, who am I kidding, Elf. I can't keep this a secret. We have to tell him right away. I really don't want to be responsible for another death." Or two.

Elf nodded firmly. "You should let Gray know about the snake." As I have said, she was quick.

It really did worry me. Snakes were dangerous, and no one expected to encounter one on an ocean liner. "This is bad, Elf. Who knows where it could end up? Do you know anything about their habits?" We didn't get many snakes where I grew up, at least not poisonous ones.

"Don't know. Don't want to know." I could see her shiver. "Thought of something. You go first, as lookout."

I went past her and scanned the hall. "Elf, what are you doing?" It was more a hiss than a whisper.

"Just in case we want to go back," she said cryptically. I had no idea what she meant by that, and I had learned long ago not to ask questions where we could be overheard.

Seconds later, she joined me, and we continued down the corridor to the main hall.

And came smack face to face with George Eversleigh, rounding the corner.

I stopped in my tracks. It was the first time I'd been this close to him. The shock on my face must have alerted him, because — to be honest — I was surprised he remembered me.

"What are you doing here?" he demanded in a grumpy voice.

"Hello, Mr. Eversleigh," I said to alert Elf.

"This is second class. What are you doing here?" he repeated.

Elf froze beside me. I stood with my mouth open. Should we tell him?

It was then he noticed the bundle I was holding. "That's Meg's wrap! Where did you find it?"

He reached forward, pleading, and I let him pull it out of my hands. "I'd know it anywhere! I gave it to her." He gazed down at it in tearful shock.

It *was* Meg's shawl! Our sleuthing had come up with the goods. The clothes must be hers too, I reasoned. Maybe we could do this without involving Renata and Roy.

George raised his eyes to mine. His voice dropped to a whisper. "Tell me. Have you found her?"

I could hear the fear in his voice. Did he think we had found her corpse? That was too much for me to bear. I couldn't have him thinking that. "I'm sorry. We haven't found her yet, but it looks promising. I found this in a cabin in second class that was supposed to be empty."

That energized him. "I was right! The bastard hid her away in some cabin. Show me!" His voice became more animated, and with people milling about, I was wary of attracting attention. I made a sudden decision.

"Of course," I said. "Come with me. It's down here."

Elf scooted ahead of us, stopped at cabin 128, and pretended to unlock the door with a key. I say pretended, because I was holding the key. She had no need of it, of course. I'd already figured out that she had rigged the lock when we left the cabin earlier.

The door came open, and George forced his way past us into the room.

He took a swift glance around; with the wrap off the bed, there was nothing obvious to show the room had been occupied. But his eyes settled on the wardrobe, and he charged for it, opening the door with his free hand. "Her evening gown!" His words held a curious blend of excitement and disappointment. He reached for the frock with one hand, fingering the silk. The other hand held firm to the wrap.

"We found that evening wrap on the bed," I said quietly. "I think there are shoes on the floor, other side." We all moved our gaze to the silver fabric T-straps beside the bed.

"I was right." His voice dropped on the last line. "She is hiding out here. But why? I never meant her any harm. I love her! She knows that. Why wouldn't she tell me where she was?"

My heart went out to him. This was clearly a man in great pain.

His hand fell from the dress fabric. He turned to face us. "Unless that bastard threatened her. I wouldn't put it past him. The way he tries to control both those women ..." He gripped the wrap in iron fists. "When I get my hands on him ..."

I didn't envy Roy. The cold fury on George Everleigh's face was something I had seen all too often on the men in my own family growing up. It had never ended well.

"I'll try to look for Meg in the hair salon, ladies' lounge, and other places women might be," I said, trying defuse the situation. "Places you can't go."

That stopped him. It was almost as if he had to interpret the words one by one. He turned slowly, eyes off in the distance. "Yes. Yes, do that. Leave Armitage to me."

With that, he stormed off.

"Well, that's curious," I said to Elf.

"What?"

"He never asked why I was looking for her. Which is strange, because I don't actually know her. She never made it to dinner that first night."

Elf shrugged. "Bloke with one concern thinks everyone else has the same concern."

I smiled. As I said before, Elf can be awfully smart for someone who can't read.

CHAPTER 11

"AT LEAST WE don't have to confront Roy Armitage and Renata." Being the bearer of embarrassing news was never fun. They wouldn't appreciate any scandal. "I wasn't looking forward to that."

"Yup," said Elf. "Pretty sure the little sis was camping out here with a bloke."

"I wonder if they'll come to blows?" It was easy to imagine George taking a swing at Roy, and just as likely that Roy would reciprocate. I didn't need to see that.

"Glad to be out of it," muttered Elf.

I took one last look around the cabin, trying to imprint it onto my memory.

"Okay. You take the keys back to your steward friend. I'll go alert Gray about the snake." I turned to leave cabin 128 for the second time in an hour. "Let's meet back at our cabin."

"Don't take too long. Nearly time to dress for dinner." Elf wagged a finger at me. "No time for hanky-panky with the purser." She giggled.

"Nor with the steward!" I shot back as we separated.

Elf had the longer journey, I expected. She'd have to track down her steward friend while he was working, and that could be in a number of cabins or decks. Me, I just had to drop by the purser's office.

Easier said than done. I'd always approached the office from the direction of my cabin or the grand staircase. Not from a second-class deck with no amenities other than personal accommodation. This ship was a maze of dimly lit corridors, with no windows to act as landmarks, of course. Not to mention, there was more than one staircase.

The carpets were a different colour too. Decor was something I tended to notice. These floor coverings here were a deep green, whereas the carpets in my corridor were black with gold. I couldn't remember ever being here before, and my sense of direction is close to nonexistent on land, let alone at sea.

After a prolonged interval of nodding to fellow passengers and strolling with confidence, I finally found a steward with thinning white hair. Or rather, he found me, standing bewildered outside a linen room somewhere.

"May I help you?" he said. His smile was warm and friendly. I was so glad we were able to offer older men employment on these ships. Young lads might be able to work the mines or staff factories, but men over fifty needed work too, and they often had little choice of employment that wasn't backbreaking.

This steward was a credit to his profession. Polite to the point of charming, within five minutes he had us standing outside the locked purser's cabin.

"Blast," I said, most inelegantly.

"I expect he is with the captain," said my fatherly escort. "Perhaps you could check back following dinner?"

I pondered that, hesitating. Dare I mention the snake? This was a public corridor. Someone could overhear, and to be frank,

I didn't know how Gray would react if I caused a panic.

I settled for caution. "Perhaps I could leave a note under his door," I said finally.

"Allow me." The steward whipped out a notepad and pencil from a pocket in his immaculate jacket. "Would you like Mr. West to contact you?"

"Yes, please. Tell him Lady Revelstoke needs to speak to him." I wanted to make it sound urgent, but not too urgent, if that makes any sense. "He'll understand."

The elderly gentleman smiled. I'm sure I must have blushed. How much did he know about Gray and me? Were our relations the talk of the staff, even after all our efforts to be discreet?

"Of course, Lady Revelstoke. Enjoy the evening."

I thanked him profusely and accepted his directions back to the grand staircase.

Hopefully, Gray wouldn't delay in tracking me down. Snakes didn't like people, I knew, so it would probably hide. Still, I couldn't help scanning the corridors for anything that looked remotely like a green curtain sash slithering along the baseboards.

Outside, I told myself. *Stop looking for snakes! Go out on the deck and catch your breath.* There was still some time to kill before dinner. I could lose myself in the sea. I left the grand staircase and strode to the heavy doors that led out to the ship's railing.

"You again," said a voice behind me. "We have to stop meeting like this."

I turned around to find Stella looking me up and down. She seemed to approve of my blue ensemble.

"I guess we both share a love of the sea," I offered.

"Too right," she said, as we moved to the rail. "I was raised by the ocean. Were you?"

"On a big lake," I said. "But yes. I spent most of my childhood playing on the docks or close by."

She smiled. "That doesn't sound like a la-di-da lady."

"Good thing I never claimed to be one," I said.

She laughed, a pleasant tinkling sound. I moved in quickly with a compliment to distract her from asking the next question.

"That is a particularly stunning frock," I said, in complete honesty. "I think maybe three women in the world could wear that and look as good as you."

"Why, thank you!" she said, beaming with delight. "Vionnet made it specially for me. Don't you just love Vionnet?"

"I'm not sure we've ever met," I said, teasing.

She got it, and chuckled.

"But obviously he definitely loves you, to create such a delightful gown. That black lace overlay is magic."

I watched her finger the fabric. "She. Vionnet is a she. Isn't that remarkable? We need more women in the rag trade. They know what feels good as well as looks good. I like how fashion is changing. Don't you?"

"Definitely. Especially after going through the austerity of the war." *Why do my thoughts always go back to the war?*

"Did you work during the war?" Stella asked.

"Yes," I said. "I drove an ambulance. My son and I lived in London the first two years, in order to be with my husband when he came home from the front on leave. Later, after Johnny was wounded, I helped to run a convalescent home."

She nodded at that, no doubt assuming I had taken a senior nursing role.

I didn't bother to add that it had been my own drafty castle, and that I had in fact managed the convalescent home. We had taken wounded soldiers and medical staff into our country estate once Johnny himself had been invalided out and sent home from France. As our location was about as far from the battlefields as you could get, we welcomed soldiers from the West Country. How could we not? It meant the world to injured soldiers to be close to family and friends while recovering from their ghastly wounds.

"We thought it would all change after the war," Stella grumbled.

"You mean the lives of women." I said it as a statement.

She flung a beautifully manicured hand through the air. "Of course. We took on so many roles during the war. Women worked in factories, offices, the fields, nursing. No longer having to choose between two occupations or being absolutely destitute."

I knew what she meant. Before the war, most young girls who needed work to support themselves or their mothers went into service as young as twelve. A life of being domestic help — no matter how menial — was usually preferable to the other option.

"I didn't mind being surrounded by schoolboys, like that Ethan. It was nice to be adored, not just lusted after. Poor chap. I really am sorry about that. I had no idea ... well, never mind. A lot of those boys were messed up after the war. They clung to you like a life raft, in a kind of desperation. I don't know what they were expecting. Forgiveness ... redemption, maybe. If I'd been a little older and wiser ... Bloody war. Well, you can't go back, that much I know."

"No, none of us can go back," I said in all honesty.

We both drifted in thought for a moment or two, very much like a moment of silence for the fallen.

"We thought things would change for us." She sounded bitter, and I had to wonder if she herself was acutely familiar with the other option.

"They will," I said. "We have the vote now. Finally. It won't happen overnight, but things will change. Women will be able to support themselves by working at legitimate jobs, and we won't have to depend entirely on men. It will take time."

"In time for the next generation, perhaps," she said softly. "Not for us."

"Maybe not." I agreed.

"Did you like working?" she asked.

I thought about that. "Yes," I said. "Very much. It felt good to be contributing to the war effort, you see. Johnny was overseas, risking his life for England. I wanted to do my bit."

Her eyes rested heavily on me, and I was aware of shrewd depths behind them. What was she thinking?

"But you're not from here," she said finally.

Her bluntness took me aback. For a moment I thought about prevaricating. Pretending I didn't know what she meant by the word *here*. But why bother being mendacious, really, when I had made no secret of my home country?

"I'm from the colonies. Canada," I said. "A place called Hamilton, close to Toronto. I've been here since 1912. I was actually escaping the bonds of family by crossing the Atlantic."

"Really?" The eagerness in her face was something to behold. Now I had her full attention. "Not an evil stepmother, I hope."

I shouldn't have been surprised that she surmised my mother had passed away. I appeared "well-bred" to her, and no mother would let a well-bred young lady travel by herself across an ocean. It was a shrewd guess on her part, and not far-fetched at all. Before the turn of the century, fifty percent of women died in childbirth, as my own mother had done. Even in our modern age, the mortality rate for women made any childbearing risky. I had been lucky myself, with Charlie's birth thirteen years ago.

"Not a stepmother. But you guessed right in some ways. My mother did die in childbirth." I turned to face the ocean. "You mentioned the lives of women. It might interest you to know that I can relate. I was escaping from a marriage the family was determined would take place."

"You don't say," she said, eyes twinkling. "So, you hopped a freighter and made your way to England alone?"

"Pretty much," I said. "Sold the jewellery my mother had left me to finance it all."

She chuckled. It was warm and rather charismatic, which surprised me. I had taken a mind to dislike her at first but was slowly changing my first impression.

I remembered an aunt giving me a piece of sound advice: *If you don't like someone, get to know them better. There are many sides to one story.*

Stella's look changed to admiration. "Thank the Lord for jewellery and the men who give us such things. But still, you took a hell of a risk."

I did, really. A young woman, landing in the docks of London with a limited supply of money and no prospects? "Utter madness, I know now. What can I say? I was young. It's amazing what you will do when you need to free yourself from an untenable situation. Getting out is all you can think of and damn the consequences." Terribly forward of me to swear like she had, but Stella seemed to approve.

In fact, she nodded. "Too right. And now you're in a position where you can buy your own jewellery." Her voice was wistful. "Hopefully one day, we all will be."

"Now, look here, Stella! I want a word with you." The voice boomed out from behind us.

We both swung around as one.

"Roy." Stella said it softly. Too softly. I could feel latent emotion behind the word, and sensed sorrow.

Roy charged forward, a man on a fated mission. "You've got to desist from this senseless baiting of Renata. It's not on, old girl. She's a sensitive thing — not as strong as you."

Stella's expression changed in an instant. "Renata, sensitive? That vicious old cow? If you knew the number of times —" Her fists clenched, and I could almost see steam coming off her head.

Frankly, I had to agree with Stella. Renata, a poor sensitive creature? Were we talking about the same woman? Could the fellow be that far gone in love?

I automatically stepped back as Roy stepped forward.

"Now, look here. This petty bickering solves nothing. Surely you can see that. You're a grown woman now, not a green girl. Behave like one." He reprimanded her like she was a child and grabbed both her fists in his large hands.

"How dare you tell me what to do?" She pulled her right hand away. "As if you're the paragon of all things virtuous. Leading innocent young women on and then dropping them like a hot potato for that … that … aging bitch with all the money."

"Innocent!" he roared. "YOU?"

"You pompous hypocrite!" Her right hand lashed out and caught him on the side of the face.

There was a stunned silence. I felt rather than heard gasps and was surprised to see that a small crowd had gathered behind us.

Time to depart, I told myself.

With quiet determination, I squeezed myself back between the onlookers and hurried to the nearest doorway. Anything to get away from that high-pitched screeching and cursing behind me.

CHAPTER 12

I CAN'T STAND to hear men and women fighting. It brings back too many best-forgotten memories of childhood. My mind goes numb, and I strive to get away. Anything to get away.

I stood still in the corridor to catch my breath and equilibrium. In only a short while, I felt a presence beside me.

"Is that a parrot I hear squawking out yonder?"

I giggled in spite of myself. Simon Leggatt observed me with a wry smile. Funny how his sense of humour seemed to match my own.

"Not far off," I said, remembering her flamboyant way of dressing. "She's definitely colourful."

"As is her language," said Simon Leggatt. "I'm learning some words they didn't teach us at Eton."

I matched his smile and made a sudden decision. "Join me for a drink? I'd like your advice on something."

His smile reached his eyes as he offered his arm. I linked mine through his.

"My pleasure. But make it my treat, please. I insist."

A gentleman to the core. Once again, I was favourably impressed.

"Shall we try the Neptune Bar? I have a passion for sea views."

We started to walk toward the bow of the ship.

"Were you in the navy during the war?" I asked as innocently as I could.

"Not in an official capacity," he said. "But I have spent a lot of time on ships. They run in the family, so to speak."

Now that was interesting. I was about to question him further when Tony's voice boomed along the corridor.

"There you are, Lucy! I've looked everywhere."

We stopped and turned. Tony looked a little put out, in that way I had seen before when things didn't go his way exactly, tickety-boo. Had we agreed to meet? I had no memory of it.

"Hullo," I said, cheerfully. "Join us in the Neptune Bar, Tony? We're going for a drink before dinner."

Tony's gaze turned from me to Simon. "Trying to pinch my girl, Leggatt? That will cost you a large brandy."

Brandy? At this time of the day?

"Sorry old chap. Didn't know she was your girl," said Simon.

"Nonsense," I said, holding my other arm out for Tony. "It isn't often I get two handsome men to run escort."

WHAT HAPPENS WHEN two men from the same school get together after many years? They slip happily into shared memories and seem to forget a third party is even there. I listened politely, with a fixed smile on my face, amused at the predictability of this outcome. Truly, I wasn't needed for this conversation. I made my excuses after one drink and slipped away to change for dinner.

It didn't take me too long. Luckily, the makeup I had applied earlier would do with a mere touch-up. Elf was nowhere to be seen, but the clever girl had laid out a beautiful dress on the bed that I could manage to get into and do up on my own. Silver T-strap shoes were on the floor, and a matching evening bag sat beside the dress. *Bless that girl.* Tonight, I would carry the blue theme over, with chiffon layers and silver sequins.

I arrived at the dining room to find everyone already seated at the table. Everyone who had planned to attend, that is. Tony, Harry, Simon, and Roy rose when I drew near. Simon signalled the chair next to his, which put me between him and Roy. Renata was missing, once more. And of course, Meg. No matter, because Stella made up for all the others.

She was wearing the same gown she had worn at the rail, but without the short jacket that had covered up her neckline. That famous cleavage was certainly on display right now. She had topped the outfit with a feathered headdress and looked absolutely stunning.

I wondered what had happened after her tempestuous argument with Roy. She seemed completely serene now, talking and flirting mildly with Tony and Lord Harry. I remembered that she was a trained actress, of course. And an acclaimed one, so obviously good at disguising her own feelings and putting on the skin of others.

Roy, beside me, was about as far away as he could get from her.

Roberts took my order, and I relaxed back, enjoying the conversation around me. I don't like to talk much between bites, but I do appreciate the friendly companionship of others.

Strangely enough, the topic of women working came up once again, in a curiously roundabout way.

I had just finished a main course of the most impossibly tender roast lamb with mint sauce. I don't remember the vegetables. I hardly ever do.

While waiting for dessert, my favourite part of any meal, conversation turned to the difficulty of getting good servant help after the war.

"Can't keep a maid for longer than a few months," complained Roy. "They all want to work in shops instead of domestic service. I blame the war."

I smiled while thinking, *Could they possibly not be happy working for the demanding Renata?*

Simon caught my eye and winked. "Do you have trouble keeping servants, Lady Revelstoke?" he said. Oh, he was a devil!

I put on my serious face. "Oh, most certainly."

Tony was quick to become part of the conversation. "How many people does the castle employ, Lucy?"

"Fifty-four," I said.

"Fifty-four!" exclaimed Stella. "How do you keep them all straight?"

"Of course, you wouldn't deal with them personally," said Roy.

"That's not quite true," I said, lifting my wineglass. "The housekeeper reports to me, as does the estate agent — I couldn't do without them — but Johnny left me in charge of the place. I take an interest in all the staff." I took a sip.

"And you ran the convalescent home during the war," said Stella, triumphant that she knew more than the others at the table. "You're a working woman just like me!"

"Yes," I said. "Things really didn't change when Johnny got home. He had caught TB at the front and wasn't in good shape. He left matters of the estate largely to me. I've been covering that role for at least a decade and will do so until my young son can take his place."

"That is definitely a full-time job. Much like being a corporate president, I would imagine," mused Simon. "Overseeing the people who do the work."

I turned to him and smiled gratefully. "That's a good way of putting it."

"Well, I think it's jolly good of you, Lady Revelstoke, but most irregular." Roy shook his head. "It's not natural. You need a man to handle the business decisions."

The smile erased from my face. "My estate agent is very capable and gives me good advice on farming and livestock. Of course, I don't involve him in the other investments that Johnny left to me personally." I toyed with the empty glass, waiting to see who would pick up on that line.

"Which investments?" queried Stella. I caught her eye, to see her smiling. Clever girl. She was giving me an opening if I chose to take it.

"Now really, Stella." Tony started to intervene. "You shouldn't ask such personal —"

"It's okay, Tony," I said smoothly, deciding to take her up on it. "Take now, for instance. The reason for this journey. I'm on my way to America to take my seat on the board of directors of this shipping line for a special meeting."

Roy made a choking sound. "You're on the board of directors of a shipping line? A woman?"

"Indeed, I am," I said, the picture of innocence.

Tony finished before I could. "Of course she is," he said irritably, right hand strangling his whisky glass. "She owns the entire line."

LATER, ON MY way back to the cabin, I gave some thought to Tony's revelation. The gasps around the table were, of course, memorable. Only Harry seemed to take it in his stride. Of course, when you are closely related to one of the wealthiest families in the world ... But it was Tony's grumpiness that took me aback. Did he — like Gray — find my financial position uncomfortable? Not that I could do anything about it, if they did. I wasn't about to give up my financial independence for any man.

It was more than keeping the estate safe for Charlie. Elf depended on me. I had her to worry about and to provide for. In fact, I'd recently changed my will to include a legacy for Elf. It would shock her, the investments I planned to leave her. And that pleased me enormously. She would never have to worry about money again.

"WHAT'S THIS I hear about Stella Burke in a yelling fight with some older dame?" Elf was on me the second I entered the room.

I explained, as best I could, the uncomfortable encounter from earlier today. And the intimate tea Simon and I had shared with Ethan's mother in the aftermath.

"Why didn't you tell me before?" she demanded.

"We were kind of busy breaking into cabins," I reminded. "Not to mention the snake took most of our attention after. It was all a surprise, you know. No time to sell tickets."

She threw a pillow at me.

We talked a bit more about the sad state of the men haunted by war and the unfeeling women who took advantage of them. To my surprise, Elf took Stella's point of view in stride. "Survival is tough on the streets. An' those lads — a lot of them want something for nothing. Can't blame a gal for trying to better her lot."

It was another harsh reminder for me that there were two sides to every story.

Elf left to join her steward friend for the night before Gray snuck into my cabin. I had changed into a particularly fetching lavender negligee from Paris that had elicited an enthusiastic response on the earlier crossing we had shared in the spring.

But before we got down to "business," I insisted we talk about business.

"Snake in cabin three thirty-four," I announced, expecting a big response.

"Not again," he muttered, undoing his jacket.

Well, that was a little underwhelming. I increased the stakes. "Out of its cage!" I said.

Gray cursed with some pretty colourful language. "How big a snake?"

Now I gulped. "Head to tip of the tail, it would stretch across the corridor."

"It got out of the cabin?" His hands stopped on the last button.

Wow, Gray was quick. Or maybe he was getting to know me too darn well.

"Elf says it did. I was sort of preoccupied, running in the opposite direction."

The jacket was off now, and he was working on his shirt. "Any idea what type?"

"The type that hisses?" I suggested.

There was a moment of grumbling as the shirt came off.

"A green one," I added. "The colour of my eyes, Elf said."

Gray harrumphed. Not sure how I was supposed to take that.

"Damned smugglers put a crew member on board again, most likely. The snake is probably African. Sounds like a boomslang, or African tree snake — quite venomous. They get a fortune for those in America." I watched as he sat down on the bed to remove his shoes. "Rich people are insane. As if they don't have enough snakes of their own in America."

"This has happened before?"

He nodded. "Usually, we find them in the kitchen, or the engine rooms. Somewhere warm. I'll alert the crew to be on the watch for it when I leave here."

"Um. You might want to do more than that. There were other baskets on the bed."

He cursed loudly.

Could it keep until morning? I could see him deliberating.

"Three thirty-four, you said?"

I nodded.

He stopped undressing and grimaced. "Damn. I won't spend the night then. Probably best to deal with this before dawn."

He didn't have to explain it. There would be fewer witnesses in the middle of the night.

"I'll need experienced men to handle them, and special equipment. And there's someone else I'll want to bring into this."

What would happen to the creatures? Would they be killed and dumped overboard? Probably best not to ask. I decided it was a strategic time to move on.

"And you have several booze bottles in three fifty-seven," I added.

He sighed again. "Not surprising. But I'll follow it up. Thanks for the tip."

"Is this a common thing?" I didn't like the idea that our employees were stealing from what I had come to think of as my ship.

"Expected," he said. "Booze especially gets pilfered. Usually, the evidence disappears before we reach port."

"Meaning ... the contents are drunk, and the bottles tipped overboard?"

"Exactly. Did it look like the bed was slept in?" Gray rose from the bed to neatly place his outer clothes over a chair.

"No, actually."

"Well, that's a positive." He went back to undressing. Only the undershirt and shorts left.

"Have you considered counting the bottles at the beginning of the journey, and then counting on the way out to see if any are missing?"

"To what end?" he said. "There are several hundred staff on this ship. Unless we catch someone red-handed, there's nothing we can do"

"Good point," I considered.

"There will always be pilfering. Always has been — always will be. Let me tell you the statistics on that sometime."

"Statistics?" I asked, still sitting on the edge of the bed.

"Not now," said Gray as he pushed me gently over on my back.

CHAPTER 13

DAY FOUR AT SEA

GRAY LEFT SOMETIME after midnight. It occurred to me the next morning that I hadn't told him about the third cabin. The one with Meg's belongings in it. This is because he kept me quite busy. But also, I still wasn't straight in my mind what it meant.

Something was bothering me about that cabin. I couldn't put my finger on it, but I knew from experience that the mind had a way of sorting itself out with time. I'd let it sit for now.

I'd slept late — too late for breakfast — and Elf was nowhere to be seen. I actually enjoyed dressing myself for a change. It wasn't often I got a break from my maid. What could she be doing? I glanced at the clock, noting with satisfaction that there was time for a little reading before lunch. I had packed a recent book by my friend Agatha Christie and happily settled down in the easy chair under the porthole.

Maybe an hour passed. I was just finishing up *The Murder of Roger Ackroyd* when Elf stormed in.

"Gotta come," she said, grabbing my lower arm. "Come *now*."

I let her hustle me along the corridor without protest. At times like this, I was given to wondering who was the lady and who was the servant. It gave me a wry smile. More than once, Tony had expressed that thought to me. Certainly, the well-dressed people who passed us en route must have wondered what could have compelled a pint-size gal in a maid's uniform to drag her fashionable employer along the corridor in such a manner.

And I didn't get an explanation.

"What —"

"Not now," she said abruptly.

Into the interior passageway, down a corridor, up a flight of stairs ... I hardly had a second to admire the beautiful art deco sconces that lit our way.

"Where are we —"

"Not *now*," she said again.

I let her guide me along the wood-panelled corridors, confident that eventually there would be some reasonable explanation. Elf wasn't flighty. She must have had good reasons for this behaviour.

We stopped outside a cabin that I recognized: the Victoriana Suite. The Harwoods' cabin. Elf knocked on the door and didn't wait for an answer. She sailed right in.

Renata Harwood sat on a small divan with her head in her hands. She looked up, eyes blurry, and said, "Oh, it's you."

I stopped, about to say something, but was almost pulled off my feet by Elf in her haste to reach the bedroom. Through the door, and —

"It's Polly," she said as she let go of my arm and pointed to the body on the floor. Elf's voice was dark with grief and broke on the name.

I didn't know Polly as well as Elf did. And looking at the body, I would have thought it was someone else entirely. She was wearing the dress our film star had worn the night before.

Crimson sequins sparkled under the cabin lights. On her feet were beautiful shoes that looked a little too long for her. This woman had bobbed dark hair. Like Renata. A slim figure, like Renata. From the back, she would look very much like Renata Harwood. Except Renata was sitting in the other room with her head in her hands, and this poor girl was on the floor with her head bashed in.

What the devil was going on?

I gulped. "Have you sent for help yet?"

"Nope," said Elf. "Waited for you."

I shifted into efficient mode. "Good decision, Elf. Okay, tell me everything you can."

She sniffed a bit, then started. "Polly didn't show up for our time off. I went hunting for her. Steward told me she'd been summoned to the Harwood's suite. I came down here, knocked on the door, then used my key —"

"What key?" I said. How could Elf have a key to this suite?

"I got keys for everywhere now. Never mind about that. Came in to find the film star swooning and Polly on the floor."

"Did you touch anything?"

"Nah. I know the drill. Wanted you to see it first before we report it."

"And Renata agreed to that?" I was slightly taken aback.

"Told her you'd take care of it, with as little fuss as possible. To your advantage to keep a lid on things, I told her. She knows you own the ship, after all."

I nodded. "Good work, Elf. You did everything well. Now we need a story. Let's go back into the room next door to work it out with Renata."

Five minutes later, we had a plan that played only slightly with the truth. We decided it made more sense to tell people that

I had arranged to meet Renata for tea in her rooms. We would tell them that Elf and I had arrived together to find Polly dead and Renata prostrate. I thanked my lucky stars that husband Roy was occupied in the card room with Tony. Last thing we wanted was a man or two taking over before I had a chance to manage things to our satisfaction.

Elf was sent to apprise Gray and the security officer of the situation, and I watched over the scene of the crime to preserve it. Which basically meant, I went over everything I could see in order to commit the crime scene to my memory.

I started from the outside and worked my way in. Nothing appeared to be out of place in the room. No drawers open, no things strewn about. The jewellery box on the dresser appeared untouched. The closet door was closed, and the bed neatly made up.

Maybe it was a result of her employment, or maybe she was naturally so, but Polly had been a tidy young woman. Her uniform was carefully draped across the bed. Her own sensible shoes were on the floor, grouped together.

The murderer had not been so particular. For to the right of shoes, tossed at a haphazard angle, lay the murder weapon. I made my way carefully around the body to look at it more closely. It appeared to be a bronze statue, about fifteen inches high, in the shape of a female dancer. The heavy base was engraved with lettering obscured by blood and hair. I shivered.

No doubt the body of the dancer had made a perfect hand-hold. I expected it had been wiped clean.

The dress Polly wore was done up at the back. She must have been able to slip it over her head without undoing the hooks. She was on her stomach with her legs splayed apart, the right one extended. One would almost think she was sleeping peacefully there, until you looked at her head.

I forced myself to examine it carefully. There was no look of horror on her face. There never is, of course. When you die, your muscles relax completely. I learned that from my war years tending to wounded soldiers. I think that's why we use the term, *finally at peace*. They look at peace. Only the Lord knows if they really are.

She faced left, and the gash at the back of her head looked nasty. Blood had pooled to the right on the floor. It was almost the same colour as her dress.

She had obviously been hit from behind. With any luck, she hadn't seen her killer and had been spared the feeling of terror in her final moments. But glancing around, I came to the conclusion that Polly had had no luck this day as it was obvious what had occupied her attention at the time of the cosh. She'd been gazing at her well-dressed self in the full-length mirror.

My heart felt bruised. Her killer would have been clearly reflected in the mirror behind her.

Renata appeared at my shoulder.

"She was like that when I got here." Renata wrapped both arms around her thin body.

"How long ago was that?" I asked.

"Only two or three minutes before your maid burst in," she said. "No more than five. I saw her on the floor and had to sit down."

I clucked sympathetically. "I'm sure. Anyone would." Except I hadn't. And Elf hadn't. "Any idea what she was doing in your dress?"

She shrugged. "I guess she was playing dress-up. Helping herself to my clothes when I wasn't there. Others have done it. It's harmless."

Well, apparently it wasn't. Because now Polly was lying on the floor, dead.

"She was a sweet little thing. Who would want to kill her?" murmured Renata.

I stole a look at her and wondered how much I should say. Poor little Polly had tried on Renata's dress. Her hair was a similar colour and cut. From the back, it would be hard to tell them apart.

The intended victim wasn't Polly.

It was Renata.

"I JUST CAN'T believe anyone would want to harm me." Renata shook her head in bewilderment.

She was sitting on my bed now, next to a magenta evening gown Elf had thought might be suitable for tonight. It wasn't. Far too flashy; I simply couldn't bring myself to wear it, under the circumstances.

Renata already looked like she was ready for the cameras. Her black hair was perfectly coiffed, and the smoky purple dress she wore had appeared in *British Vogue* just last month.

After Gray arrived, I had taken Renata back to my cabin while the ship's authorities did their work. I knew they would be checking over the crime scene, retrieving the murder weapon, and of course, removing poor Polly's body. No need to put Renata through all that.

Elf had gone to fetch Roy from the card room. We had a few moments alone, and I didn't plan to waste them.

"No one? You've not made any enemies? No jilted lover, or mother of a jilted lover, like the woman who confronted Stella?"

Renata looked at me blankly. "I can't think of anyone on this ship. Except perhaps Stella herself."

I had thought of that too. Could Stella be so vindictive that she would whack Renata over the head? Seek her out specially to do so?

The fact was, this murder looked unplanned. A spur of the moment strike of passion that wasn't necessarily intended to kill. With a weapon that happened to be handy.

"You're sure you didn't see Stella in the room?" Of course, what I really meant was, had Renata invited Stella to meet her there.

She frowned. "Of course not. I would have said."

I felt it best to soft pedal. "I know you weren't on those kinds of terms."

"We weren't on any terms!" Renata waved a careless arm. "The woman is a lunatic."

"Exactly," I murmured.

I tried to think of circumstances under which Stella could have wielded that statue. Perhaps, if she had gotten into a row with Renata, she would be infuriated enough to swing the weapon. I could see her committing a crime of passion. But to cold-bloodedly track Renata down in her cabin, and strike her from behind without saying a word? It didn't fit with my image of her.

There would be words first. *Oh yes, there would be plenty.*

I couldn't rule Stella out, but she did seem unlikely as the murderer. I wondered if she had an alibi.

Elf entered the room in her usual abrupt manner, which meant kicking the door open with her foot and letting it slam behind her.

"Where's Roy?" Renata sounded excited. I smiled. This surely was a woman deeply in love with her husband.

"He insisted on going to the crime scene." Elf sounded like the penny crime novels she devoured. "They want you there too. More questions with your husband present."

Renata rose immediately.

"Would you like me to come with you?" I said.

She shook her head. "Kind of you, but no. I'll be fine."

Rats, I thought. I would have liked to have been a fly on the wall during that interview.

She turned gracefully at the door to wave goodbye. Her pretty, madeup face relaxed for a moment, which made her look younger and vulnerable.

"Thank you for staying with me," she said to me. "I mean that sincerely."

I like to remember her as she stood there that day, in the doorway. I truly do think her gratitude was genuine.

CHAPTER 14

WHEN WE GOT back to our cabin, I made a pronouncement.

"Elf, I'm having second thoughts. We need to find out more about Polly. It sure looks like Renata was the intended victim, but we can't be positive. Polly could have known something or been a danger to someone. We need to explore all possibilities. Do you know anyone among the stewards who might be a good friend to her?" Or rather, had been a good friend. I should be using past tense. Poor Polly.

Elf looked thoughtful. "Mary. Been around for a few years and bunks with her."

Elf was also having trouble with tenses.

"Can you find Mary and bring her back here? I know it means we'll have to tell her ..."

"Crew will know already," Elf said firmly. "They always do."

In a way, that was good. It made my job easier. "I feel awful about this. We need to do something, Elf. That poor girl ... I can't help feeling she was an innocent, caught up in something that shouldn't have been her business. That it was all just bad luck on her part, or unfortunate timing."

"Polly didn't deserve this," said Elf. "Not for anything. She was a good girl."

I turned to sit down on the foot of the bed and voiced my thoughts out loud. "I don't trust Gray to ask the right questions of a female steward, nor, if I'm honest, to even think of questioning her. But who better to know what Polly had been about, or what she might have witnessed? Hopefully, this Mary will feel it's okay to tell us gossip she wouldn't tell the authorities. Polly could very well have talked to her about things she saw or overheard."

"Sounds smart. I'll get Mary. Back in a jiff." Elf blew through the doorway in her characteristic take-no-prisoners way.

I took advantage of the time to attend to necessities in the loo.

THE DOOR WHAMMED open about five minutes later. Hard to explain how she does that, but it doesn't seem to matter which way a door opens; when Elf takes charge of it, it announces her presence in a big way.

"HERE SHE IS," yelled Elf.

I watched a tall, thin young woman follow Elf into the room, at least tall compared to Elf. She was probably not up to my height. Mary had curly red hair and a cute snub nose that was too small for her face. Her hair had been bobbed, and it looked as if she had been struggling with it ever since. Her steward's uniform was well-starched, and she wore a delicate silver cross on a chain around her neck. *Catholic and Irish, I'll bet, with that colouring,* I thought.

She entered the room cautiously, looking first left, then right. For a moment, I wondered if Elf had told her about the renegade snake.

"Don't be dawdlin'," Elf coaxed. "This is the boss lady. She's all right." Elf then turned to me and waved an arm. "This here is Mary, Luce."

I winced as I had done so many times before. Maids simply didn't call their employers by first names, let alone a nickname.

Mary looked up at me and gave me a genuine smile with slightly crooked teeth. Her whole face came alive. "Heard so much about you, m' lady. Elf speaks highly."

Irish Catholic indeed, with that lovely accent! She did a little bob at the knees.

"Don't need to curtsey, Mary. She ain't like that." Elf, yet again, was speaking for me. Once again, I was beginning to think I wasn't needed for this conversation.

"Please sit down, Mary." I pointed to a chair by the porthole. As she passed closer to me, I could see from her eyes that she had been crying. "You've heard about poor Polly, I take it."

"Oh yes, my lady. It's horrible." She plunked down on the chair, then drew her knees tightly together. I could almost hear the nuns back in Canada instructing me that I should be able to hold a penny between my knees every time I sat down.

"Yes, it is horrid. That poor young girl. It makes me so angry. That's why I want to do something about it, if we can."

"We gotta find her killer." Elf plunked into the other chair. "And you can help us."

"How?" asked Mary. She sat, wringing her hands, as a red blush spread across her face.

With no chairs left, I sat down on the edge of the bed, also pulling my knees together. "Elf tells me you knew Polly as well as anyone. What can you tell us about her background? Where she came from?" I knew enough to start with easy questions.

Loyalty was always an issue with young women, particularly when reputation was at stake. Mary could address this question without having to comment either positively or negatively on Polly's behaviour.

Mary answered with a bob of her head. "She was an orphan girl, put out to service. Like me. I think from Liverpool."

I nodded. It was a common enough story. So many babies ended up as orphans. Too many women died in childbirth, leaving an infant behind, and a husband unable to cope. Not to mention, some poor girls found themselves without husbands, having to give up a newborn baby for adoption in order to keep their jobs.

"Started as a tweeny maid in a big house, she told me. But then a lad she knew — footman, I think — told her about steward opportunities on ships. Coming from Liverpool, she had a special feeling for the sea."

Elf was quick to add, "Head stewards like to hire pretty girls with no ties. No harm in it. Passengers go easier on you if you're a looker."

My own mouth formed a thin line. *What an unfair world.* I had read that people gave more credit to women who were good-looking. For some unfathomable reason, the average person seemed to think pretty to look at women were smarter and more virtuous than plain women. I wonder if the same prejudice held true for men.

I wondered also, if Elf had come up against this unfair world in her youth. While she was the dearest girl in the world to me, I knew for a fact she would never have called herself pretty. I thought she was wrong in that. When Elf smiled, her face just beamed, and it was impossible not to be infected by her zest for life. But perhaps it was her experience on the other side of things that made the advantages of prettiness more apparent.

I needed to focus. We had learned something: Polly didn't have a family. I asked Mary if there was anyone I could contact.

"Don't know of anyone," said Mary. "We were her family, she used to say." She gave a little sniff and wrapped both arms around to hug herself.

It broke my heart to watch her. I realized with sadness that Mary, as an orphan, might be in the same situation. No one to contact but her friends on this ship if something were to happen to her.

"She didn't get any letters from anyone?" I asked, hopefully. "Maybe from the orphanage?"

Mary shook her head. "Couldn't read or write."

That wasn't unusual. Girls were put out to service as young as twelve. Some even earlier. You had to earn your keep as soon as you could.

I pulled myself back to the task. "We need to find a reason why someone would feel compelled to do this terrible thing to her. Did she see something she shouldn't have? Or was there something in her past that might have followed her here?"

Mary's hazel eyes went wide. "I thought ..."

Elf interrupted. "Polly liked to dress up, right?"

Mary sat forward. "Aye. Was always donning the ladies' togs when no one was looking." From her voice, I had a sneaking suspicion Mary admired her but was too timid to admit such a thing to us, or to do the same.

"Taking a risk, she was, but no one could tell her anything," Mary continued. "'Just a bit of fun,' she'd say."

"And I'm sure it was," I said smoothly, to put Mary at ease. "I'm sure she meant no harm in it. But it was a pretty bold thing to do, all the same. Was she that daring in other ways?"

This new aspect of Polly's personality was a revelation. It could explain why she was a danger to someone.

Mary's forehead creased in thought. "Not especially. She didn't drink or naught. Just, she had a love of pretty things, is all. And film stars on the ship! Well, that was a dream, to go through their closets. She would report back to us girls, all important like."

"What about blokes?" asked Elf, taking over. "Was she mad about the blokes?"

"Nah, not really. She was a quiet girl, not a tease. She didn't get dolly-eyed about the steward fellas on the ship. Not like some." Mary sniffed her disapproval.

"Was there anyone special in her life?" I coaxed.

"Well, none on *this* ship that you'd notice." Mary hesitated, as if she'd just thought of something.

Elf caught it right away. *This*. "You can tell Luce. We want to catch her killer, that's all."

"Anything might help," I added quietly.

Mary turned her attention to Elf. "Jus' something she said once. I think she liked older men. Always going on about film stars, how 'mature' they were ... not like the young blokes that pester us. That sort of thing."

Elf leaned forward. "And?"

I was impressed. Elf seemed to have a sixth sense for interrogation.

"Well, something else I heard," said Mary. "Gossip, so's I don't know for sure. One of the other stewards told me he heard

Polly left the last company she was with because of a man." She leaned forward. "Had a pash for a passenger that the head steward kenned to."

Even Elf was hushed at that.

"And was it reciprocated? Did he say?" I put it as carefully as I could.

Again, she hesitated. Then she leaned back in her chair and nodded. "But she never said nothing 'bout it. And I never saw her, but she was a good girl."

I hadn't known Polly had changed ocean liner companies! But no wonder. That was instant dismissal, mixing in a — shall we say — *personal* way with passengers. When it came to matters of morality, all of the transatlantic vessels depended on maintaining a spotless reputation. A hint of anything close to sexual favours being exchanged, for money or other, would cause the first-class passenger list to shrink to nothing. It couldn't be condoned. Ships like this one absolutely depended on the enormous fees charged for first class.

Polly's infatuation could have been chaste. She and her love interest might never have gone beyond dreamy-eyed romantic to carnal. We'd never know that for sure. But any personal relationship with a passenger was a big no-no.

This was an interesting bit of new information that might help us. Polly had demonstrated a preference for older men. From what I had seen, she had been a sweet-looking girl. Not alluring in a conventional sense, perhaps, but nice-looking. Could she have fallen into the same trap on this voyage?

Unscrupulous men will take advantage of innocent young girls, especially those a station or two below theirs. And girls, for their part, are sometimes desperate for attention, and innocent like newborn lambs. It was a story as old as time.

Poor naive girls. Had I ever been that young?

There wasn't much else I needed to ask Mary at the moment. I thanked her very much, and Elf sent her on her way.

She waited until Mary was out of sight, and then slammed the door shut before speaking.

"Watcha think? Polly got a thing for the film star's hubby and 'e didn't say no? Film star catches them in the act and bops her on the head in jealousy?"

"Possible. Except hardly in the act. She was fully dressed when she was bopped." Good grief! I said *bopped. Have a little respect for the poor girl, Lucy*. Elf's language was rubbing off on me in ways that were not exactly admirable.

"Maybe she was dressing in the film star's clothes to excite the old man," Elf suggested.

Yuck. Where does Elf come up with these ideas?

Best not to ask …

"Well, it's a possibility," I admitted. "I'm not ruling anything out at this point. But in truth … after talking to Mary, I'm leaning toward Renata as the intended victim. It makes a lot more sense. Many people have it in for film stars. I can't see a simple girl like Polly attracting murderous enemies, can you? And there's no slighted boyfriend in the picture, from what we've heard."

Elf came to join me on the end of the bed. "Nah. Plus, can't see the hubby chancing a fling with Polly, either. Why would he? Obviously head over heels about the film star. Even Polly said that, and she saw them together in private."

"Good point," I said. They had seemed truly devoted to each other, in the times I had seen them together.

"You want me for anything more?" Elf said.

"Not particularly," I said, with only half my attention. "Why?"

"Thought I would follow Mary down and skulk around the other stewards. See what the scuttlebutt is."

"Sure," I said, with a thin smile. "How appropriate. Do you even know what *scuttlebutt* means?"

She hesitated. "Gossip?"

"It means that now. It's original meeting was a cask that contained a ship's daily drinking water supply. *Butt* means cask, *scuttle* means a hole drilled through something. You know how you can scuttle a boat by poking a hole in it? Only in this hole, they'd put a spigot. The sailors last century would hang around the water cask and yak away. Like a tea kettle in an office now. Hence gossip."

Her brown eyes went wide. "How do you know this shite?"

My turn to shrug. "I read it in a book. See, you really should let me teach you how to read."

She just grumbled and left the room in a rush.

One day, I thought, *one day, I'll make her sit still long enough to learn her letters.*

I'd missed lunch, as well as breakfast. This was not a good thing. I need to be fuelled regularly. With any luck, I could catch the kitchen making sandwiches for tea. It wouldn't be a problem because they know me. I always make it a policy to visit the crew and staff to introduce myself.

But I had a second reason for visiting the kitchen. While I couldn't do a lot for poor Polly, Meg was still very much in my mind. The kitchen was on the same floor as the first-class dining room, for convenience. The short distance meant food would stay hot while being served. Perhaps I could do some sleuthing of my own down there.

It's always easy to find the main kitchen on a ship. Simply enter the first-class dining room and look for the double doors that serving staff walk through with their trays. By the time I got to the dining room, tables had already been set for dinner, and the room was virtually empty. The kitchen, however, was bustling. I watched in fascination until someone appeared in front of me.

"Good afternoon, Lady Revelstoke! This is indeed a pleasure. Can I help you?"

I looked up into Ronaldo's warm brown eyes. I knew him only by his first name. He was one of the pastry chefs — a gentle grey-haired soul who had also been widowed. Hence the empathy we felt for each other.

"Hungry," I said simply.

"I'm icing little lemon cakes right now. Will that do?" He turned and gestured to the pastry station.

I groaned in joyous anticipation. "Wonderful! Cake is better than sandwiches."

He laughed with pure enjoyment. "We are so sympatico."

I watched as he iced one right in front of me. He held it in his left hand, swirling the glaze with almost loving tenderness. It was hard not to drool, I was salivating so much.

"Here you go. Couldn't be fresher." He balanced it on a frosting knife until I managed to snatch it with my fingers.

"Oooh, heavenly," I said between munches. "This may be the best thing I've ever eaten."

Ronaldo's eyes twinkled. "You always say that, and it always does my heart good. Have another."

I did have another, and then a third, all the while practically swooning with pleasure. Ronaldo beamed with the compliments. Honestly, chefs are the sweetest people on the planet to please.

All you have to do is praise their culinary creations. If only other men were that easy to make happy. I thought of Tony and all his vices, none of which actually made him happy.

After I'd overindulged, Ronaldo introduced me around to some of the younger kitchen staff who were new on this voyage. I attempted to remember their names by repeating them out loud. It was a little trick taught to me by my mother's sisters. People warm to you if you call them by name, and one never knew when one might need a midnight snack.

Which reminded me: *snack, snake*. Gray had said snakes might be drawn to warm environments, like engine rooms and kitchens. I kept my eyes alert for any slithering movements along the floor.

When the young folk went back to their stations, I turned to my host. "Ronaldo, I have another reason for coming here. We've been trying to find a young lady who has gone missing. We very much fear she's been seduced by an older man."

"Oh, that is not a good thing, Lady R. Not good at all." He shook his head, most disturbed. Now, there was a decent man. If I recalled correctly, he had daughters himself.

I said the next bit carefully. "I was wondering if second class had a private dining room like first class does. Some place they could be left alone, yet still be served. I expect he would want to impress her."

Ronaldo shook his head. He looked thoughtful. "No. I can't think of any place that would give privacy. That poor girl."

"Thank you." I touched his upper arm. "I must ask you to keep this confidential. Just between us. Her relatives are frantic to find her. It's such a touchy situation, I'm sure you can understand."

"Of course, my lady! If I hear anything, anything at all, I will let you know."

Ronaldo would understand the fate that could befall a young woman who lost her reputation in such a way. It was so unfair. A woman would be destroyed by such behaviour, whereas the man she was with — well, he would hardly suffer at all. This world is hugely unfair. I hope we can make it a better place for all in the future.

Something brushed against my leg. "Yikes!" I yelped.

"Tiger!" Ronaldo scolded. "What are you doing out and about at this time of the day?" I looked down to find a small marmalade cat winding between our legs. "I'm sorry, my lady! Usually, the cats stay out of the way until night, when they do their … um … hunting. But this one is especially friendly." He reached down to pet it, scolding all the while. I wasn't supposed to see the treat he pulled from his pocket to feed the dear thing, of course. Cheese, I think? No wonder it came out of hiding. I wasn't the only one beholden to Ronaldo.

I thanked him sincerely, then retraced my steps to the double doors. *Cats don't like snakes*, I told myself. And without doubt, the feeling was mutual. If Tiger was omnipresent, there's a good chance the boomslang hadn't taken up residence in the warmth of the kitchen. But just in case, my eyes swept the floor for anything green, one last time.

CHAPTER 15

ELF FUSSED ABOUT me as I dressed for dinner. The frock we decided I should wear this evening was dove-grey silk crepe, with discreet beading. Nothing flashy or provocative. Elf knew I had chosen carefully with respect for Polly, but even so ...

"Seems strange, dolling yerself up when ..." her voice cracked.

"I know," I said, full of sympathy. "But I have to go. It seems heartless, but we need to pretend things are normal. We can't draw attention to the fact that something has happened until they give us permission."

"Normal," Elf muttered. I understood exactly what she meant. *Nothing will be normal for Polly again.*

Probably not for Renata, either. How do you live with the knowledge that someone else has died wearing your clothes, and that you yourself might still be in danger?

As Elf smoothed out my hair, I contemplated that.

Under the circumstances, Renata had seemed uncommonly brave while discussing it all. She hardly seemed to recognize that she herself was likely still in danger. Even when I asked who might want to harm her, she brushed it off, almost as if she didn't believe it could be true. Perhaps she was more of an innocent than

I had thought? One could still have a history with men, and yet be naive about other things, I suppose.

I made my way down to dinner, a few minutes early, all the while wondering when the urge to scan every corridor for slithery green things would finally leave me.

Roy was sitting at the table by himself. I was a little surprised to see him there. He spotted me, shot up from his chair, and pulled out the one beside him. I smiled, secretly satisfied that I'd have a chance to talk to him alone.

"Renata didn't feel up to it," he confided.

I started to position my wrap along the back of my chair, then felt a chill go down my back. Cold? Ghosts? I changed my mind and instead swept the shawl over my shoulders.

Roberts turned up at my elbow to take my drink order and explain the choices for dinner. I smiled up at him, yet secretly wondered if he sensed phantoms here too.

All the vacant chairs. First, Meg. Now Renata, if only for one dinner. And somewhere in this ship, poor Polly's chair would remain empty. I wondered who, beyond the ship's staff, would grieve for her? Was there anyone back home? A girlhood friend? A priest or minister? Perhaps someone at the orphanage where she had lived?

Those thoughts led me even deeper into sorrow. Dead bodies don't last well on a ship. Usually, a burial at sea is necessary for the safety of all remaining. I felt uncommonly sad, thinking of it.

Maybe I could do something to help when I got back to England. Purchase a gravestone for her, perhaps. I'd ask Elf.

The drink appeared at my side. I seized it, nearly downing the thing in one go.

"I'm glad you came," Roy said. "They want us to keep things as normal as possible, of course."

"Yes," I said, glad to have my thoughts interrupted. "I gather we're not supposed to say anything."

I expected the captain's seat would stay unoccupied tonight as well. Both Gray and the captain would be engaged in managing the scene of the crime with their top staff.

Renata knew about Polly's murder, and I hadn't expected her to make an appearance. But of course, Stella wouldn't know. I assumed she was waiting for the dining room to fill before she made her entrance. And sure enough, a few minutes later she appeared at the door with a good-looking young man who steered her over to another table of male admirers. She didn't even pause for a glance our way. I guessed she wasn't joining us tonight. And why would she? Surely a table of adoring young men would provide a much better audience for her obvious charms than our stodgy group.

I had to admit she looked stunning in a shimmery turquoise sheath, which equalled her vibrant personality.

"I see our peacock has flown the coop for now."

I turned to my left, surprised to see Simon Leggatt about to sit down in the chair beside me. How did he manage to materialize there without my seeing his approach? Then I remembered what Tony had told me Leggatt had been involved with during the war: "*Something very hush hush.*"

Mr. Leggatt no doubt had hidden talents.

I recovered myself and smiled broadly. "You'll have to settle for this old hen." I tipped my cocktail glass to him.

Oh dear. Alcohol had loosened my tongue. I had momentarily left him speechless. I could see he was struggling to think of something gallant to say, so I decided to make it easy. "Forgive me. That remark puts you in a terribly awkward position."

"Lady Revelstoke, you are by far the most attractive woman in this room, never mind at this table." He spoke very low into my ear. "I was congratulating myself at having arrived in time to sit next to you."

Well, that put me firmly in a position of gratitude. Definitely a gentleman, our Simon Leggatt. I didn't even have time to compose a response before he added, "Now what are you drinking — I'll order another."

"A Sidecar," I said.

"I don't know that one."

"Cognac, Cointreau, and lemon juice," I said. "Made famous by the Ritz Hotel in Paris, I believe. Invented sometime during the war. Quite civilized, I'd say, but lethal."

"Then I'll have one myself." He smiled and signalled the drinks waiter over. "We'll both live dangerously."

I felt a shiver go through me. A rather sensual shiver that ended where it shouldn't. Something about that man put all my senses on alert, in a very disturbing way. It struck me that Simon Leggatt was the rare sort of fellow who could indeed be a danger to me and my ordered life.

The low voice beside me took me out of my reverie. "Tony Anderson seems to think you're his girl."

"Tony Anderson is clearly misinformed," I said clearly. "There has never been even a hint of an understanding between us." I turned to him. "Tony was my husband Johnny's friend, actually. They were officers together in France and remained close after. I would call him a family friend. My son, Charlie, calls him Uncle Tony. He was good to us after Johnny died but has been somewhat absent of late."

Simon was watching me closely, as if hesitating to say something.

"And yes, I know about the gambling. You don't need to tell me his faults. My maid, Elf, does that daily. She doesn't like him much." I threw back the end of the Sidecar from my glass. "Of course, calling her a maid is a trifle optimistic." It seems this was becoming my standard line to explain our relationship.

He chuckled. "I look forward to meeting this interesting companion of yours."

Our drinks arrived, and I grabbed for mine.

"If you spend any time with me, you will," I said, moving the glass to my lips. "She'll insist upon it."

"Then I look forward to it," he said evenly. *Was that a hint of future plans*, I wondered?

"Poor man," I said, keeping the conversation light. "You have yet to see what Elf can do with a knife."

He laughed out loud. "And I assume you don't mean to roast fowl." He picked up his glass. "To Elf," he said. "May she always be there at your side." He took a sip.

"Good show! Here come the others," said Roy, to my right.

Tony appeared in the doorway with Lord Harry, and they made their way over. I could see both had been drinking hard.

Tony was first to speak as he plunked down across from me. "Gad, Lucy, you are a sight for these sore eyes." They did look sore too. *Bloodshot* might be more accurate. "Where are the other pretty birds?"

I nearly choked on that, so close it was to what Simon had said. Men seemed to have a universal language for appraising women, young and old. "Only me tonight. Renata took a pass, and Stella is seated over there." I pointed to the table of adoring young men.

"Then we are doubly lucky to have you," Tony said gallantly. Lord Harry merely giggled.

It occurred to me that I was a little lonely for female company this trip. The staff had tried to balance the numbers at our table — Renata, Meg, and Stella should have been sitting with us, but all were missing tonight. On my last voyage, I had made friends with a delightful middle-aged American couple with whom I'd stayed in touch by letter. I missed Florrie's easy company this time out. The attention of men, although flattering, can get wearing after a while. Often, one feels like a ball being fought over in some kind of sport.

More drinks arrived. Roberts attended to Harry, then to Tony, and lastly to Simon. The class hierarchy was certainly in play tonight. I listened to the three of them banter back and forth about the menu and then turned to Roy.

"I have a rather unique question for you. What can you tell me about boomslangs?"

He looked startled. "Tree snakes? Nasty things. Very poisonous. Got one of my houseboys in the old country. Bites you, and then the venom takes hours to work. Anticoagulant, as I remember." He took a deep breath. "Very dangerous. Not unlike black mambas, another wretched creature. Boomslang males are a pretty green and have huge eyes. They climb trees ..."

"What do they eat?" I asked.

"Lizards, birds, eggs, and frogs — they'll even eat each other." He turned to me. "Bloody cannibals. Godawful things, snakes. Why on earth are you asking about them?"

Good thing I had thought of a reason. "I heard two men talking about Africa and thought of you. The word stuck in my mind." That seemed to satisfy him.

"Unusual name, yes. *Boom* means tree in Afrikaans, and *slang* means snake. It's perfectly logical, really."

I was satisfied. This little conversation had served a purpose. Roy had indeed lived in Africa. It was doubtful he could know so much about the snakes there if he hadn't, let alone the meaning of the words in Afrikaans. This made it likely he was at least partly who he claimed to be.

I gave myself kudos for putting two and two together. At the same time, a harrowing thought occurred to me. *He had lived in Africa ...* and knew a lot about boomslangs. Rumour was he liked money and had little of his own.

Could he be the snake smuggler using cabin 334?

CHAPTER 16

DINNER FINISHED WITH an absolutely delicious crema catalana, which I knew to be similar to crème brûlée. Coffee had been served and brandy, for some. Soon the band would start. I didn't like to wait around for that. Watching others dance brought back too many memories of Johnny.

"Anyone up for a game or two?" said Tony. "Lord Harry? Armitage? How about you, Leggatt?" He looked hopefully across the table at Simon, who shook his head.

"I'll join you. Sure," said Roy.

"Why not," said Harry.

They all rose at once. I saw Tony hesitate, wondering what to do with me, since once again the men seemed keen to desert me.

Luckily, Simon Leggatt picked up the hint. "Would you care to stay and dance, Lady Revelstoke?"

I shook my head politely. "It's been a long day."

"Then let me escort you back to your cabin."

Tony gave him a hail-fellow-well-met smile with some sort of approving male hand gesture, then turned to go. I watched, amused, as the three men tottered off together to the card room. All had been drinking so heavily, I was pretty sure any card shark would make a meal of them. But that wasn't my problem.

I toyed with my coffee cup. I had my own concerns. Nothing I could do about poor Polly at this point. I'd express my deductions to Gray later when we were alone. But there was still Meg's disappearance to be sorted out. Something bothered me about our conclusions yesterday. I had planned to do a little sleuthing after dinner, and here it appeared I was going to be marched back to my cabin by a male protector.

Not to worry. My mind was already concocting a plan …

"I understand you have an estate in Wiltshire, Lady Revelstoke."

I was brought out of my reverie by that pleasant male voice.

"Yes, although I'm really only the caretaker. My son, Charlie, inherits when he comes of age. He's nearly fourteen and away at school."

"I am also from the west. Shropshire, to be exact. We're almost neighbours."

"Fancy that," I replied. "How nice that we share something in common." And at that, I had to smile. Sheep! That's what we had in common. The West Country and Shropshire are populated primarily by sheep.

"Do you live there now?" I asked.

"Alas, I don't get much opportunity. My work is primarily in London."

"And what work do you do, Mr. Leggatt?" Oh, I can be a devil when necessary!

"Call me Simon," he said. "I have a government job. Quite dull, I assure you."

A giggle escaped me. Dull? *You'll have to do better than that, Simon Leggatt.*

The band had started up. I made signs to rise, and Simon was on his feet in an instant, pulling out my chair.

"Do you hear that?" he said, as I started away from the table. "They're playing a waltz."

"'The Merry Widow,'" I said automatically. "By Franz Lehár." How fitting. I had to smile. It was a small band, but they played it well. That sweeping tune had always filled me with an almost spooky mixture of hope and longing.

"I do love a waltz," he said earnestly, touching my arm. "Just one dance? Please?"

I hesitated, turning to him. For a moment, he looked like an eager young boy. I was reminded of Charlie, and it did something to my heart.

I smiled and relented. "Why not?"

He laughed and pulled me over to the wooden dance floor in front of the bandstand. I slid into his arms. My left hand automatically went to his shoulder, his own to my waist. We fell easily into the three-four waltz tempo, drifting smoothly together under his lead. He began with an easy flow, back and forth, until he was sure of me. When the music picked up speed, he started to twirl us, and soon we were soaring into a full Viennese waltz, using the whole dance floor. At that point, others started to join us.

Oh, what a whirl! Tempestuous but controlled, Simon moved us with such abandon that I giggled out loud as we passed other couples. The song returned to the sweet theme, and I was floating, almost breathless, filled with the most glorious feeling of freedom and joy. I hadn't felt so alive in years!

When the song came to an end, everyone whooped and clapped. I was smiling from ear to ear.

"That was fabulous!" said Simon. "Where did you learn to dance like that?"

"The Knights of Columbus Hall in my hometown," I said wryly. "All the aunts in attendance, plus the Holy Ghost, to make sure we didn't stand too close. Although I think the dragon aunts could have managed on their own without a deity. How about you?"

"Mrs. Gore-Smith," said Simon, eyes twinkling. "She taught Saturday morning dancing lessons in the village hall. Mandatory attendance for me and all my mates. Asking ladies to dance was a necessary adult obligation, according to my old man. He would say, 'Gotta do your duty, boy.' I actually loved it but was smart enough not to ruin a lad's reputation by saying so."

The band had switched to a slow romantic song. Simon sensed my awkwardness and steered me off the dance floor.

I understood what Simon said about "doing one's duty." Sometimes, like tonight, dancing can be an utter joy. Other times it can be pure torture, if your partner is holding you too close and you don't want to be in his arms. Still, to be a good wife and hostess at social gatherings, one had to dance with a myriad of your husband's friends and noble acquaintances. Some not so noble, as it turned out.

I shivered, remembering how much I had enjoyed being in Simon's arms. What was I to make of this?

So deep had I been in my own thoughts that I missed our departure from the dining room, and passed by the card room without even a notice. With a start, I realized we had entered the main foyer, whereupon Simon paused, waiting for instructions.

"I'm on the promenade deck," I said, pointing toward the grand staircase.

We continued walking, in quiet companionship. Simon had a trait given to few men, in my experience. He seemed comfortable with silence.

As we strode the final corridor to my stateroom, I resisted the urge to ask him where his cabin was located. Usually, men will tell you without being asked. "Ah, I'm not far from you," they'll say, or "I'm one floor down." Anything to keep the conversation going.

I was reminded of the expression: Still waters run deep.

"Here we are," I said. I opened the cabin door, gave him a goodnight smile, and retreated within. I might have closed the door a mite too quickly, as this man seemed to have my mind warning *danger*. Simon Leggatt messed a little too much with my equilibrium.

Elf was nowhere about. I assumed she was off with her steward friend. I also knew that I would be alone in the cabin tonight, as Gray would be preoccupied with poor Polly's death.

That suited my purposes fine. I sat on the bed for about five minutes, calculating it to be enough time for my escort to retrace his steps along the hall and out of sight. Then I picked up my bag and slipped out the door, closing it quietly before turning.

And coming face to face with Simon Leggatt.

"Merda," I hollered, clutching the fabric at my chest. "You scared me."

"My apologies. I think we should talk," said Simon. Up until now, he had seemed the ultimate gentleman … quietly attractive, smoothly harmless. I could see it was a good disguise. Right now, he looked as solid and resolute as a giant mastiff.

I stood facing him, trying to catch my breath. "You've scuppered my plans," I admitted. Not waiting for a reply, I swung around, opened the door, and ushered him in.

I plunked myself down on the bed. When the door closed behind him, he looked this way and that, frowning slightly.

I had a sudden brainwave. "Let me guess. Did Graham West put you up to this?"

It would be just like Gray to appoint a substitute guardian when he himself couldn't be in place.

Simon smiled sheepishly. Finally, a break in the bulldog countenance. One hand went to his forehead to sweep back his hair. "Guilty as charged. He asked me to keep an eye on you. Which was truly a pleasure. You dance divinely."

I sighed. Earlier, Gray had said, "There's someone else I want to bring into this." That someone was without doubt Simon Leggatt. It made me wonder yet again exactly what professional title and occupation Mr. Leggatt held in the real world.

"Tell me first. How do you know our purser?"

He shoved fists into his pants pockets, hesitating a beat. "I served with him during the war."

That made me sit up. According to Tony, Simon had done something hush hush for the military back then. I knew Gray had been in the navy during the war but assumed he had been a common sailor. *Exactly what part had he played?*

I gulped. "Then it seems I may have underestimated Mr. West enormously. Would you agree?"

"Fine way to put it," he said. And that was that. No elaboration. I felt like an ingenue standing behind the curtains, peeking out at the adults.

"How did you skip to thinking I might have night plans?" I asked.

Once again, he grinned. "Little things in your behaviour. Comes down to experience. Or maybe bloody-mindedness."

That made me smile. "Would you have stayed outside my stateroom all night?"

"Not sure." He took the chair under the porthole. "Probably not. An hour, two maybe. Thanks for saving me the time."

I groaned audibly.

"So. What did you have in mind for us?" Simon said. He glanced at his watch. Waited.

My heart was beating a jazz rhythm. What to do? It was late at night. What possible explanation could I have for sneaking out of my cabin after just being dropped off here?

My first thought was I could make up that I was on my way to a romantic rendezvous. But that would never do. Since Gray had sent the man here for my protection, it was obvious the romantic rendezvous wouldn't have been with Gray himself. *It wouldn't do, Lucy*, I told myself. No way did I want to worry either man about competition that didn't exist.

What else could I plead? Drinks with married friends in their cabin? If so, why didn't I just have Simon walk me to their cabin in the first place? That wouldn't do either.

I was out of ideas. And when that happens — when all else fails — I usually opt for the truth. If Gray trusted him ... well, there was a good chance he would expect me to do the same.

I came clean. In a roundabout way.

"Do you know what happened this morning?" I asked. That way, he could tell me.

"I know about Renata Harwood's sister going missing, and I know that her steward has been murdered," said Simon.

I let out the breath I had been holding. "That makes it easy. You know as much as I do then. Well, almost." I took another breath. "I've been doing a little sleuthing with my maid. We managed to get a set of keys —"

"I won't ask how," said Simon. His eyes twinkled.

"Good man. And a list of empty cabins in second class." I looked over to see how he was taking it. *Sardonic* might be a good way to describe that smile. "Thoughts being …"

"The sister might be hiding out there with a man." Simon's brown eyes drilled into mine. "Good reasoning. What did you find?"

I chuckled. "Smuggled snakes in one cabin, half empty booze bottles in another. Gray knows about them."

"Gray?" he said.

Rats! How could I be so foolish as to only use his first name? And worse than that, a nickname! I could feel the blush coming. "We go way back."

He smiled. "I sense an interesting story there. In fact, I gather it might explain some unique skills West demonstrated during the war. Are you Canadian, like him?"

"Yes," I said. "I was born there. Can you still hear my accent? I've been here since before the war and am told I've lost most of it."

"Just a hint left. But continue, please, about the cabins."

Good! I was relieved to put aside the past for now. "At the third cabin, we hit pay dirt." I leaned forward. "We found a few items of Meg's clothing in the wardrobe. But no evidence of a man sharing it with her."

"Well done. You've identified the clothes as hers?"

This is where I decided to tread carefully. "Yes. An evening dress and a shawl. Shoes on the floor. Thing is, something keeps bothering me about that cabin, something I can't quite put my finger on. I wanted to have another look at it tonight. That's where I was going when you found me out."

Simon rose gracefully. "You have keys still?"

I pulled myself up. "Em, not exactly. But we won't be needing them."

He gave me a thin smile. "I shall wait and see then, shall I?"

Only one in a hundred men would let me off the hook like that, I mused.

As the door closed behind me, Simon said, "Better lock it. I hear there are unscrupulous people on this voyage."

I punched his shoulder with my fist. He guffawed with delight.

Walking down the hall with Simon Leggatt certainly gave me ambivalent feelings. I was grateful for his company on this mission, in a general way. Gray had vouched for him, which counted for something. It would be good to have another person, someone extremely intelligent with whom to share my sleuthing thoughts. No question, he was good company. On the other hand, that ambivalence. *He was good company*. Too good, in some ways.

Keep your eyes on the prize, Lucy, not on the man! I told myself.

It was a somewhat uncomfortable walk to cabin 128. Down the corridor, into the main foyer, down two flights of stairs. Simon accepted my lead as a matter of fact, opening doors where they needed to be opened. There are a lot of doors on a boat, of course.

I knew the reason why. Icebergs may have taken down the *Titanic*, but the one thing we fear most on a ship is something quite the opposite: fire. Heavy doors help to contain a fire so it doesn't spread before staff can put it out. Or at least, that's the hope.

I stole a look at my companion, trying to put my feelings aside and observe him dispassionately. As before, he had opted for nondescript appearance. Kitted out for dinner in the accepted white tie and tails attire, but nothing to make him stand out.

Tony always dressed in the height of fashion, wearing his hair and clothes in a way that appeared somewhat flamboyant. In contrast, Simon Leggatt managed to blend in with the scenery. It was a rather particular talent.

I had to ask myself: *What was it about the man that made him so darn attractive?* Yes, our dance had been wonderful, joyous, and almost wild. I had seen another side of him that was so different from the quiet statesman or diplomat, or whatever the heck he was … daring, and very, very attractive. Maybe it was something about confidence — that he didn't seem to care or even register what other people thought.

I also liked the fact that he didn't need to fill in space by talking. That was a rare trait indeed, and not just among men.

"Down this corridor," I said, with a small hand signal.

He followed my lead, whistling quietly.

I stopped in front of cabin 128 and tested the handle. Good old Elf! She'd obviously rigged the catch to render the door unlockable. Chewing gum and a paper wedge?

"Well, hello there!" rang out a voice behind us. "We're your next-door neighbours!"

Oh no! My blood froze. I don't know what made me give the handle a swift pull shut, whether it was conscience or self-preservation. Whatever, I acted without thinking.

We had checked the hall for people, but of course couldn't anticipate that someone might exit their cabin at exactly the time we were going past. It was impossible to hide the guilty look that must have been on my face.

Luckily, Simon took immediate command. "We're the Leggatts," he said, reaching out a hand.

It took less than a moment for me to realize how clever he had been. That was a cue for me to play the part of his wife. *Oh, you are quicker than a wily fox, Simon Leggatt!* I thought to myself.

"Bert Crocket," said the portly man with the big smile and no hair. "From Boston. And this here's my wife, Ginny. Come say hello, Gin."

I would have known he was American by the way he pronounced his hometown: Baaston. Or from the way he made introductions including their first names. No Brit of lofty social standing would do that. I smiled and moved my gaze to "Gin."

She was a pretty woman dressed in the height of fashion, with elaborately arranged caramel hair and a few more pounds than was considered fashionable. I liked her smile.

"Pleased to meet you," she said happily. "Isn't this a fabulous ship? It even has a beauty parlour!"

I beamed at her. Now I knew how the hair was so beautifully maintained. And to think some board members of the Empire line had claimed the salon would be a "waste of space." All men, who would never turn down adding another bar or card room, of course.

"I've used it myself," I said to make her feel comfortable. "Do check out the shop adjacent to it. It's worth browsing through as well."

She nodded appreciatively.

"We were about to take a turn around the deck before bed. Nothing like a good walk in the night air to make you sleepy, I always say. Would you care to join us?" He looked at us eagerly. I felt a moment of panic. Did it show on my face?

"We're turning in now," said Simon, with a determined smile.

Bert grinned back and winked. I could just imagine what he thought Simon had in mind, and I could feel the blush creeping up my face. Luckily, the notion of hanky-panky seemed to bypass his wife.

"Delightful meeting you," I said to her.

"Yes!" said Gin. "Maybe we'll see you for lunch or dinner?"

"We'll look for you." Simon managed a polite head bow. He held the cabin door open for me to walk though.

I scanned the floor frantically. *No snakes*, thank the Lord.

The moment the door shut behind us, Simon started apologizing.

"I'm terribly sorry about that. I didn't know what else to do."

Ah, the universal language of men! They knew what to say to put others of their kind offside. I turned away from him. "He was rather insistent."

"Putting up a front at the door is quite a different thing from having to maintain a conversation over time. I didn't want to take the chance." That one hand went to sweep his hair back again. It appeared to be a nervous gesture. I found it quite endearing that our Mr. Leggatt wasn't as stoic as he attempted to appear.

"You're a good sport, Lady Revelstoke."

"Call me Lucy," I said. "After all, we are husband and wife."

He grinned sheepishly. "Yes, that came at the spur of the moment. I couldn't think of any respectable reason for the two of us to be ... at this time of night ... well, you understand. Thank you for playing along. Good thing we're staying in first class, otherwise things might get a bit awkward."

My turn to grin. He meant we were unlikely to run into the Crockets again. And yes, if Tony got a hint that I was in fact being introduced around as Mrs. Leggatt, *awkward* would be the mildest of terms.

I sat down on the end of the bed. "Here's the penny tour. You'll see an evening dress in the closet. George Eversleigh says it's Meg's."

Pause. "Eversleigh?"

Darn! Simon didn't miss a thing. I cursed under my breath. Somehow, we hadn't got around to all the details of yesterday's adventure. "I didn't have a chance to tell you. George Eversleigh was also looking for Meg. You missed that scene the first night."

"Heard about it," he said. "Jilted lover, or some such."

"Mr. Eversleigh saw me in the corridor outside this cabin, leaving with a shawl. He claimed it was Meg's and demanded to see the room here. In retrospect, it was a bit of good luck for me. It meant I didn't have to confront Renata and Roy myself with the evidence."

"So, Eversleigh identified the shawl."

"And the evening dress in the wardrobe there." I pointed. "Her shoes are beside the bed."

Simon opened the wardrobe door. The gown was still hanging there, I was relieved to see. I watched him finger the material.

"Are we sure this is Meg's? How much do men know about women's clothes really?" he murmured.

"Well, he had no trouble identifying the shawl, since he was the one who purchased it for her." Yes, I was amused. For some reason, it felt good to one-up my companion on facts. Perhaps I felt the need to justify my amateur sleuthing.

"Ah! Not likely to make a mistake about that, then." Simon nodded. He bent over, pushed aside the dress, and reached out with one hand to snatch something from the bottom of the wardrobe. "Here's her handbag."

It was an evening bag, actually. A lovely thing that would go with the frock hanging above it. The skirt of the gown brushed the floor of the wardrobe and might have covered the bag. "We didn't notice that in our haste." I had been occupied with the shawl on the bed.

"It was pushed back a bit. Shall we open it?" Simon handed me an expensive, slim, silver-coloured clutch bag covered in sequins. A memory came back to me quickly, from the hair salon. This was Renata's bag, the one she had described to me in detail, right down to the monogrammed clasp. The bag she had accused Meg of taking without permission.

I took it almost reverently in my hands. Here were contained some of the most personal items of a woman's possessions. Inside, I could expect to find a handkerchief, perhaps with initials, a powder compact, her favourite lipstick ... all those things that define us as individual females. Things we value and touch over and over ...

I opened the clasp.

Empty. No wait. One thing. *How odd*, I thought, as I drew out the crisply folded notepaper.

I felt suddenly cold. Premonition overwhelmed me, as it had done in the past. And this I knew: Never before had it been wrong. I looked up at Simon, the piece of paper dangling from my fingers like something too ghastly to hold. "You read it." My voice was hoarse.

The way his eyes drilled into mine confirmed what I was feeling. He came forward, took the note from my hand, and read aloud.

My life is miserable. I can't go on. Forgive me. Meg

CHAPTER 17

"A SUICIDE NOTE." I said it softly, not wanting to believe it.

"Seems so," said Simon. He refolded the note carefully.

The grim reality of this discovery made my heart feel like it was weighed down with stone.

"She threw herself overboard?" I could hardly manage to say the words.

"It looks that way." Simon came to sit beside me on the bed.

"I feel so bad for her. What could have made her so miserable?" He paused, reflecting. "We'll probably never know."

I thought about that for a moment. It seemed even more pathetic — to take your own life and leave the people who mourned you with no reason why.

"The thing I don't understand is, why did she hide the suicide note in a handbag?" Simon puzzled. "Why not just leave it on the bed?"

"I can explain that," I said. "This is Renata's evening bag. Meg borrowed it from her sister without permission. Renata told me yesterday, when we were in the hair salon. She was quite irate about it." I took a deep breath. "I think Meg wanted Renata to discover the note. She knew that when her belongings were collected by her family, Renata would reclaim the bag."

"Ah. I can see that," said Simon.

"Plus," I continued, "if you leave a note on the bed, it will most likely be found by a steward. You know what people are like, with shocking news like this. Knowledge makes them feel important, and they would hardly keep it to themselves. Word gets around pretty quickly among the staff and crew. Probably Meg was thinking of her family, and didn't want there to be hurtful gossip." I swallowed. "It's what I would do."

Simon nodded solemnly.

The weight of the air in the room seemed oppressive. "First, poor Polly dead. Now Meg. It's almost too much to bear."

Simon reached into a pocket and came out with a handkerchief. He handed it to me. "Do you think their deaths are related in some way?"

I made to stifle the sniffles. "I might have done before. I don't see how now," I said, before blowing my nose most ungracefully. "Meg wouldn't have killed Polly. If she had, it would be in her note."

Simon nodded. "Smart girl, to link the two of them that way. I did have thoughts along those same lines. Remember, though, that Meg disappeared the day before Polly was killed."

Ah. That clinched it. "No connection between the two events. The timing is wrong." I wiped my nose and scrunched up the handkerchief. Should I give it back? Dirty? No, of course not. My goodness, common sense was eluding me this evening.

There was no other conclusion to make. I had to accept that Meg committed suicide because she was desperately unhappy. But oh, I didn't want the mystery of our missing Meg to end this way. I had hoped for a happy ending, a romantic one. Two lovers running off to be together ...

"Why is life not like books?" I looked over at Simon with childish longing in my voice. He put the tragic note down on the bed beside us, picked up my hand, and cradled it in his.

"Maybe that's why we like books so much," Simon said kindly. "They make right of the world. Order from chaos. They provide endings that satisfy us, and that we can understand."

We stared at each other for a moment too long. I let my eyes drop to my lap as I puzzled what to do about this attractive man who seemed to mirror my own thoughts so poignantly.

From the corridor came a commotion. Angry voices became louder as they drew near. I snatched my hand away from Simon's at the sound of the door opening.

Roy Armitage entered, pushing his way past George Eversleigh. Both looked ready to commit murder.

Roy stopped dead when he saw us perched on the bed. His already outraged face turned a brighter red. "What are you doing here?" he demanded.

I sat with my mouth open. I seemed to be doing a lot of that lately.

It was obvious what must have happened. George had caught up with Roy and confronted him about the shawl, and Roy had demanded to see where it had come from. The older man was still in his dinner jacket, so I expect George had found him in the card room or had staked out the hallway outside the Victoriana Suite waiting for Roy to return.

"Come in," Simon said. "Be quiet and shut the door behind you." Really quite amazing, how he did that. Perhaps it was the low bass of his voice, or maybe the uncompromising tone. But without raising the volume at all, his words had an element of command that you dared not ignore. Military intelligence, indeed.

"Now look here, Leggatt —"

"Shush …" Simon ordered.

George closed the door. Simon was on his feet now, the folded note in his hand. Again, I marvelled at how an average size man could transform himself into such a formidable commander.

"What I'm about to show you is strictly confidential, for now. We just discovered this. I haven't had time to inform the security staff."

He looked at George, and then back to Roy, as if making a decision. Then he passed the note to Roy.

I understood this. George might be the one who would suffer more, but Roy was next of kin.

Roy opened the note and read, while George stood shuffling from one foot to the other impatiently beside him. I heard Roy curse under his breath, and then he passed the note to George.

"Bloody hell. What am I going to tell Renata?" Roy muttered.

A wail came from George that shook me to my shoes.

"Hold it together, man," chided Roy. "For God's sake."

Simon interceded. "Before we jump to conclusions, can you confirm for me that this is Meg's handwriting?"

Roy nodded slowly. "Looks that way."

"And you, Eversleigh? Can you confirm this?" Simon was nothing if not thorough.

George fingered the note and nodded. "It's even her notepaper. I recognize it. She's written to me before."

"Do you have any of those notes with you on this ship? We could compare conclusively."

"Yes. In my cabin." He looked up, and the pain on his face

was hard to bear. "But why?" cried George. "Why was she so miserable? Why didn't she tell me?"

"Maybe if you had stopped hounding her," said Roy.

That was cruel. I had to wonder: *Why did Roy hate George Eversleigh so much?*

There was a pause of silence before the explosion.

"Hounding her? How dare you! I loved her! Which is more than you can say, you ... you ... heartless cad!" His left hand still held the note, but his right hand went to a fist, and I braced for blows.

Knock knock.

We all went quiet.

Knock knock again.

"*Hello? Everything all right in there?*"

Oh no! It was our neighbour from the next cabin, Mr. Crocket, back from his night walk.

I stood quickly, put my hand up to silence the others, and went to the door. I opened it just enough for him to see my face.

"Thank you for checking, Mr. Crocket. I'm sorry we disturbed you. I'm afraid we've received very bad news about a young lady friend of ours. These kind gentlemen came just now to tell us, and we're all rather grief-stricken." I opened the door more than a foot so he could see in and swept a hand back to the others. George was obviously stricken, still holding the note.

"I am so sorry," said Crocket. "I'll leave you in peace." He hesitated. "If I can do anything to help —"

"Thank you for your kindness," I said, shaking my head slowly.

I raised a hand to my eyes as if to wipe away tears, which in fact were close to forming. He retreated with a soft "Goodnight."

Phew. Back in the room, I rested my forehead on the door for a moment to recover my equilibrium.

"Bloody brilliant," said Roy, with one clap. "Have you ever considered acting?"

The sheer audacity of that statement gave me strength. Actresses did not have the best moral reputation, to put it kindly, and for that suggestion to be put to a countess ... Well, if Tony had been here, it would have been pistols at dawn for sure! I pushed away from the door, finding it hard to hold down the giggles.

"Well done, Lucy," said Simon.

"It had to be me, I figured." I retraced my steps to the bed and sat down again. "Mr. Crocket is a good sort who wouldn't back down until he knew I was out of any danger."

"Good call," said Simon. "And now, gentlemen, I believe we should take our leave. I'll take care of the note. And please, I must insist that you keep this matter to yourselves for now."

"I have to tell Renata," Roy objected. "How can I not?"

"He has a point, Simon," I said. "She is next of kin, poor thing, and I don't know that any of us are such terrific actors that we could pretend nothing had happened tonight."

"I couldn't," said Roy.

"Yes, you may tell Renata," Simon agreed. "But please insist that she keep this to herself until the proper officers have been notified. Now, leave quietly, please. We'll follow later."

"You first," George said to Roy.

"So be it. You'll be in touch tomorrow?" Roy addressed it to Simon.

"Of course."

Roy nodded to me and left the cabin.

No sooner had the door closed behind him, but George came alive.

"You have some sort of authority here, I take it? On this ship?"

I was a bit taken aback that George would do the asking instead of Roy, and at the same time, I wondered why nobody had asked before. Neither man had questioned Simon's insistence that he be the one to keep Meg's suicide note.

"Yes," said Simon simply. No explanation.

Now that takes guts, I thought to myself. Most people feel they have to fill in silence with explanation. Not Simon, apparently. He demonstrated a level of confidence I've never felt.

The two men measured each other with their eyes until George eventually nodded. Once again, I was witness to the unique language between men.

"It's late. I'll want to compare the handwriting in this note to the one in your possession. As soon as possible would be best."

"Certainly. We can do that right now. I have a few. Where?" asked George.

"I can meet you at your cabin after I walk Lady Revelstoke back to hers. I'm very sorry, Eversleigh. I know this must be horrendous for you."

George moaned in pain. I was reminded of that story of a great lion with a thorn in his paw. "Have you ever been in love?" He directed the question to Simon, who paused before answering.

"I was very fond of Mrs. Leggatt," he said carefully.

George snorted. "Fond of! Oh man, that's not even a close second! I mean, utterly mad with it. Like the air she breathes is the only thing that keeps you alive. Have you?" He gestured to me now. "Do you know what I mean?"

I nodded in earnest. "Everyone deserves to experience it once. I did."

George hung his head. "You never knew her. She was … one in a million. Sweet, fun-loving, clever — a lot more clever than that painted hussy sister of hers. I just can't believe she's dead." With that, he turned and dragged himself from the room.

CHAPTER 18

SIMON MADE NO effort to leave the bed. "We'll wait a short while before departing. I'd like to make sure those neighbours of yours are well-ensconced within."

"They're not my neighbours," I reminded him. "This isn't my cabin."

Simon cursed under his breath. "My apologies. For some reason I think of this entire escapade as your business."

Well, it sort of was, I had to admit. If Simon hadn't laid in wait for me outside my stateroom, I would have been on my own tonight. He wouldn't have experienced the last scene with Roy and George, let alone been a party to the reading of Meg's suicide note.

That note. It made me so sad.

"I wonder if Meg knew how much George loved her," I said wistfully.

Simon agreed with me. "It's hard to imagine someone being so loved yet feeling the need to end their life."

"I have to think she was unaware. Which makes me even more sad that she never experienced the kind of love George talked about."

Simon seemed deep in thought. It occurred to me that he wasn't just a man of action, as much as I had seen he could act instantly if needed. Still waters, as they say. Finally, he said, "When you spoke of your similar experience, were you thinking of your husband?"

I nodded. "We met on an ocean liner, before the war. I was only eighteen, eager for adventure, regardless of the risk. 'Stark reckless like a baby,' Elf would say."

"Ah yes. Graham West also spoke of the inimitable Elf. Tell me more about her, how you came to be together," Simon asked.

For a moment, I was taken aback. Then I remembered — it wasn't Gray I was with tonight. Simon had not yet met Elf. *How could I be feeling so close to this man, when he hadn't even been introduced to my dearest friend?*

"Elf is short for Elfreda. Technically, she's my maid, but in truth, she's more like a sister. She was with me on that first transatlantic crossing from New York City. I ..." I hesitated, not quite sure how to put it. But then emotion got hold of me. "I wouldn't know what to do without her. She helped me nurse Johnny when he was dying. He wouldn't have anyone else. She took charge of my young son, Charlie, when I was so full of grief I couldn't cope. And she was at my side day and night to keep me alive during that first year when all I wanted was to fall asleep and never wake up."

I felt Simon watching me. When I turned to meet his eyes, he nodded with sympathy. "I know what it's like to lose those you care about the most."

Of course he did. I'd forgotten his own history. "I'm so sorry. The flu was so tragic and unfair," I said. "Is it any wonder we don't trust the future? As if the war wasn't enough. To survive that, and ... I'm sorry you lost your wife and child. Gray lost his only sister. She was such a sweet thing." The flu had taken a few of my family members back in Canada, but luckily not Elf or Charlie. Johnny had already been sick with TB, so we had retreated to relative seclusion in the country.

"Tell me about West. You've known him for many years, I take it."

Uh oh. How did the conversation turn to this? I would have to be careful not to reveal too much about my past. *Say enough to satisfy him, but only that.*

"We grew up together on the east side of Hamilton. My older brother, Paolo, was his best friend. We all played together back then, when they let me. Gray and Paolo are still in touch." I paused, searching for words. "It was one big surprise when I met up with him on this ship last June, after all those years. Felt almost like having my brother close, you understand? Funny, how easily you can fall back into old relationships, old habits. Like calling him Gray, instead of Mr. West."

Simon smiled. "It does seem silly, addressing each other by formal names when you were kids together. Did you know Elf back then too?"

I smiled in remembrance. "No. Elf was a byproduct of my one day in New York prior to the voyage. She and her knife got me out of a jam, so I returned the favour and hauled her along with me on the ship to England."

"As your maid." Simon seemed amused. "Is she a good maid?"

"Appalling," I admitted. The thought of it cheered me up. "Luckily, she has other, more essential qualities."

"Such as?" he asked.

Again, I hesitated. "Loyalty. Courage. Abundant energy. And a great throwing arm."

He laughed at that, while shaking his head.

"Plus a mouth that can make prospective suitors go dead white on the doorstep."

"In shock?"

"More in fear." I pushed myself off the bed. "Speaking of which, can we go now? Elf will be waiting. I'm very late getting back to our stateroom and have more reason than you to dread that mouth of hers."

IT WAS IMPOSSIBLE to retreat from the room without being seen, as it turned out. At least, without being heard. Simon pointed to the Crocket's cabin and put a finger to his lips, as the door had been left ajar. I succeeded in quietly pulling our door closed behind me without Simon noticing that it remained unlocked. Not sure why that seemed important to me at the time. Something still niggled at me, no doubt.

Elf was indeed waiting up for me when I reached our stateroom. That girl has ears like a Labrador retriever. Before I could say goodnight to Simon in the corridor, she had the door open.

I took firm control.

"Mr. Leggatt, this is Elfreda, my maid. Elf, this is Mr. Leggatt, who also sits at our dinner table. He was kind enough to walk me back."

"How do you do?" Simon gave her a wry grin.

"Pleased ta meet ya," said Elf. She gave him the once-over in that special "Elf" way. "You coming in?"

She addressed it to him, but I answered for both of us.

"He was just saying goodnight. Thanks for the escort, Mr.

Leggatt. I'll see you at breakfast, no doubt."

He smiled warmly. "I'll look forward to it."

Elf was all over me after the door closed behind us. "Who's the new guy? What's he up to? Where's Lord Poncy-face?"

"Tony — don't call him that — was last seen in the card room, probably down to his undershirt and trousers by now. New guy is an unofficial temporary replacement for Mr. Mason, only much more of a bigwig. By luck, he happens to be travelling on this ship to Washington for something hush hush. Gray knew him in the war."

Her eyes lit up. "He's in on the doings, then?"

"Yes. We can thank Gray for that." My voice held an edge.

Now came the hard part. I had to explain what had happened during the last hour, and soft-pedal the fact that I hadn't waited to include Elf in my sleuthing.

I started at the end and worked backwards.

"Meg left a suicide note." I proceeded to tell her the sad contents.

"Bloody hell," said Elf, eyes wide. "She did herself in, after all."

I nodded. "Simon found the note in her evening bag at the bottom of the wardrobe. I expect we missed it because it was mostly hidden by the skirt of her evening gown."

I waited for Elf to explode at the fact that we had visited the cabin without her. Which only goes to show that sometimes I am a Dumb Dora and can miss the salient point completely.

"Simon?" she said, one eyebrow rising.

Oh golly. First-name basis. How to justify that to Elf without pointing to a developing intimacy?

"He's from Shropshire," I said. As if that explained anything.

"They do things differently in Shropshire?"

"It's all those sheep," I mumbled somewhat incoherently. "You don't call a sheep by its last name."

"You are goin' completely bonkers, you know that, Luce?"

In retrospect, I thought that went pretty well.

"Shush and let me tell you the rest." I retold as best I could about Roy Armitage and George Eversleigh at each other's throats, neighbour Bert Crocket knocking at the door, and the four of us crowded into that little cabin. I strategically skipped the part about Simon claiming we were husband and wife.

No matter. The remonstrations came anyway.

"You should have waited for me," Elf scolded.

"There was no more room in the cabin," I countered.

IT OCCURRED TO me later that I hadn't told Elf why I wanted to revisit cabin 128 in the first place. So much had happened in the last hour that I'd let it slip my mind.

Basically, it was to check if the bed had been slept in. And if so, to put it as delicately as possible, if it had been slept in on both sides.

I guess that didn't matter anymore. Or did it? Why did it bother me so?

As I lay in bed unable to sleep, it occurred to me that I still had questions.

If Meg had intended to commit suicide almost immediately, why had she taken an evening dress, shoes, and wrap with her to cabin 128?

Why would she do that? Yes, some suicides like to look their best going out, but that's usually because they know they will be found. Meg threw herself overboard. She didn't intend to be found, and she hadn't changed into those clothes. So why bring them?

Turn it around, Lucy, and think of yourself.

Why would I bring an evening dress to a secret cabin?

Oh, my goodness. Of course it's clear. Our original idea was on the mark. *She had a rendezvous.* Isn't it more likely she'd brought her best duds to impress a man? And — now I had it — perhaps that man hadn't shown up.

She'd waited and waited for him. He didn't show up, and that's why she was miserable. This could also explain why she left the suicide note in that cabin instead of in the family suite. He might be the one to find it, and she wanted the man to know that he was the cause of her misery.

Who was he? I had to know. Would he revisit the cabin? Could we station someone there to see if he tried to enter it?

I got up from the bed to grab a pen and paper. I had to get this recorded before I forgot any of it. Feverishly, I wrote it down: the scene in cabin 128, the suicide note, and my conclusions. First thing in the morning, I would report it all to Gray.

First thing, I said to myself as I drifted off to sleep.

Except I forgot the old adage: Man makes plans while God laughs.

CHAPTER 19

DAY FIVE AT SEA

I DON'T KNOW what possessed me to wake up so early. It couldn't have been later than five. Dawn had not yet broken when I rose up from the bed. Elf was still out cold, which suited my plans.

No one would be about at this time in the morning except for kitchen staff. I wasn't going anywhere near there. Still, I knew time was of the essence.

More important, I didn't want to wake Elf by taking several minutes to dress, so I snatched my magenta silk kimono from the chair beside the bed, donned my mules, and slipped out of the stateroom making no more noise than a mouse on Christmas Eve.

It was daring, yes. A lady did not appear in her nightclothes outside her cabin. But I was fairly sure the coast would be clear for the next half hour. I just needed to be quick.

No one was in the corridor. I swept through the grand foyer and reached the main staircase without seeing a soul. Down I went to the deck that contained cabin 128.

It would only be a quick visit, and it would relieve my mind immensely. It all centred on the bed. Something told me it was still important to determine how soon Meg had died.

Had she gone overboard that first evening? In the night? Or perhaps the next day or night?

The bed had looked pristine. Men might be fooled by that, but I knew any woman could pull a bedspread up and tuck it tightly so as to make the bed look newly made. We're all taught that at a young age.

However, it's simply impossible to disguise the creases that come from sleeping in sheets throughout the night.

Had the bed been slept in? And if so, had it been slept in *on both sides*?

I raced to cabin 128, ready to do a quick check of the sheets, knowing that if they hadn't been slept in at all, Meg had not made it through the first night.

My hand hit the door handle and pushed with one motion as I checked behind me to ensure there was no audience. Then I scooted inside.

"What?" A male voice stopped me dead.

George Eversleigh sat on the edge of the bed, holding a carpet bag in his hands. He was dressed in tweeds for breakfast (not night attire like me) and appeared to be wiping away tears.

"What are you doing here?" His voice cracked with emotion.

My mouth opened and closed. Opened again, and finally words came out. "I wanted to check if Meg's bed was slept in." *Best to be honest*, I thought. *Especially since I'm a lousy liar.*

"Why?" His hands hugged the bag now, as if holding on for dear life.

I leaned back against the door. "To see if she ... died ... the first night." I didn't say, to see if she had been with someone in bed that first night. That would be too cruel.

He got up from the bed and signaled with his head. "Be my guest."

I walked swiftly around to the other side of the bed and threw back the bedspread and top sheet. Perfectly ironed. No creases.

"No," I said, deftly replacing the covers. "She didn't sleep here."

He only nodded. Then he sat down on the bed again and lifted the carpet bag to his lap. "Armitage said I could have her things here. Surprised me. Didn't think he had a heart at all. I thought it would be best to come down before anyone else was around." No need to ask why. The poor fellow was beside himself with grief and wouldn't want to show it.

I nodded. "I thought the same. Better to be discreet." It was awkward. I didn't know whether to sit down beside him or race from the room. But he seemed to want company, and I know how it is to lose the one you care most about.

"There was no doubt about the note? The handwriting matches?"

George nodded. "Leggatt agreed. I met him this morning. He's taken her ... note and the others to the purser.

"Can't believe how this could go so wrong. If only I'd known she was miserable. I would have told her in advance about the booking." He wiped an eye with one hand. "But why? Why would she be in such a state?"

I merely shook my head and waited for him.

"I meant to surprise her on this ship. Hoped to rekindle the romance. She'd been so busy lately, in London, and after I took the job in Manchester last winter ..." He paused, finally looking up at me with deadened eyes. "I hardly saw her all spring and summer. Long-distance romance wasn't working for her, she said. This move to America with Renata was what she wanted, a chance in a million to see the world. I thought, if I showed up by surprise on this ship, she would understand how much she means to me. We'd have all this time together. I might even be willing to find a job in America, if that's what she wanted. But I didn't even get a chance to see her." A burble left his throat. "She never even knew I was here."

"I'm so sorry," I said softly, resisting the impulse to hold his hand. I was acutely aware of time marching on. "We should go now, if you're ready. The staff will be around soon."

He rose heavily from the bed holding the bag as if it contained treasure. I wondered if the evening dress would still carry the smell of her. A whiff of perfume ... perhaps more. I remember when Johnny died, for months after I kept his dressing gown beside me on the bed where I could cradle it in my arms, just to keep some of the smell of him with me.

I coaxed George out the door finally, and closed it shut behind me. The corridor was quiet, so I hastened him down the hall. Somewhere behind me, I thought I heard a door open, but didn't look back to check. Too late now to do anything about that. My goal was to get back to Elf before the staff began their working day. It wouldn't do to get caught outside my cabin in my nightwear.

I left George in the main foyer looking utterly bereft.

IT'S THE STRANGEST thing, when you appear to be alone yet feel like you are being watched. The hallways were completely quiet, and yet ...

I stood still on the stairs, all senses alive to any movement.

Nothing, and then ... was that a soft footstep behind me? Or simply ship noise? Ships are rarely quiet. Air leaks through the portholes and doors leading to the deck. Waves create sound as they collide with the hull. Even on the upper decks, you can hear some noise from the great turbines and propellers that whoosh us across the sea.

I paused on the stair for a minute or two, considering my options. Even though I could summon no proof, I couldn't shake the suspicion that someone was following me. Imagination or a sixth sense? I had learned to pay attention to such premonitions, if you want to call them that. Whether it was something I was born with, or something learned through my — shall we say — unusual upbringing, being able to spot danger is second nature to me. Almost a second sight.

I didn't dismiss it. Instead, I leaned back on my training. *Never lead an assailant back to your home or cabin.* Instead, create a merry chase, which will hopefully force your stalker to show himself. And then — if threatened — scream like hell.

It was a lesson given to me by my late mother. "Whenever you're in trouble and can't overpower your assailant, never just yell *help*," she had instructed me and my brothers. "Yell 'FIRE'! That gets the most action, because a fire might endanger anyone who hears the cry, not just you."

I smiled at the wisdom of this. On a ship, fire is the one thing we all fear the most.

I carried on up the stairs but went up past my floor to the uppermost deck. I paused at the top of the stairs, listening. Yes, soft footsteps, I would swear it. I looked back, and the footsteps stopped, out of sight. Someone knew what they were doing. That revelation alone made me nervous.

Was the killer on to me? Had I given away my interest in sleuthing? I opened the door to the main foyer and dashed to the double doors that led to the deck.

My plan changed as I hit the cool air outside. Stupid to try to confront my stalker when I was alone and had no weapon. Instead, I would lose him and return like a ghost to my cabin. With Elf, I'd be safe.

It was first light. I whipped down the outer corridor, past several common rooms on the port side, and slipped through to an outdoor reception room behind the first smokestack. The sign read Veranda Café. Dawn was breaking, but I took no time to admire it or the decor and instead raced around the potted trees and tables, keen to get to the starboard side of the ship.

From there, I dashed down to the second set of doors leading to the interior. I didn't pause to hear if I was still being followed. The staff would be busy soon, and I needed to evade them as well.

Luckily, I had donned slippers instead of shoes. They made little noise. I started down the centre staircase, when drat! I could hear stewards — at least two — coming up from the lower decks. *What to do? What to do?* I groaned silently. Why hadn't I taken the time to change into day clothes before venturing out on this foolish errand? If found on the stairs in my negligee and kimono, they would assume the worst — that I had slipped out of my lover's cabin in a desperate effort to get back to my own undetected. How soon would it be before that shameful gossip was gleefully repeated in the staff lounge? For there was no doubt that I would be recognized: In an effort to foster collegiality, I'd gone out of my way to make myself known to the staff.

I quietly retraced my steps to the top of the staircase, ready to dart out onto the open deck if necessary. I listened. The happy chatter continued for a short while, and then I heard a door swing open and then close.

Silence. *Thank goodness.* The stewards had exited to another level. Now I made a mad dash down the stairs to reach my own floor before any others could spot me. It was a close thing. Just as I reached the door to my corridor, more voices, this time female, reached me from the stairs below. As quietly as possible, I stepped through to the hall.

And I nearly made it. I was halfway down the corridor to my room when I saw a female steward about to enter another cabin. This is when I thanked my lucky stars that I knew the ship well. I knew, for instance, that a linen closet took the place of an interior cabin, only a few steps ahead of me. I slipped into it to wait for silence.

I leaned against the wall of linen shelves, holding the door open barely an inch with both hands, so I could hear. More voices came from farther down. Hell! People were rousing. Hopefully they were passengers on an early morning constitutional, rather than stewards looking to enter my sanctuary in search of linens. What on earth could I use as my excuse for being there? I thought feverishly, but nothing brilliant came to mind.

I wasn't sure how long I stood there, listening and cursing silently as the two men continued their conversation. The halls were coming alive now. I groaned, hardly knowing which would be worse — coming face to face with a stalker? Or being discovered and branded a loose woman by ship's crew?

Finally, the corridor went silent. I poked my head around the doorway, and then scooted as fast as I could to my cabin. As quiet as a phantom, I slipped inside.

Nothing had changed in my time away. Elf was still snoring lightly, so I slipped off the kimono and returned to my bed. Within minutes, I was fast asleep.

SOMEONE WAS THUMPING on the door. Knock, knock, knock … pause … knock, knock—

"Hold your horses," hollered Elf. I opened one eye to see her vault across the room.

The door opened a few inches. Elf stuck her head out. "You! Watcha want?"

"The purser wants to see her nibs right away," said the uncultured voice.

I opened a second eye at that.

"The purser can damn well wait. It's only … not even … what's the time, Luce?"

I reached for my watch on the bedside table. "Just gone ten," I said. And then, more loudly, "Tell the purser I'll be down in twenty minutes."

Elf slammed the door in her particular way that leaves no doubt of her intentions. "What's this about?"

"No idea," I said, rolling out of bed. "Help me get into something."

"Sure, but I'm coming too."

"No need, Elf." She was already laying out clothes on the bed. "I can manage."

"Bollocks. I'm coming. You ain't fit to beard a pussy in a basket let alone a lion in 'is den."

Bollocks, indeed. I knew what she was like when she got in this state. Elf would be coming, whether I liked it or not.

What could Gray possibly want with me so early in the morning? Did he have news about Polly's murder?

With that thought, I scrambled into my clothes.

"WHAT COULD THIS be about?" I muttered to Elf as we scampered down the hall. It was front of my mind that I had been followed early this morning, but Gray wouldn't know about that yet.

All sorts of people were up at this hour. The last breakfast sitting was over by now, even for those who had lingered over coffee. I nodded to several couples returning to their rooms.

It was mainly couples in first class, I mused. Couples of all ages, aside from the odd single upper-class fellow like Tony, or the well-off widow like me travelling with a female companion. Second class was different. Lots of salesmen and single men travelled across the Atlantic on business, but they tended to inhabit the second-class cabins.

The door to the purser's office was closed. Elf whacked the thing in her characteristic boisterous style as I stood back. When it swung open, I was surprised to see Simon Leggatt standing there. He signalled us to enter.

I was nervous, I have to admit. Gray sat behind his desk with a deep frown on his face. Which broke the second he saw me.

At first, I thought he was having some kind of fit. He stared right at me, hiccupping, sputtering, trying to catch his breath. Good heavens, was he angry with me? Had he heard about my waltz with Simon last night? Even Elf seemed puzzled by his expressions.

Finally, I realized he was trying not to laugh, trying so hard that his face went puce. The control broke. He bellowed like a demented donkey. On and on, he roared with laughter until tears rolled down from his eyes.

I was utterly bewildered.

Eventually he stopped, reached in a pocket for his handkerchief, and blew his nose. All this time, Simon stood to the side, hands in pockets, with a wry smile on his face.

"You dun it this time, Luce," said Elf, shaking her head.

"You dun it all right," said Gray, still wiping his nose. "'A cabin of ill repute' — that's what he said." And that set him off with one last guffaw. "You. Lucy!"

Even Simon chuckled this time.

Gray shot a glance and grin at him. "By all that's holy, Leggatt, I haven't laughed so hard in all my life."

"What?" I was baffled. "What cabin? What are you talking about?"

Gray was out of his chair now. "You! Running a cabin of ill repute next to that Crocket man."

"Wha'?" said Elf. I was speechless.

"First, you're in there at night with three men, making one hell of a racket, the Crocket fellow says. Then you come out an hour later with, supposedly, your husband. Then you sneak back in your negligee early in the morning and come out twenty minutes later, again in your negligee, with a man who is not your husband."

"You can see how it looks," said Simon with a smile.

"Bloody hell, Luce. That's where you got off to." Elf looked at me in shock. "Pottier than a hat full of pixies," she said, shaking her head.

"Oh God," I said. "Someone find me a chair."

Someone did, and I plunked down into it. Those darn Crockets!

I thought I'd heard a door open behind us this morning when I left the cabin with George. My mouth was dry, but there was nothing to it. I had to spill everything, as Elf puts it.

A few minutes later, the whole story was out.

"Can I have a drink of something?" I said, waving a hand at my parched throat.

Simon handed me an engraved silver flask. Brandy, the good stuff. I'd have settled for water or coffee, but a gal has to take what's on offer. I chugged it down.

"That's that," said Gray. "No bed slept in. Meg overboard the first night. Poor Eversleigh."

"Bloody fool, you, Luce," Elf scolded. "Shouldn't have gone alone. Why didn't you wake me up?"

"And that would have helped," I retorted back. "Two women and one man coming out of that cabin in our nightclothes!"

Gray shot into another peel of raucous laughter. I handed the flask back to Simon, feeling caught in the act like a wayward schoolgirl. Although *wayward* was the last word I should be using.

"Can I go now?" My voice was pathetic.

"Not so fast," said Gray, growing serious. "This fellow Crocket could be a problem. He obviously feels strongly about the … er … situation. We need to make sure we squelch this story. Both for Lucy's reputation, and the reputation of the shipping line."

Good Lord! I hadn't even thought of the shipping line. If word got around that we condoned sordid behaviour, the respectable classes would desert us in an instant! For a first-class ocean liner, it would be catastrophic.

"Any ideas, Leggatt?"

"As a matter of fact, I have." We all turned to face him. He looked at me and smiled. "We tell him the truth."

"The truth?" I echoed.

"We take Crocket and his wife into our confidence and tell them the whole truth: A young woman has gone missing in first class, and Lady Revelstoke, who owns this ship, was helping us search cabins to find her. We don't have to give the missing woman's name, of course. No need to involve Renata Harwood."

"That's brilliant!" said Gray. "What about the suicide? Do we reveal that?"

Simon cleared his throat. "I think it wise. It will establish that the search is over, and there should be no further disturbances to the affected parties. It will give a sad closure to the affair."

"That's clever," I said, truly impressed with this man's thinking. "The Crockets will be more likely to keep the secret if they know it causes pain to people still on board. They seem like decent people."

Elf grunted. *Too decent by half*, she'd be thinking, to report on the clandestine activities of others so quickly.

"I have an idea," I said, perking up. "Why don't I invite them to have tea with me in the first-class rooms? They won't have had the opportunity before, I expect. It would be a treat for them, plus establish that I really am who I am."

"Capital idea, Lady Revelstoke!" said Simon. "They'll be overwhelmed. I can inform them after I make our explanations."

Once again, I turned to Simon. *How interesting.* He was taking the lead on this, which explained why he was in this room when we arrived here. Some sort of agreement had been made between the two of them, vis-à-vis the sharing of security in the wake of

Polly's murder. Golly, I wanted to know more about the roles these two men had played in the war.

I guess using Simon as messenger also made sense from a personal point of view, since he had played the part of my husband at the cabin. It would add to the "secret agent" aspect of it all.

"Four-thirty in the main foyer on the promenade deck," I announced, rising from my chair. "Tell them to meet me there." I turned to leave.

"And Lucy," Gray's voice carried after me. "If you are ever that short of money, let me know." He pealed off in laughter again.

"Smarmy bugger," said Elf.

JUST AS WE reached our cabin, Elf snickered and said, "Lucy is too posh. We need to think of a doxy name for you."

"Dry up," I said, punching her in the arm.

It was nearly time to depart for lunch, and as I had missed breakfast, well, this was a gal on a mission. Only the essential touch-ups would be attempted.

"I'll start eating the furniture if they don't feed me soon," I mumbled. It's hard to talk sensibly when you're applying lipstick.

Meanwhile, Elf was doing her best to annoy me.

"How about Fanny?" she yelled from the other room.

"No."

"Lulu?"

"NO."

"Fifi?"

"Elf, do you have a death wish?"

"What's she talking about?" asked Tony.

Tony?

"Where did you come from?" I accused, peeping my head around the water closet door.

"Here to escort you to luncheon, my dear," he said. "Renata seems to be avoiding me. And you and I haven't seen much of each other this voyage, don'tcha know."

Now who's fault is that, I nearly said out loud. With two gorgeous actresses to take up his attention …

Tony threw himself into the chair beneath the porthole and crossed one leg over the other. "What's this about Fifi?"

I left my ablutions abruptly and came out of the loo to put a stop to this nonsense.

"Elf, not a word if you value your life." I shook my hairbrush at her in a most threatening manner.

"What the devil are you two talking about?" asked Tony.

"How 'bout Popsy?"

"Elf, I'm going to kill you!"

"No, you're not." She grinned widely. "But I'll lay off for now." She giggled in a wholly uncharacteristic Elf way. "Wouldn't want to shock the poor gent."

"Honestly. The poor fellow," I said to Elf. "Look what you've done to him. A confused mess. Come on, Tony. We've got a meal to hunt down, and I'm so hungry I could eat a cow."

"I believe the expression is, I could eat a horse," Tony corrected. He vaulted up from the chair.

"But I like horses. Couldn't eat one of those. Cows, less so."

We exited the stateroom together.

CHAPTER 20

"DON'T YOU LOOK a peach today," Tony said, when we were out of earshot.

"Thank you." That was the nice thing about Tony. He always made me feel good about myself. Not to mention, I was rather pleased with this new outfit. Emerald-green is a favourite colour of mine, and this dress was bias cut, with more of a waistline than most these days. I fancied the deep v neck and flutter sleeves.

"I like that frock. It shows off your …" He stopped, fumbling for words.

"What? What does it show off?" I knew very well what it showed off, but I wasn't about to let him off the hook that easily.

"Figure. All those curves."

"Too many? You don't think I should try the Banting Diet?" I feigned horror and disappointment. This was fun, teasing him.

"God. No! You look perfect. I mean that. You have a smashing figure, Lucy."

I could feel myself blush. There was only one way to answer this. "Why thank you!" I said. "I work hard to keep each part well fed."

Now he chuckled with delight. Good. That had been the plan, after all. Distract with merriment. I let him work through the heavy chuckles in his own time.

"Good God, Lucy, what a mouth you've got on you." He shook his head.

"All the better for feeding the rest of me. Which reminds me. I hope they have something yummy for dessert."

Tony continued to shake his head.

We accessed the grand staircase, descending to one floor below. So many folks milled about in the main areas at this time of the day, it was almost festive. I waved to several people I recognized and nodded to others.

For a moment, I considered telling Tony about my morning stalker. *Should I?* But what good would it do, really? Of course, I could be entirely wrong. I didn't actually see anyone. And wouldn't that be embarrassing, if I were questioned by the authorities! I could just hear them, muttering *Another hysterical woman, wanting attention*. Even I had to admit it could have been my imagination, and all the men would be sure to point this out. For that reason alone, I'd held back telling Gray this morning.

And Elf — well, I knew better than to worry her. She'd form an iron cordon around me so fast that I'd have no freedom at all.

Interesting, this dilemma women have regarding safety vs. freedom. I've heard young women admit they feared reporting even something as horrible as rape, because it would cause their fathers such grief and fear, they would feel compelled to restrict their daughters' freedom entirely. What a sorry trade-off for the poor girls. I hope things change in future.

"Did you hear Stella is giving a performance before dinner tonight?" Tony seemed almost smug with the telling.

"No!" I exclaimed. This indeed was news. "Tell me more."

"In the music room. A scene from her stage play, *Salome*, followed by cocktails after."

"Oh my. Isn't Renata's nose going to be out of joint?"

"I'll say. After all, she was the original Salome years ago. Not likely to show up, is my guess. I've already got money on it." He commenced whistling a jaunty tune.

Honestly. What these men wouldn't bet on. It was the curse of our class. If there was one thing I had learned marrying into the upper classes, it was that men needed occupation. If not physical work, then something meaningful to do, not just play all the time. Men like Tony got lost to vice so easily. No estate to run. No profession to follow, and — after the war — not much use to anyone. Filling in time by drinking and gambling and worse. Some years ago, I read a profound statement by someone ancient but wise: Everyone needs something to do, someone to love, and something to look forward to.

Ain't it the truth, as Elf would say.

We reached the table to find just Roy Armitage and Lord Harry, already seated. Simon would be held up, I knew, working with Gray. And once more, Renata had stayed away. Our numbers were dwindling with each meal, I noticed sadly.

"Will Stella be joining us?" I said to no one in particular.

"She seems to have permanently joined that group of sheiks over yonder," Harry said, gesturing.

We all gawked. Yes, there she was, in scarlet splendour, holding court with the young men in question.

I had to smile at Harry's description of them. One could be tempted to blame Rudolph Valentino and his famous role in *The Sheik* for a lot of questionable fashion in young men these days, and some cultural expressions to boot. *Sheik* was the modern term describing a sexy, jazz-loving young man who parted his hair in the middle and slicked it down.

In contrast, *clubmen* were synonymous with the top hat, cane, black silk jacket over a white waistcoat, and white gloves. Tony was much more of a clubman. In fact, I happened to know that he belonged to *three* London gentlemen's clubs. Which just goes to show how much time he had on his hands to waste.

Roberts came to take our orders, and I settled back to anticipate the nice fillet of beef I knew would be coming.

Tony sat on my left, engaged in spirited conversation with Lord Harry about the latest test match. I didn't have much interest in cricket, so I turned my attention to Roy. As it turned out, he had been anxious to talk to me.

"I don't know what to do about Renata," Roy confided. "I can't get her to come out of the cabin, not even for dinner."

Uh oh. Renata might be sharper than I had given her credit for. "Is this because of Polly?" I asked.

Roy leaned one elbow on the table and turned slightly to face me. "Yes. The death of that poor girl has scared the living daylights out of her. Seems to think she'll be next."

Now this was a predicament. *What to do? Should I tell Roy my thoughts?* That Renata had indeed been the target, and Polly the unfortunate mistake?

"Perhaps you could speak to her?" Roy seemed in earnest, and I hated to cause him any more stress.

Better to say something positive. Could I come up with something? *Think, Lucy!*

I took a breath. "Perhaps she doesn't realize that the safest place for her to be is with other people. For instance, at dinner.

If you are beside her, and I am on the other side of her, surely nothing will happen. The attack on Polly happened in your cabin when the poor girl was alone. Surely the most dangerous place for Renata is alone in her cabin."

The relief on Roy's face was something to behold. "By Jove, you've got it! I'll tell her exactly what you said. And make sure that I don't leave her side for the rest of the trip."

I smiled, trying to imagine Roy turning down a game at the tables after dinner. "Or at least ensure she has company if you do go off for a bit. I can be called on for short periods."

"Capital!" Roy said. "You are a gem of a gal, Lady Revelstoke. Beauty and brains. Understand why the other men are after you."

Now that I couldn't let slip by! "What other men?"

"All of them. Tony Anderson certainly makes his intent clear. And Leggatt was asking about you yesterday. Even that poncy Lord Harry has said a thing or two."

Good heavens! I didn't need Lord Harry expressing any kind of interest. But Simon asking after me was certainly intriguing.

"Thanks for this little chat. Done me a world of good." He made a gesture of tipping an imaginary hat.

We smiled at each other. "I'll hope to see you both at dinner tonight," I said cheerfully.

Our plates arrived, and I spent the next several minutes in happy consumption, as did my companions.

Coffee had just been served when Stella stopped by our table on her way out. She pulled out a chair next to Harry, across from us.

"Miss me?" she asked, giving the men a crocodile smile.

"Always, darling," said Tony. He raised a glass to her.

I could hear Roy growl beside me.

"Have you heard I'll be giving a performance of *Salome* in the music room today?" She addressed the table but had eyes only for Tony.

"Heard and recorded on my heart, dear lady. I wouldn't miss it for the world." Tony winked at her and drained the glass he had been holding. Roy growled again, and I feared he would say something very rude.

"We're all looking forward to it," I said quickly. "That's a stunning dress you're wearing. House of Drecoll?"

Her eyes dashed over to me. "Nicely spotted, Lady Revelstoke. And I'd venture a guess that you're wearing the same. From the Spring collection, if I remember correctly."

I smiled back. Now we were on equal terms.

"I do like these new styles. Much easier to get into," Stella said.

"And out of," muttered Roy. I smothered a laugh.

"Nowadays, it's so hard to get maids, particularly those who might be willing to travel away from England. I didn't bring anyone with me on this voyage, and you have no idea how daunting it can be, having to dress oneself."

"Anytime you need a hand …" Tony said.

Stella whacked him with her fingers. "Oh, you!"

I managed a wry smile. Renata may have been avoiding Tony, but clearly Stella had a different agenda.

As they carried on with flirty banter, I slipped into a world of my own. It was the talk of maids that did it. Yes, it was hard to get female servants these days after the war. Respectable young women wanted to work in stores or train to be secretaries rather than become domestics. I couldn't blame them. Much more exciting, wearing nice frocks to work every day instead of the same old thing day in day out, a starched black and white uniform. Mixing with the public gave young ladies an opportunity to meet eligible young men in a way that living in the confinement of a great country house didn't allow. Not to mention, the life of a domestic servant was rife with hard labour and endless criticism.

Which brought me to Elf. Our unconventional meeting had been one of the truly best things ever to happen in my life, up there with giving birth to Charlie, my son.

Elf and I first set eyes on each other in a back alley in a seedy section of New York City, a few years before the war. She'd tried to pick my pockets, and I, in turn, had put her into a headlock. Needless to say, she was shocked at my street smarts and amused when I told her how I got them. You might say, I'd "inherited" them from my relatives.

Luckily, her knife-throwing skills had managed to get us both out of a perilous jam. But I was painfully aware that manslaughter, even when justified, has consequences. It seemed sensible to get us both out of the city fast, so I claimed her as my maid and hauled her onto the ship I had planned to use as my way of escaping the family back in Canada.

We'd landed in England with hardly any baggage, and without a destination in mind, but no matter. I'd picked up a fiancé while at sea. One with a title, even.

Dear Johnny. How good he was, to both of us. He found Elf endlessly amusing, and she, in turn, adored him, in her irascible manner.

Stella's raucous laughter brought me back to the present. With a start, I realized Roy had left the table some moments ago. I decided to follow his lead.

As I looked back from the doorway, it was clear Tony and Stella hardly noticed I was gone.

During this time of the day, I didn't worry about being followed. Passengers loitered in every corridor, and staff rushed past, intent on their duties. Cheery talk accompanied me as I nodded to everyone who passed. In fact, the idea of a stalker was second to my main concern at the moment.

I walked back to the cabin, observing the floors of the corridors all the way, trying not to think *snake snake snake*. Gray had said he thought they would seek out warm places, perhaps the kitchens or engine rooms. I had already checked out the main kitchen. That was enough. I would studiously avoid engine rooms in the next while.

When I got to the cabin, it was empty. Well, poop. Where was Elf?

Speaking of Elf, something she had said was gnawing at me. What was it, exactly? Back in Gray's office. Hell, I just couldn't put my finger on it. *Wait and it will come*, I told myself.

I didn't feel like being alone and still had some time to kill, so I turned around and strolled back to the library, where I spent a very pleasant two hours by myself.

Sometimes, when things got to be too much for me, I'd lose myself in books. The deaths of Meg and Polly weighed on me greatly. Throwing myself into the skin of a fictional character can be a welcome respite from an unfriendly world.

I loved the ship's reading room. It had bookshelves full of all the latest novels by authors like Agatha Christie and Dorothy L. Sayers, plus many of the old classics. Jane Austen. The Brontë sisters. Wilkie Collins. Trollope. I personally made sure the library was well-stocked.

There were also reference books. I headed toward that collection of tomes now.

I like history. Actually, I love delving through historical times, which shows what a hopeless romantic I really am. In this case, I wanted to renew my knowledge of *Salome*. The play had been written by Oscar Wilde, a favourite of mine, but of course he had researched it from historical sources. Stella's performance of Salome was known for being somewhat risqué (okay, scandalous), but I was more interested in the historical background at the moment.

My own recall was a little rusty. I paged through the index to find the real story of Salome. There it was ... I started reading.

"The Dance of the Seven Veils is believed to be the dance that Salome performed for her stepfather, Herod."

Yes, I remembered this. Something about demanding the head of John the Baptist, but I'd skip over that. Too grim. Now, this part was interesting.

> In some ancient religions, a goddess is required to descend into the underworld. She passes through seven gates on her way, and at each must give up a piece of jewellery or symbol of royalty.

Hence the seven veils! I'm not sure I ever knew that. I read on.

> It is no coincidence that the number seven was significant to ancient people. Exactly seven heavenly bodies were visible in the night sky, before the advent of the telescope: Sun, Moon, Mercury, Venus, Mars, Saturn, and Jupiter. Many religions feature seven major gods, and the number seven appears in many myths.

Fascinating! We also have seven days of the week. I wonder if that is related?

I'd never realized the significance of the number seven: *all the heavenly bodies that were visible to the human eye.* This research would make for lovely conversation at tea with my guests, the Crockets.

And to think I was born on the seventh of August. How fun! I'd have to tell Gray. Perhaps he would insist that I dance the seven veils myself. I chuckled. That was more likely to lead to hilarity rather than passion.

Enough research. There was still time to spare, so I went over to the fiction shelves, looking for something fun to read. Yes! I was in luck. There was a copy of one of my favourites, *The Secret of Chimneys* by Agatha Christie. I'd read it before when it first came out, but that was a few years ago. A big smile crossed my face, as I settled in to read about Anthony Cade, one of my favourite fictional heroes. Often, I had fantasized about being his love interest, the charming Virginia Revel, who impulsively marries enigmatic Anthony, not knowing who he really is.

I spent another hour swept up in the tale, until I managed to pull myself away. I can really lose myself in a book. No matter, I'd take it with me and read more later.

When I got back to the stateroom, Gray was waiting for me. He'd let himself in with a master key, no doubt. One of the perks of being senior staff. He sat on my bed, poring over papers. I was secretly relieved to have cleaned up the cabin before leaving for lunch. Elf and I are not the neatest housekeepers.

"What do you think? Are these the same handwriting?"

Ah. He was looking at the suicide note and comparing. Simon had implied he was obligated to share the love letters written by

Meg to George with the purser.

I sat down on the bed beside Gray.

"I'm no good at this stuff," he said, giving me the papers from his hands. "You're a woman. You know how women write. Do these look to be by the same hand?"

"Let me see," I said. Believe it or not, I had some training here. Not that it was something I would boast about in public. But anyone in the family who had artistic talent had been schooled young in the art of forging handwriting. Which also meant you were pretty good at detecting same.

I took a long, close look at each letter and the suicide note. Then I turned the suicide note over, to examine the back. No jerky movements that I could see.

"See this *M*, the way the first sweep of the letter curls? Hard to copy that. And to trace it almost always results in tiny jerky movements, which an expert can detect by looking at the depressions on the back." I showed him.

"Also look here. All the capital *M*s are the same, on all the pages. Same with the *I*s, which are particularly hard to copy. Everyone has their own style. I'd say it's pretty conclusive. If I had a magnifying glass, I could be a hundred per cent sure. But even so, I'd say ninety-five per cent." Actually, I was one hundred per cent sure in my own mind, but it's always wise to leave an opening, just in case.

"That settles it. Meg committed suicide. Damn, but that makes me feel sad," Gray said. "Not to mention, I don't relish the paperwork."

I shivered at the thought of how this would be reported, both officially and by journalists. No question, this would be juicy fodder for the gutter press. Poor Meg. And poor Renata. Does one ever get over the suicide of someone close to you? And who could be closer than a sister?

"Damn, the time," said Gray, rising from the bed. "I'll try to be here late tonight, if you want to send Elf away."

I smiled. "Elf won't mind." In truth, she wouldn't. A certain steward kept her attention most nights, in the cabin I never told Gray about. That secret would remain between Elf and me.

"Speaking of Elf, did you ever find the snake?"

"No," he said, with a glimmer of a smile. "It hasn't made an appearance. Now why did you say 'speaking of Elf'?"

"Because she asked me to ask you. It's far too much of a biblical reference for her."

"Serpent in paradise? Poor Elf. I will endeavour to widen the search for it." Gray leaned down to kiss me. "I've a meeting — must run. Enjoy the performance tonight."

"Will you see it?" I asked.

He shook his head. "Doubtful. I hate paperwork."

I stared after his back as he left. Gosh, it was a nice back. Wide and strong at the shoulders, narrowing to … *oh, snap out of it, Lucy.*

Gray had indeed been preoccupied and in a hurry. He'd left the notes on the bed. I gathered them up and put them in the top drawer of the chest, for safekeeping. We might have to show them to the American authorities once we reached shore. If not, at the very least, I would make a point to return the love letters to George. Of all people, I knew how much letters from a deceased loved one can mean.

Meanwhile, I had to prepare for my engagement with the Crockets. By now, Simon would have made the invitation to tea. I wonder if he planned to accompany us? I'd never thought to ask.

This arrangement was full of tricky timing. I would meet the Crockets at four-thirty and planned to give them tea and a tour of the first-class rooms. The problem was, Stella's performance started at six. A reception and dinner would follow immediately. There wouldn't be time for me to go back to the cabin to change for dinner without rushing the Crockets. And that would never do. I truly wanted them to feel welcome.

The solution was twofold: Dress for dinner now, and invite the Crockets to Stella's performance, as my guests!

Oh, they would love that. Yes, I would be somewhat overdressed for late afternoon, but that in itself would increase the glamour for the Crockets. And as owner of the ocean liner, perhaps it wouldn't be out of place for me to go whole hog, as we say back home.

First, I had to let Simon know about the change of plan. The Crockets would come with us to Stella's performance. Then I needed to make reservations for both the Palm Court and the music room. Both of these arrangements could be made through the purser's staff.

I hit my hand to my forehead. Gray had just left here! If only I'd thought about this before.

There wasn't a second to waste. I dashed from the cabin and tore down the corridor. With any luck, I'd catch him before he reached his office and bolted the door behind him.

CHAPTER 21

I COULD HARDLY believe it, but luck was with me. Double luck, as it happened. Simon was just arriving at the purser's office when I did. All was taken care of swiftly, and I returned to my cabin with a clear conscience and contented heart.

Now to address the important things: Whatever should I wear?

I hummed to myself as I thumbed through the wardrobe. Let's see … I wanted something smashing for tonight. Something new, at the cutting edge of fashion. To my delight, the couture collections of late 1927 and Spring 1928 were bringing change. Styles were starting to transform from the dead straight silhouette of recent years to something more shapely, draping the body. Needless to say, this suited my curvy figure much better. Where was that new wrap gown in purple and silver? Eureka! My hands reached for it.

"What the dickens are you doing?" Elf scolded from behind me. Where had she come from? I hadn't heard the door open. "Gimme that. You'll only wreck it."

So much for her assessment of my abilities. I handed it to her and stepped back obediently.

"Heard you danced up a storm with that Simon fella last night."

"Now, how did you hear that?" I asked, turning to face her.

"Dining room stewards," she said, thumbing through my lingerie drawer. "Said it was sublime."

I couldn't stop the hint of a smile. *Sublime* seemed to be the servant class word of the month. Even I couldn't be sure the exact meaning. Beautiful? Uplifting? I'd have to look it up.

"Surprised me. Haven't seen you dance since Johnny …"

"Surprised me too," I said truthfully. "We danced a waltz. It was actually fun." I'd like to repeat it, I nearly said, but caught myself in time.

"You goin' to that performance of Stella's?" Elf asked.

"Uh huh," I murmured.

"Not fair," Elf grumbled. "Why can't she do it for all of us? Why just the nobs?"

I felt an imaginary whoosh of air hit my face. Imaginary, but still potent. *Why, indeed?* Elf was right. Here she was, the biggest stage and silver screen follower I knew, and she and others like her were being left out. All because of some outdated class system.

As she laid my garments and accessories on the bed, I found myself steaming about the inequities of life in England. Yes, we had a class system in North America, but as my uncles had once told me, it's based on money. You could work hard, make money, and therefore better yourself and your family. And if you managed to earn enough money, you could buy your way into the upper classes. Here in England, your station in life was pretty much established at birth, and accents gave that away.

Our way wasn't perfect. But it was better than a birth lottery, I believed with all my heart. You can't help who your parents are. Why should they determine whether you start out with a huge advantage in life? It wasn't fair.

Which led me to a brazen idea. I made a sudden decision, one that put a big smile on my face. "Elf, did you pack that ritzy black number we bought for you last June in New York?"

Her head shot up. "The one from Bloomingdale's?"

"'All Cars Transfer to Bloomingdale's,'" I quoted from the ads we had seen there, everywhere, on billboards and even delivery wagons. "Yes, that's the one, at Fifty-ninth and Lexington. We spent a bundle there, as I recall."

"I got it," she said, voice quivering.

"Then put the damn thing on, Elf. You're coming with me!"

The joy on her face was something to behold.

THIS WAS GOING to be a rather daring stunt to pull off. Not only was I sneaking second-class passengers into the music room, but my maid as well! Tony would choke on his own air.

Not that Elf didn't look pretty darn swell in that little black dress. We'd managed to get it at quite a discount, her being so wee in all dimensions. It had been a leftover from last season. I had to smile in memory. Elf was in awe … of the store, of the chic salesclerk, and of the dress. She'd fallen deeply in love with the soft material and the fringed hem, which was cute as a button on her. Never had she tried on anything so "swank," as she'd put it.

Now I felt like a big sister as I watched her roll her long hair under and pin it in place in front of the mirror. Elf hadn't embraced the latest bob style of shorter hair. Without saying a word, I took one of my own feathery hair combs and positioned it right at the back of her head in the hair folds. Yes, those may have been tears in her eyes.

Elf looked the part, all right. Only thing is, I'd have to tell her to keep her mouth shut, else ruin the whole disguise.

"What's she gonna perform, do ya know?" Elf asked me.

"She's doing the dance from *Salome*, I believe. The one with the veils. Everyone says it's the wasp's ... whatnot." I said, searching for lost words.

"What?" said Elf, buckling up her one pair of petite dress shoes.

"The wasp's ... wings? You know. That expression."

She stared at me. "You gone loony?"

"The ... the ... I don't know. You said it the other night."

Light dawned in her eyes. "The *bee's knees?*"

"That's it." I snapped my fingers. "See? I was close."

"Except wasps sting like a bugger. It's supposed to be describing a good thing." Now she frowned. "Say the *cat's meow* instead and stay away from creepy crawlies."

"The dog's dinner. The moose's goose." This was starting to be fun. "The bunny's butt."

Elf just groaned. "You're gonna embarrass me tonight. I just know it."

"I'll just say you taught me everything I know." I picked up my evening bag and gestured for her to follow.

WHEN WE REACHED the grand foyer, all sorts of people were milling about, waiting for entry to the ballroom. The air of excitement seemed almost tangible.

Simon had no trouble spotting us, or rather me. He smiled widely and turned to the couple beside him, to beckon them our way.

As they approached, I saw the eyes of my guests beam with pleasure.

"Oh, Lady Revelstoke, this is thrilling!" Ginny Crocket

effused. "Mr. Leggatt has just explained about Stella Burke!"

I smiled, with a slight fear that she might just bubble over. Her husband, on the other hand, could hardly take his eyes off my evening gown. At least, I think it was the gown that captured his attention.

"How good to see you both." I said it quite sincerely. How nice, when one can actually say what one truly feels. "Let me present my dear friend, Elfreda Evans, who is travelling with me. Elf, this is Mr. and Mrs. Crocket from Boston, but I expect they will want you to call them Bert and Ginny." I winked at Ginny.

"Oh yes, please do," said Ginny.

"Playstaameetyaaw," Elf said. I think. It was hard to tell with the accent she had put on, which I assumed had been an attempt at posh, but sounded more like a prize sow attempting to speak Welsh.

"She's from the West Country," I said hastily, as if that should explain everything.

Simon made a choking sound.

"Delighted to meet you," said Bert Crocket. "Gee, that is a smashing frock, Lady Revelstoke."

"Thank you. Please call me Lucy. I must return the compliment because Ginny, your gown is beautiful. Is it possible I may have seen it in *American Vogue*?"

She just beamed. "Yes! I got it specially for this trip."

"Fancy you spotting that," Bert said, shaking his head. "Women know the darndest things."

I was touched. Both Bert and Ginny had made a special effort to wear their very best attire for our adventure.

"I thought we might have a quick cup of tea in the Palm Court before the performance. It's just down this corridor." I gestured with an arm. "The sea is fairly calm right now, which should make things easy for Miss Harwood on stage. With any luck, the weather will hold for a few more hours."

"Might be a jim-dandy," said Bert, with robust enthusiasm. "We could be in for an adventure."

"Oh, do you think so?" Ginny sounded anxious.

"The captain assures me that we've changed our path to avoid most of the storm," I said, looking to Simon for confirmation.

"We may catch the outer edge of it," said Simon, far too truthfully. Drat! My goal was to reassure them, not create more alarm. I attempted to give Simon a warning slap on the arm but hit air instead.

"Hard to predict entirely," he continued. "But truly, the captain is a good man who knows his business."

"He certainly does!" I said with a smile. "We're in excellent hands. Cheerio! Time to move on." I can be determined when I need to be. With brisk speed, I whooshed our party down the corridor, toward the Palm Court. Ginny walked on one side of me, with Elf on the other. The men closed in behind us.

"I've never been on this deck before," enthused Ginny. "It's so opulent. All this brass and wood." I watched her sweep one hand across a particularly ornate pillar with circular brass trim polished to reflection.

"There are more than thirty different types of wood used in decorative ways throughout the ship, from all around the world," I said, turning my head to face everyone. "The marquetry is particularly remarkable, I always think. In these days of industrial-made goods, it's almost a relief to see beautiful handcrafting. A nod to the past."

"Definitely first rate," said Bert, nodding his approval.

I had to smile. If the hallways were enough to impress our guests, entering the Palm Court would be like slipping into another world.

"What sort of power does this whale of a ship have?" Bert asked.

We were drawing near our destination, so I stopped walking to answer the question. I had the impression this was some kind of test. The tall businessman humouring the little lady, perhaps? Needless to say, I leapt to the challenge.

"Horsepower? Over one hundred thousand. One of the most powerful ships in the world," I said with pride. Truly, I found the engineering of these new ships a marvel. "The *Victoriana* has three stacks and four propellers, each about the size of a three-storey house, but the real improvement has been in fuel. Older ships were coal driven. We use bunker c oil now."

"Ah," said Bert, obviously impressed. "Good business move. Huge savings in manpower, of course."

"Yes," I said reluctantly. "The loss of those jobs for good working men is something I feel bad about. In part, that's why I fought to increase staffing on the ship above the engine rooms."

"More than one crew member for every two passengers, I understand," Simon added. "Quite remarkable." I could have kissed him.

We resumed walking.

"Here we are," I said, gesturing to the entryway on our right. The large doors had been swept back to reveal a wide expanse of luscious green.

"How beautiful!" exclaimed Ginny.

It was. Originally it had been called the Veranda Lounge, but recent changes had seen that lounge actually move outside onto the promenade deck to take advantage of warm summer weather. I'd found my way through it this morning, on my mad dash to escape the stalker. This room had experienced some decor improvements, with the addition of many potted plants and palm trees. Hence the new name, Palm Court.

The lounge looked well-attended. I said a few words to the steward at the entrance, who escorted us to my reserved table.

We settled into plush green seats around a round glass table. Painted vines and tropical flowers graced the walls, framing a cerulean-blue waterfall. These beautiful landscapes formed a backdrop for the profusion of natural plants for which this reception room was noted. Next to me, a gorgeous flowering hibiscus was in bloom. Aspidistras, philodendrons, and other greenery surrounded us like miniature hedgerows. A great deal of care had been taken to provide privacy between the tables.

"It feels like a tropical oasis!" Ginny said.

I had to smile. While I wasn't personally acquainted with the tropics, it did occur to me that one was more likely to find an oasis in the desert.

I made a point to put Ginny on one side of me and Elf on the other. Bert settled in beside his wife and next to Simon, which would enable easy conversation between the men. This suited me fine. It also put Simon sat next to Elf, with the two of us forming a rather protective shield around her. So far, she had governed her mouth with astonishing discipline. I prayed it would last.

"We should have ample time for a cream tea," I assured, placing my small evening bag on the glass tabletop. "There is no need to worry about seating for the performance as I have arranged to have chairs held for us at the front. One of the perks of being an owner of the ship."

"I'd like to talk to you more about that," Bert said eagerly.

"I've never known a woman to take an interest in business, let alone become an investor. Is your own family in the transportation business?"

Oh bugger, I thought with alarm. This cut too close. In no way did I want to talk about my own family's businesses, being that they were largely illegal! My hope had been that Simon would keep Bert occupied with conversation during tea, so I could talk fashion with Ginny. Somehow, fashion seemed the most innocuous and therefore safest topic of discussion.

Simon seemed to sense my panic, and did what every clever diplomat would do. He asked Bert about his own businesses.

There is nothing so charming as a man who directs the conversation toward you. Bert accepted the bait with grace and enthusiasm. I was safe for several minutes.

I signalled the steward to take our orders for tea. Happily, both Ginny and Bert enjoyed the beverage, and I knew the cream tea here would be a treat. It always is for me.

"The men have exclusive use of the smoking rooms. I always think it so unfair," I said, drawing Ginny into my confidence. "Not that I want to go in there! But honestly, it irks me to think that there are places women are still restricted from entering. I hope that changes with these modern times."

Ginny nodded her agreement. I was glad to see she took a modern perspective on these things.

"However, we women tend to monopolize this room, and of course the Ladies' Lounge. And I must say, this is probably my favourite. Along with the reading room, of course."

"You're a reader?" Ginny asked eagerly.

"For my sins," I said. "Particularly mystery novels. I love the intellectual challenge of following clues to the killer's identity.

Not to mention, there's something satisfying about seeing justice done, don't you think?"

Ginny looked thoughtful. "I've never thought of it that way before. But you might be right. My father is a lawyer, you know. Justice ... yes, no doubt, our system of justice has been constructed by men. The laws and our court system were designed to satisfy men, as they view the world. Women might see justice in a different way."

I tried unsuccessfully to raise an eyebrow. "That's extremely astute of you, Ginny." Truly, I was impressed. I had thought her rather a hothouse flower.

She smiled her thanks. "Generally, I like novels written by women. I relate to them more."

"So do I," I replied.

Our tea and scrumptious bakery delights arrived at the table. The three-tiered plates of crustless sandwiches, scones, and small tartlets made quite a display. Our steward put one tray in front of Bert and Ginny, and another close to Elf.

"Traditionally, one starts with the sandwiches on this bottom plate — there are egg, cucumber with cream cheese, and fish paste, I believe. Then one moves to the scones, which are my favourite. The usual procedure is to split them and liberally apply cream and jam." I pointed to the pot of Devon cream. "Then the top dessert layer is a final treat."

"It's all a treat," exclaimed Ginny. "I never eat like this at home, especially between meals. I'll never fit my wardrobe by the time we reach shore."

"Then you'll simply have to buy new gowns," I said with a smile.

"The Brits sure know how to live," Bert said, reaching with both hands.

We all waded in to the jolly feast, and for a while nothing was heard but happy mmms and munching. Everyone seemed to enjoy the Darjeeling tea, but I didn't indulge. People shake their heads when I say tea without sugar is vegetable soup, and I prefer mine left in the pot. The stewards know this, and always bring me water instead.

It took me a few moments to notice that Ginny had stopped mid-motion, with her hand in the air. And that both Bert and Simon had stopped eating and were staring. All were looking at Elf.

Oh dear. I'd forgotten about Elf. Darn. What was the one thing I'd neglected to coach Elf on for this adventure in first class? Table manners.

Here's a sad truth I've learned about many good folks who spent their formative years scrambling for food and never having enough: They rarely get over it, no matter how much their circumstances improve. If food is available, their instincts tell them to wolf it down before others, equally desperate, can grab it away.

Elf was doing just that: eating as if she were ravenous. I was reminded of a chipmunk in the fall. Her mouth was full to overflowing, and each hand held more edibles. It almost broke my heart to see how quickly Elf was stuffing her face.

I jogged her arm with my elbow to break her concentration. Her eyes went wide as they registered the astonished audience.

"She missed lunch," I said evenly to the others.

Simon covered another choke by clearing his throat.

"Try the lemon tarts," I said to Bert. "They're really quite feisty."

TEN MINUTES LATER, we had cleaned off the plates and sipped most of the tea.

"Shall we wander down to the music room? It's nearly time," Simon said.

More excitement! We all rose.

"I can't thank you enough," Ginny said to me. "This is such a thrill! And to think she'll be on stage in New York, and we will have seen her first."

"Have you seen the movie version of *Salome* with Renata Harwood?" I asked.

Ginny shook her head. "Bert didn't think it was appropriate." She tittered and leaned in close to me, as the others walked in front of us. "Really, aren't men amusing? Here I am, a mother of four ... as if I don't know the facts of life."

I nodded my agreement.

Men are astonishingly naive in the strangest way, I wanted to say. Feeling the need to protect us from seeing a woman in scanty attire ... as if we women haven't seen our own bodies in the nude, every single day of our lives!

"Convention is a powerful motivator," I said instead. "We're pulling out of Victorian times but not quickly enough, in my opinion."

It was hard not to feel a frisson of excitement when we entered the corridor. It was busy with first-class passengers dressed in their finery, chatting happily as they made their way to the grand staircase. We all headed down a few decks, the ladies lifting their long skirts to avoid tripping. Yes, skirts were shorter now, thank goodness. But most respectable matrons wore their evening dresses to the ankles or just above. Stairs were a particular menace to those uneven scarf hemlines, as I had discovered to my embarrassment while visiting a friend's country house one night. Poor Elf. We all learned a few new words when I landed on her.

I was guiding our small party to the correct foyer when a voice rang out behind me.

"There you are, Lucy! I've been looking all over for you." Tony frowned. "Hello Leggatt."

Oh dear! Not another confrontation. I stepped in quickly. "Mr. and Mrs. Crocket, please let me introduce Tony Anderson, third son of Viscount Helmsworth."

I had guessed correctly. In my experience, Americans reacted enthusiastically to making a personal acquaintance with aristocracy. Ginny Crocket's eyes went wide as Tony extended his hand to her.

"Oh, Lord Anderson! This is such an honour." She positively bubbled.

"No need for the title," Tony said, beaming at her. "Call me Tony."

I had to smile. Of course there was no need for the title. As third son, Tony didn't actually have one.

"Bert Crocket." Bert thrust his hand to Tony, and they shook vigorously.

"The Crockets joined me for tea," I explained to Tony. I carefully omitted that they were second-class passengers. I also failed to mention why Simon had accompanied us.

"We're only travelling in second class, so it's delightful of Lady Revelstoke to invite us here today!" Ginny Crocket enthused.

I groaned inwardly. So much for my keeping their status under wraps. The best laid plans of mice and …

"We're all excited to see Stella Burke perform," I blurted out, before Tony could say something awkward.

"Right ho," said Tony with a boyish smile. "Count me in for that."

Ginny giggled.

I gestured for us to continue walking. It was important we not be late.

The music room was really a small theatre that sat about one hundred. The stage area contained a lovely baby grand piano and enough room for a small stage play or musical ensemble. The piano had been moved aside to make more stage floor area available, and a gramophone was positioned with the horn facing the stage.

I directed everyone down to the burgundy velvet upholstered seating at the front where a crew member had thoughtfully placed Reserved signs. For the most part, the men fell in where they wished, but I made a point of placing Elf to one side of me and Ginny to the other. Elf, in particular; I wanted to isolate for her own protection. Her mouth was finding it pretty hard to maintain the upper-class disguise.

"What brings you to America?" Bert asked Tony. "Business or pleasure?"

"Definitely pleasure," said Tony, turning to face us. "All those Tom Mix films, don'tcha know. Have an urge to see cowboy country. Maybe ride a trail or two."

"Oh, do you ride, Mr. Anderson?"

"Does he ride …" I said under my breath. All the sons and daughters of English lords are taught to ride from the age of four, it seemed. They rode to hounds at an uncommonly early age. It wasn't the kind of riding Ginny was thinking of, but I knew from experience that Tony had a good seat on a horse.

I listened to him explain about the stables "back at the old pile," the breeding program, the horses he preferred, his first pony …

A steward came up beside me, cleared his throat, and handed me a note.

I thanked him and opened it quickly. For a moment, the room seemed to sway.

CHAPTER 22

"OH DEAR," I said to my guests. "Excuse me. I'll be back in a minute."

I rushed over to the stage stairs and made my way up to where I could see the stage manager waving at me from behind the curtain. We disappeared from view for a few moments and had a short conversation.

"You're sure?" I said finally. "She didn't send word to anyone?"

He shook his head; I could tell he was on the verge of panic.

"I'll try to find her. Leave it to me," I said, thinking fast. "Wait five minutes. Then make an announcement that there has been a delay, and that we'll let everyone know the new schedule at dinner."

He relaxed immediately, with the burden of decision taken off his shoulders. Meanwhile, I couldn't shake off this feeling of dread. I hoped to heck there would be a new schedule, and that we would know what it was by dinner …

One more thing to take care of, and then I would return to my friends wearing a grim expression. It was impossible to keep this completely confidential. I would try to speak quietly to Tony and Simon, but of course our guests would overhear.

The men stood up when I returned, and then so did Ginny and Elf, who crowded close to hear better.

"It's Stella," I found myself explaining. "They say she never turned up. I promised the stage manager I would check her cabin, but there's been a delay. We had to send someone to the purser's office for her cabin number because no one here knows it."

"Four forty-six," said Tony.

Both Simon and I gaped at him.

He had the grace to look embarrassed. "She doesn't like to drink alone."

Elf eeped and Ginny gasped.

Well! We all let that set in. Bert cleared his throat about a dozen times. Simon, as usual, was silent.

I shook myself out of it and said, "I must go." I turned to the Crockets. "I'm so sorry. This hasn't turned out as I had hoped. Tony, could you be a darling and look after our guests for the next while?"

"Of course," he said, turning on the charm. "How about a little tour? Would you like to see the first-class lounge and dining room? We can find a drink along the way, I'm sure."

I slipped away as they expressed their delight.

I HURRIED TO find cabin 446, trying to keep the rising fear out of my head. Yes, she could be ill. But Stella would never deliberately miss a chance to perform before an audience. She wasn't the type to let people down in a fit of pique, I would swear it. She would drag herself to the stage, if necessary.

This meant she was either so ill she couldn't walk, or …

I hesitated in the grand foyer.

"This way," said a familiar voice coming up beside me.

Elf? How quiet she was! I didn't even know she had followed me.

Just a minute. Stealthy Elf. Could it be? I had a whole new thought about this morning's early adventure, but it would have to wait.

Tables turned, and I now rushed after her as she dashed down a softly lit corridor. It occurred to me that we didn't have a key. Not that Elf couldn't work her magic, if necessary.

440. 442. 444. 446 ... Elf grabbed the door handle and pushed. Unlocked. She held the door to let me enter.

I stepped into the room.

The first thing that hit me was the smell. I knew that smell of sick as it brought back haunting memories of dying men on stretchers and cots. I almost turned back, hesitated, then scolded myself for being a coward.

Stella lay on the floor, face down, with her head to one side. Her beautiful costume for the Salome dance had been donned. I hoped she was merely unconscious — perhaps she'd had a few too many pre-performance drinks, but I feared she would never give that dance again.

I felt, rather than saw, Simon at my side.

"Followed us, eh?" Elf said.

I placed one hand on the wall for support. He dropped to the floor on both knees, beside Stella, took her pulse, then looked at us and shook his head.

My nose took me in another direction. I looked over, following the vomit trail. It led from her mouth to the chair by the porthole.

"Poison?" Elf asked. She crouched down beside him, without a care for her beautiful dress.

I turned away to avoid looking at the ghastly tableau. Even though it was too warm in the room, I shivered, not even entertaining the thought of suicide. Stella had been on top of the world when last I saw her. But more importantly, no one would deliberately welcome a death like that.

Simon sat back on his feet and nodded.

"Strychnine?" Elf suggested. There was always an ample supply of pesticide on a ship. For the rats, of course.

"Cyanide, I'd guess," Simon said. "See the skin colour."

I forced myself to look. Poison wasn't something I had much experience with, but even I could see her skin had a subtle cherry-red stain.

"See how she tried to drag herself to the door." Simon was on his feet now, pointing to the vomit trail. "Look at her hands."

I turned away instead. "Simon, what is happening? Why would someone kill her?"

He was quick to answer. "She saw something or knew something. At this stage, I think she was an incidental nuisance. Not the original intended victim. Someone who had to go because she knew too much. Maybe she tried a bit of blackmail. Do you know her well enough to accept she might try that?"

I turned back, reluctant. "Yes. Yes, that wouldn't be out of character. She grew up poor."

He shook his head sadly. I wondered if he was thinking the same thing I was. There are a lot of things we forgive the poor.

Elf, meanwhile, had been carrying out a subtle search of the room. "No suicide note," she said. "Two cups on the side table, one with lipstick."

Her last companion had been a man. We all must have thought that.

"Elf, will you go find the purser?" Simon said. "Kindly explain and ask him to send crew to act as guards."

She nodded. "You'll stay with her."

"Of course." He stood up. They meant me, I realized.

She pointed to the edge of the bed and ordered me to sit. I did as told, knowing she wouldn't leave the room until I acquiesced.

Simon came to sit beside me on the bed. He took my hand in both of his but remained deep in thought for several moments.

After a while he said, "Amazing how one gets inured to the smell."

"Odour," I corrected automatically.

He laughed quietly, but with an edge that seemed to break the fragile ice around us.

"It's been a long while since I've been in a room with a dead person," he said. "I'd forgotten. But it comes back to you." His voice trailed off.

It sure does, I thought to myself. *Your senses seem almost enhanced in the presence of death.*

He vaulted up from the bed. "Let's leave the room. I can bring those chairs into the corridor."

I rose, and went to hold the door open, trying not to look at poor Stella. Simon picked up the first wooden chair with both hands and deposited it against the outside wall next to the door. I watched as he went back for another, then closed the door gently behind him.

It felt a little better in the hall; at least I could breathe. I sat in the quiet corridor beside him, with my hands folded neatly on my lap. Safer to keep them there.

"How long has it been since your husband died?" he asked carefully.

"Four years," I said. "No, closer to five."

"Do you miss him still?"

"Every day." This was something I could talk about. A topic other than murder. Something I knew for sure.

"My wife died nine years ago. Our baby daughter, two weeks before." He stopped for a long breath. "Time is cruel. I can hardly remember what she looks like now — looked like. My wife. But I can hear her voice. And I miss the essence of her still, if you know what I mean."

"I know." I looked down at my hands.

"Do you think you'll ever marry again?"

For some reason, the question didn't make me uncomfortable. It seemed to flow with simple ease. And to be honest, it was a relief to speak plainly.

"I don't know. I don't have to. Johnny left me pretty well off. But I can't imagine being alone forever …" It was true. I had a wonderful friend and a sweet lover. Would that be enough for me throughout the decades to come?

I could feel him struggle with the next words

"I want to dance with you again …" his voice trailed off in almost a whisper.

The air around us seemed to lack oxygen such that my heart was struggling to keep a steady beat. So much said through only a few words. I reached for his hand and held it in mine — I couldn't help it.

It seemed to give him energy. He squeezed it gently.

"I wanted this post in Washington. I sought it out, worked hard for it." There was a quiet power behind his voice now. "God knows, this isn't the time or the place. But now …" He rose from the chair, stuck both his hands in his pocket, and turned away.

"If I were going back home instead of a two-year posting, I'd ask to see you again."

I chose my next words carefully and spoke with measured precision. "There is no reason to expect I won't be in England two years from now."

I met his eyes and found it hard to look away.

"I haven't felt this way in years," he said simply.

Voices in the distance brought us out of the uneasy reverie. Elf came into view with Gray and two young stewards I didn't know. Simon dropped my hand and hurried to open and hold the door for us. Gray nodded to Simon, then directed one of his fellows to take photos with the camera he held. At any other time, I would have salivated over that camera. But the subject of his photography today left me unenthusiastic.

"Definitely poison," said Simon. "Probably cyanide."

"Self-inflicted?" said Gray. He went over to stand beside Simon.

Simon shook his head. There was a comfort and rapport between them that was obvious to me. This wasn't the first time they had worked together, of course. A lot of trust had been built in those navy years during the war, no doubt.

"Two glasses," I managed to squeak out. "Only one with lipstick on it. Her own, I think." I felt comfortable saying that because I had seen her wear that colour before and because it looked very much like a colour and brand I used myself for special evenings.

"So, her killer was a man," said Gray. "It has to be a man."

I let that set in to see if it felt right. It didn't. I frowned.

"Not necessarily." I looked over at Elf, who was watching me thoughtfully.

Her mouth was set in a grim line. She nodded slowly. "Not all of us wear lipstick. Not on the job."

Men wouldn't know that, of course. As far as I could tell, men just saw a woman as pretty or not pretty, without even recognizing that it might be cosmetics that made a difference.

Simon decided to make it clear for Gray. "Obvious cosmetics are frowned upon for the service class. At least in the many great homes where they are trained."

"You're saying a female steward did this?" Gray couldn't keep the horror out of his voice.

"Not at all," Simon rushed to explain. "It doesn't seem likely. Why would a film star share a drink with a female servant?"

That was it, of course. The thing that would make her guest most likely a man. Not only that but a man she knew and trusted. Either that, or a friend. Who else would Stella invite into her cabin for a drink?

Oh dear. Tony had been there at some point, we knew. Or at least, Simon, Elf, and I knew it. Tony had offered us her cabin number, with the comment that she didn't like to drink alone. Would the others bring this up? Should I?

But I simply couldn't believe Tony had anything to do with Stella's murder. What motive would he have? There had to be a motive.

Oh Lord …

"Ethan's mother," I said suddenly. My skin was tingling all over. "She doesn't wear lipstick."

"'Course she doesn't," Elf said sagely. "Her type hates painted ladies. Specially now, after her son done himself in. Considers all those makeup things tools of the devil."

"And Stella would invite her in because …" I thought fast.

"Maybe she felt badly about the way things ended in the corridor."

"Trying to explain ... make amends." Simon got it immediately.

"Who is Ethan?" Gray demanded.

We three stared at him. Oops, I'd forgotten — it was Simon who had been with me at the time Stella had been accosted by Ethan's mother, not Gray. Elf had gotten the full story out of me some time after our cabin fiasco with the snake, but I guess no one had informed Gray of that sad episode.

Elf stepped up. "Bloke who done himself in over Stella, who dumped him."

"A young war veteran," I explained. "Survived the war, only to ... well, die by his own hand. Stella treated him rather callously, broke his heart. Ethan's mother was still in deep grief and confronted Stella outside the dining room, in front of us and a small crowd."

There were a few moments of silence, as we let all that set in. *Please God, no, don't let it be her. She has suffered too much already.*

"But why would she do away with Polly?" Elf blurted out. "Doesn't make sense."

Pause.

"Elf, you are brilliant!" I felt much better and sat up straighter. The others were looking at me, waiting. "Polly was dressed in Renata's clothes, not Stella's. She was killed in Renata's bedroom, not here. Why would Ethan's mother even know Polly, let alone have any reason to kill her?"

"A vendetta against film stars?" Gray suggested. "She meant to kill Renata?"

"Nah," said Elf, with almost a swagger. "You gotta understand women. She'd go after Stella first if she was of a mind to kill. Why take a chance on getting caught before you can take out the one doxy you really hate?"

"She's right," I admitted. "Women are single-minded. You don't find many females who kill multiple times. We murder someone specific for a cold, hard reason."

I could think of a few people in my time that I wouldn't have minded murdering. Unscrupulous men who take advantage of innocent young girls. Those who deny us agency and give us a bad name if we refuse their advances.

Gray looked over at me and said, "You look ready to drop. Go to your cabin, Lucy. Leggatt can bring me up to speed on anything else. Do you two need an escort?"

Elf snorted.

I shook my head. No escort needed for us. Really, I wanted to be by myself. To think. Elf at my side was almost like being by myself, so that didn't count. And I wasn't afraid of anyone following me if Elf was there.

Wait a minute ...

Thoughts came tumbling over me, falling into place. I left Stella's cabin without a word. Which didn't mean I had nothing to say.

When we got to the main foyer, I voiced my suspicions out loud.

"It was you this morning, wasn't it, Elf? Following me. You can tell the truth. I'm not angry. In fact, I'm touched in a way."

She grunted. "Killer on the loose, and you, a good-lookin' woman. I needed to know you'd be safe."

Her simple explanation did something lovely for my heart. Dear Elf. *I always need to know you're safe too*, I thought.

I nodded. "You're right. It was foolish of me to go alone, in retrospect. I should have taken you. But I'm glad it wasn't the murderer following me." I shivered. At least that was one bullet I'd dodged. "How did you get back to the cabin so fast?" I asked. Elf had obviously been feigning sleep when I entered the room.

"You lost me quick. Figured out you were onto me, so I skedaddled back."

I nodded again. "Did you see anyone else on your return journey?"

"Not a soul."

We walked with a purpose, almost in lockstep with each other. "No more procrastinating, Elf. This attack on Stella signals that the killer is getting bolder, which means we must too. Time to put our whole energy into discovering the truth."

"For Polly," said Elf.

"For Polly," I repeated. We sped up our pace.

When we reached shore, these crimes would be turned over to the authorities. Whether they would treat them as individual crimes or linked, I didn't know. Suffice it to say, they wouldn't have the insight I did, being on the spot. My inside knowledge from talking with both Renata and Stella would be overlooked completely when we reached shore. Men don't know how women think, and the authorities have a tendency to dismiss us.

This is where I had an advantage. I owed it to Polly — and Elf — to try my best to expose her killer, at the very least. And that should lead to Stella's killer.

I thought about Ethan's mother. She was the obvious suspect for Stella's murder. I could see her wanting Stella to die, but it didn't explain Polly. What possible reason would she have for wanting to kill Polly?

No, I simply didn't believe it could be her.

Instinct must have taken over (or Elf) for I found myself standing in front of our cabin door. Really, one had to marvel at the human mind. I had managed to walk the whole way back without ever taking in my surroundings.

"First dibs on the loo," said Elf. She scooted through the door ahead of me, on a mission.

I walked into the room and threw my handbag on the chair. And stopped dead.

It was something from earlier. Something that had stayed in the recesses of my mind, that I hadn't been able to put my finger on. I stared down at the chair. *At my handbag on the chair.* Then it came to me. I walked to the wardrobe and drew open the doors.

My clothes were hung with care on individual hangers. This was Elf's domain. I could see they were arranged by time of day: morning dresses, afternoon ensembles, and finally evening wear. Shoes were perched in pairs on the floor of the wardrobe.

I heard a flush, and then Elf peeped her head out. "You okay?" she quizzed.

"Elf, where do you put my evening bags?"

She sniffed. "You don't want to be going nowhere now. I'll order some grub for the cabin."

I held my irritation at bay. "I'm not thinking for now. But they're not on the floor of the wardrobe."

"Nope. That's where shoes go. You don't mix shoes with purses. No one does that. They might get dirty." She sniffed at the idea. "You put them in drawers, of course. Or on that high shelf in a wardrobe, if you can reach it. I can't." Elf retreated back into the water closet.

Meg's evening bag had been on the floor of the wardrobe. *Why would she do that?*

I felt that chill again as I picked up the small handbag I had thrown on the chair and returned to the wardrobe.

Yes, the top shelf was empty. Poor Elf was simply too short to reach it. But I could and did. Placed there, the bag was an easy reach for me, as it would be for most women.

Including Meg. She was a similar height to me. So why?

It simply didn't make any sense that Meg would put her evening bag on the floor of the wardrobe.

Now I just had to figure out what that meant.

CHAPTER 23

THERE WERE TOO many unexplained things. Because of that, I was haunted by the feeling that a very clever person had engineered an extremely complex crime that had gone wrong somehow. I needed to put everything in order to make sense of it all and try to find a motive that linked all the events.

First, I needed a pencil. There was one on the small table, along with monogrammed Empire line paper. Most people would use it to write to friends and family at home. Probably no one else had employed these in the quest of solving murders, I thought wryly.

I sat down in one of the side chairs and thought of my friend Agatha Christie. What would she suggest?

That was easy. I could almost hear her voice. *Look for motive, ignore the smoke and mirrors, and write down what actually happened.*

What happened first? *Work it out, Lucy.* I made a list.

1. *Meg went missing the first night.*

What we knew for sure: No one had seen her since.

Well, actually, that wasn't true. No one *admitted* to having seen her since. There — Agatha would be proud of me.

However, we did find a suicide note in her handwriting. That was a fact. We confirmed it by the love letters George produced, and I really couldn't think of any reason he would have to lie about that.

All evidence pointed to Meg having committed suicide. But since no body had been found, could one truly consider this closed?

Moving on, what happened next?

2. *Polly was murdered.*

Here's where I'd been somewhat haunted. Polly was struck from behind while dressed in Renata's gown. From behind, she was similar in size and had similar hair to Renata. Because of this, everyone assumed Renata had been the target. And most likely she had been.

But the other possibility couldn't be dismissed. What if the target had actually been Polly herself?

It seemed inconceivable. Everyone said Polly was decent and sweet. Here was a girl with no money to speak of, and no apparent boyfriend. Our talk with Mary had confirmed that.

Far more likely that Renata would be the intended victim; Renata, who had gone through men like water, trampled on others to get to the top of her actress trade, and left lots of disgruntled people in her wake. It was logical we would focus on her.

But …

This was where I could hear Agatha clearly in my mind. *Who actually died? Who would have reason to kill her?*

Had we been misdirected all along?

Okay, keeping that reasoning in mind, could I think of any reason why Polly would need to be removed? Had she, as I had once mused, seen something she shouldn't have?

Something inside me started to quiver. For in all my concentration on what happened to Meg and Stella, I'd completely overlooked what had happened the second morning. I'd forgotten the gossip Elf had been bursting to tell me when I got back from breakfast. Here's what really happened, in order:

Meg went missing.

Polly found hair dye hidden in Renata's cabin.

Polly was murdered.

Could that be the reason why Polly was murdered? She found out that Renata was dying her own hair, instead of going to the ship's salon? But why would Renata do that? And more, why would it need to be a secret?

I was starting to go in circles in my mind. *Keep to the plan*, I told myself. *Keep that point open and move forward*. What happened next?

3. *Stella was murdered.*

Now, this is one that could be believed. Too many people had reason to murder Stella. People like the poor grieving mother of Ethan, who had committed suicide. Stella, like Renata, had left a trail of men with broken hearts. Also like Renata, Stella had no doubt stepped on a lot of people to get to the top.

I remembered my older brothers telling me: *Never mess with the emotions of men. Men are dangerous.*

Was it a man who poisoned Stella? Usually, poison is seen as a woman's weapon, but it was a method of murder that was close to pristine. No blood spatter, as Elf would say. No sound of a gunshot to alert people. You could poison a person, watch them die, and wait until the middle of the night to dump them overboard, and no one would be the wiser. Was that the intent with Stella, and our murderer's luck ran out because she was discovered too soon for the rest of his plan?

But back to the list. I needed to add a few things that bothered me, that might be related. So, I rewrote the list, including the new points.

1. *Meg went missing the first night.*
2. *Polly discovered hair dye in Renata's rubbish bin.*
3. *Polly was murdered.*
4. *Meg's suicide note was found in an unoccupied cabin.*
5. *Meg's suicide note matches the handwriting on her previous love letters to George.*
6. *Stella was murdered.*

Was there anything else that disturbed me about this case? Things that didn't add up? I called it a *case* because I was trying to follow the logical reasoning of Agatha's fictional detectives.

Yes. Meg's purse was found on the floor of the wardrobe. Elf had said no woman would do that, particularly when there was a shelf within reach. *Meg could reach it.* So, who put it there?

One more thing. *The salad days comment.* Why did Renata not recognize the passage "my salad days" for what it really meant? This really bothered me. Such a simple thing, easily overlooked, and yet …

Why, as I was sitting here, did the character of Anthony Cade come into my head?

Anthony Cade, the star of Agatha Christie's *The Secret of Chimneys*, who had disguised himself as an adventurer, when he was actually someone else entirely.

I sat back in thought. It was coming. Slowly it was coming to me, and the story I was seeing virtually took my breath away. If I was on the right track — dear God, if I was right — it all came down to this:

Meg missing.

Stella murdered.

Anthony Cade.

I felt cold excitement. Cold, because what I had deduced was so cunning and so fiendish that the sheer cruelty of it sent shivers down my spine.

Did everything fit? Yes, Polly's death fit. The matching handwriting fit. My goodness, if I was right, our discovery of the suicide note may have inadvertently prevented another murder! Why? The suicide note put George off Meg's trail, and that was critical to the killer. Otherwise, George surely would have become another victim.

And Stella? The reason was obvious. It explained why Renata looked afraid rather than annoyed when Stella sat down at our table the second night. Having worked on stage with Renata, she was a risk. Even though it was years ago, Stella couldn't be a tablemate without getting too close to Renata. *Too close!* They didn't want anyone close.

It also explained why Renata had excused herself from eating in the dining room after that second night. *She didn't want to run into Stella.*

People from the past ... they had to be avoided, *at all costs.* Even if it meant murder.

It made me realize — Good Lord! Tony could be next. Yes, it had been years since Renata and he had known each other, and they hadn't been as intimate as I had first thought. But when you stumble across a tiger …

It's possible the murderers — yes, *murderers* — would just lie low until the ship made shore. But could I risk it? Could I risk Tony?

No, I had to do something. Had to get proof. But how? For I'd definitely need it. Imagine the outrage. The consequences of making such an accusation were so great that I would need concrete proof to convince just about anyone else.

Then I realized I could get proof. Serendipity had proved to be on my side for once. Elf's penchant for film stars would give me the proof I needed, if my theory was correct.

I hoped it wasn't. It would be so much easier if I wasn't right. But I knew in my heart …

It was risky, yes. But necessary. I was reminded of that phrase I once heard that went something like this: The only thing necessary for evil to triumph is for good men to do nothing. *Good women, too*, I thought wryly. For just like men, there were good women and bad women.

I had to keep going. There was one more thing to check, and then I would make my move.

The photo would do it — Elf's photo, the one I had watched Renata sign in the hair salon. I was absolutely certain it was her handwriting. I had watched her sign it with my own eyes.

What a stroke of luck that Gray had left those love letters behind. They had been written weeks, and perhaps months before, by Meg.

Elf was still in the loo, but it was easy to find the photo

of Renata. Elf had placed it on the chest of drawers beside the wardrobe, where she could admire it each time she passed by on her way to freshen up.

I picked up the photo from the chest, then opened the top drawer, where I had stashed Meg's love letters. I put all of these on the bed and sat down to compare.

How fortuitous that Renata had written "May your dreams come true" on the photo! I could compare that *M* to the signature on each love letter written by Meg. One by one, I stared at the *M*s, turning each note over to double-check in the way I had been taught by a master forger.

They all matched.

My heart raced. Everything fell into place.

And that's when Elf thudded out of the loo.

She stared at my face for a few moments, and then her eyes went wide. "You've got it, haven't ya? You figured it out."

"Salad days," I said, with glazed eyes.

She crossed to the chair and sat. "Spill," she said, and waited.

"On the second day of the trip, when I was talking to Renata on the deck, she remarked on the slenderness of a girl who'd asked for her autograph. I said we'd both looked like that in our salad days, and she said, 'I never eat salad.' Something about her remark stayed with me, and I've just pieced together what had bothered me.

"Elf," I said, rising from the bed. "If I commented on our salad days, what would you think I meant?"

She shook her head slowly. "You don't want to lose weight. Look good as you are."

I smothered a chuckle. Elf had strong views about my personal appearance, and no qualms about sharing them.

But mainly I smiled because Elf had made the same interpretation as Renata. Which was interesting as my comment hadn't referred to the actual eating of salad. *And that was the clue to it all.*

"It's a quote from Shakespeare," I explained. "Salad days. Cleopatra says it at the end of Act One, referring to her younger days with Julius Caesar, when she was 'green in judgement.' That's what I meant — our younger days."

"Never heard that before."

"Yes. And neither had Renata, apparently. Which is very strange, don't you think?"

Elf looked over again, this time with a confused look on her face.

"Think about it," I said. I waited the requisite ten seconds for Elf to catch up. She did it in five.

Elf gasped. "She played Cleopatra in the West End!"

"Exactly," I said. "What do you make of that?"

Elf stared at me with horror on her face.

"Listen to me," I said, leaning forward. "I've been following Agatha Christie's advice. *Ignore the smoke and mirrors. Focus on what actually happened.* Not hearsay, but what we have seen with our own eyes. And what was that? What was the first thing that happened that we both actually saw?"

A pause.

"Polly died," said Elf.

"Good girl. Remember what you said at the time? 'But why Polly? Why did she have to die?' And I said, 'I expect she saw something she wasn't supposed to see.'"

We both stared at each other.

"Oh God, Elf, I've been such a fool," I said now. "It was right before my eyes all along." Or rather, on a deck beneath this one.

I shot up to my feet, arms swinging. "The hair salon, Elf! There's a hair salon on this ship! That's why Polly had to die."

"What? Watcha mean?"

I headed to the door, turning back to answer. "She saw the hair dye bottle, Elf. No one was meant to see it. Why would Renata touch up her own hair in the stateroom when we have a brand spanking new hair salon right on this ship? One she visited only the day after?"

Elf sat with her mouth open.

I answered my own question. "She wouldn't, of course. She would go to the experts. Any film star would."

"But she didn't," Elf insisted. "Polly was sure she did it herself in the stateroom."

I sucked in a breath. "Somebody did. Somebody dyed her own hair in that stateroom for the most obvious reason ever. *She didn't want anyone to know she was doing it.* Don't you see, Elf? *It wasn't Renata.*"

I saw the light come into Elf's eyes, and then the shock. "It was Meg," she said, almost breathlessly.

Meg, who had mousy brown hair, not black, like her older sister.

"Meg. She cut her own hair and used the black hair dye so she'd look like her sister!" Elf's voice grew in strength.

The pieces were falling into place with brilliant clarity.

"Similar build, similar height. Even their eyes were the same colour!" I said. "Remember when they first arrived on the boat? Roy called Meg 'Sparrow.' I recall seeing them side by side and thinking Meg was the dull, black and white sister, whereas Renata was resplendent with colour."

"Meg, all madeup to look like her sister," said Elf with awe. "Just like I make you look different with makeup."

"You can do a lot with hair and makeup," I agreed. "But it would still be risky. Work out the rest of it, Elf. Why was Roy horrified when Stella first joined us at the dinner table?"

Elf didn't hesitate. "Because Stella knew Renata way back when!"

This was the spanner in the works, a simply horrible act of fate. This whole intrigue had been carefully planned to take place not at home in England, but on an Atlantic crossing to America. Why? Most likely, the convenience of getting rid of a body at sea. *They just didn't expect to meet anyone on board ship who would have more than a passing acquaintance with Renata.*

And even though time had passed, and the resemblance was good, it probably wasn't good enough to fool a person who had worked with her years ago. It might be easy to resemble a sister, but infinitely harder to think like them all the time. Talk like them. Eventually, Stella would discover the imposter.

"And that's why Stella had to die," I concluded.

First Renata. Then poor Polly. Then Stella. And George could have been next, for quite a different reason: He knew *Meg* too well. So well that it wouldn't take much for him to see through the disguise.

It was a pattern that would persist for the rest of Roy's and Meg's lives — this knocking off people who had been close to Renata. And it had to stop.

I could stop it. I could go to Gray right now and present the case to him. But first, I had to warn Tony.

"Elf, Tony could be in danger. It was a long time ago, but he and Renata ..."

"He knew the real Renata too," interrupted Elf.

"Tony told me he thought Renata was avoiding him! Which was strange after the warm welcome she gave him on deck, when they first arrived. If only I'd put two and two together sooner. I need to warn him." I was pacing now. "I'll do that right now. Elf, can you track down Gray? Bring him up to date? Use your steward friend to find him if you must, and if you can't find him, go to the captain. Tell them I've gone to warn Tony."

"Right," she said, hopping up to her feet. The boat shuddered, and she nearly took a tumble. "Storm's coming," she said.

I walked deliberately to the chest of drawers, opened the bottom one, and took out a small shoe bag. It wasn't empty, and it didn't hold shoes. I hung the braided cord around my wrist and picked up a shawl to drape over it.

"You takin' Bessie?" Elf said, eyes wide. She knew what was in the bag. A small, but lethal, revolver.

"Yes." I turned at the door. "And Elf …"

"Yeah?"

"Be careful."

CHAPTER 24

I DON'T KNOW why I said that last bit. Elf would be safe in the company of Gray. No one could suspect she knew the truth of our murders.

Tony was the one in immediate danger.

I had to find him, but where would he be? Last thing, I had left him with the Crockets, and he was going to get them drinks. How long had it been since we parted in the music room? I couldn't be sure ... my time sense had been corrupted by the shock of discovering Stella. But surely by now they would have finished imbibing, and Tony would have escorted them back to the second-class dining room in time for dinner. They wouldn't want to miss dinner.

Which meant that Tony was probably at dinner himself. So that's where I would go.

The storm was getting louder, whistling through cracks in the portholes and outer doors. Inside, the hallways were unoccupied, which told me that my sense of time had been right. Everyone was already seated and enjoying the meal. I took a turn at the foyer and wound my way to the first-class reception rooms and through to the dining room. I walked through the double doors, waving a hand at the attending steward to signal I didn't need his help. Just a few steps into the room told me what I needed to know. It was a sobering sight. Lord Harry sat at our table, looking very alone. No Roy, Renata, Simon, or Tony.

I felt my heart skip a beat.

Think, Lucy! Where was the next obvious place Tony could be? Perhaps the smoking room? I spun around, retracing my steps to the smaller room two doorways down. The smoking room was male domain; no women were permitted within. I poked my head in nevertheless and was greeted by silence. Empty.

His cabin. That was the next place on my list. Luckily, I knew where that was located. Early in our time on board, Tony had said he'd managed to book the same cabin as last time. That last time was in June, and I'd had reason to visit his cabin then. I knew exactly where it was.

Tony's cabin was on the same deck as mine, but on the other side of the ship. I rushed down the corridor to the centre hall, crossed over, and made my way farther down.

For a moment, I lost my balance. The ship seemed to lurch to the right, just enough to trip me up. I grabbed for the handrail, praying that Captain Miller had kept us far enough north to escape the worst of it.

I passed a grey-haired steward on the other side of the corridor, hand also on rail, who smiled and nodded his head. When I got to Tony's cabin, I knocked heavily on the door. "Tony?" I knocked again. Nothing.

"Are you looking for his lordship?" came the soft voice behind me.

I cursed silently. Tony was the son of a lord, but he wasn't a lord himself. Only the eldest son could claim that title. But as I had seen before with the Crockets, word got around about his father, and Tony made no effort to correct misconceptions.

"Yes," I said. "Tony Anderson?"

The boat shuddered again. We both dived for the handrail.

The steward smiled. "You've just missed him. He asked me for directions to the Veranda Café, not five minutes ago."

My mouth flew open. Why on earth would Tony go there at this time in the evening? He didn't even know where it was, apparently. "But it's closed now, surely."

"That's what I told him. And with the wind picking up, who wants to be on the deck tonight?" The older man just shrugged. "He had a note in his hand, if that helps."

I thanked him and made to rush down the corridor, with my hand ready to grasp the handrail at any moment. *The note. Someone had arranged to meet him there.* I quickened my pace.

I already knew the Veranda Café. I'd run through it earlier in my quest to lose the follower who turned out to be Elf. The outdoor café was tucked away behind the first smokestack, in a sheltered spot. This forward positioning was not by chance. Anywhere on deck was likely to be affected by smoke from the bunker C fuel burned to power the ship, but one had a better chance of clean air toward the bow of the ship.

Tonight, with a storm building, thick smoke was the last of my worries.

Who had summoned him? It had to be Renata, or rather Meg writing as Renata. She was the one person, other than me, who Tony would go out of his way to meet.

If only I was on time. I couldn't be too late ...

I raced into the grand foyer, thanking my lucky stars I had chosen my newest wrap dress to wear tonight, which didn't restrict my legs in the way of a slim chemise. I turned left and carried on out the doors to the promenade deck. The wind hit me square in the face, and I had to gasp for breath. Out here, the pounding of the waves against the hull made a threatening roar that Thor himself would have been proud of. I grasped the inner rail to keep myself upright as the ship lurched in time to the waves.

Twilight had come, although masked by thick clouds. Soon it would be pitch black, with only the ship's artificial light to guide my steps. No one shared this side of the deck with me. The rain had turned from drizzle to light drops, not yet worthy of a tropical storm, thank goodness. Fine droplets hit my face as I pulled myself along to the other side of the middle funnel.

At last, I reached the sheltered spot between the stacks and dove into the area that housed the Veranda Café.

The wind died immediately, whistling around either side of the great stack. The sound of the waves diminished, and I was sheltered from the rain.

"Bloody hell," said a voice. "What is she doing here?"

It took me a moment to take in the scene. I seemed to have been transported to a tropical garden or a jungle. Rich with dark green, several tall palm trees shared space with other, more traditional flora I couldn't make out in the moment. The almost unbroken expanse of broad leaves would provide shade from the sun during hot days, although now they were wavering in the little wind that made it around to the lee of the funnel.

Meg sat shivering at a café table. Roy stood behind with a handgun trained on Tony.

"Oh God, Lucy." Tony groaned and shook his head.

"Put your gun down, Lady Revelstoke," barked Roy.

"Not on your life," I said coolly.

Roy stared at me as if I'd gone dumb. "If you don't, I'll shoot Anderson. Don't think I won't."

"And if you do, then I'll shoot Meg. Simple, isn't it?" Probably I was shaking, but that could have been the movement of the ship.

"You must be mad," said Roy.

"Of course I'm mad! But not in the way you mean." I held Bessie steady, at eye level. "Never give up your weapon. First rule of the family. Or didn't you know about my family? Perhaps you don't have organized crime where you come from?"

All three people facing me looked astounded. This was the first time I'd ever admitted my criminal background to anyone other than Elf and Johnny.

"Put it down," Roy repeated slowly, "or I'll shoot him and then shoot you."

Roy still couldn't believe I had the stomach for this showdown.

I smiled, and it wasn't nice. Time to drop the countess mask. "You really don't want to call my bluff. My godfather had me shooting targets from the age of eight. Forewarning: I aim for the head." I took a breath. "And don't think to switch your aim to me. I'm already trained on Meg, and I'll take her out immediately if you point it this way."

"Roy, she knows! She called me Meg." Meg was rocking back in her chair now, arms clasped around her chest.

"Yes, I worked it out. It was damned clever, I'll give you that. Getting rid of Renata so Meg could take her place." I kept my arm steady. "What I don't understand is why? Why did you do it, Roy?"

He gave me a crooked smile. "Have you any idea what it's like to be married to a woman like Renata? The whole world must revolve around her, every moment of every day. It's ..."

"Exhausting?" I said, hoping to keep him talking. If Elf could get to Gray, or if a crew member came our way ... Maybe we could get out of this without anyone dying.

"Soul-sucking." His face turned dark. "Yes, she was good to look at. And I got fooled by that. The reigning sex symbol of stage and screen ... oh, she looked the part. But do you know, she had no use for sex at all? Can you believe it? She could hardly stand to be touched!"

Tony groaned. "The sex symbol who doesn't like sex? That explains it ..."

I nearly laughed. Doesn't it just figure that Tony would leap upon the reason why he had been rejected way back when. But what a bombshell! If the gutter press ever got hold of that news, her reputation as a screen siren would have been completely derailed, as well as her career.

Roy wasn't finished. "Stay with her long enough and you discover there's not a brain cell in that head. It drove me mad! *Roy, get me this. Roy, how does this look on me?* She demanded to be worshipped. Demanded! My God, I had to tell her she was beautiful ten times a day! I was bored out of my mind."

"And then you met Meg."

His look softened as he glanced at her. "She came home from school to live with us. It was like a dream and a nightmare. She looked so much like Renata when she did the same things to herself. And here she was, younger, a thousand times smarter. I couldn't help myself."

Meg smiled back at him. It was almost as if she glowed from within. *Check your empathy,* I told myself. *They don't deserve it.*

"You fell in the love with the younger sister," I said, keeping my voice hard. "Tied to Renata, and yet it was Meg you wanted all that time." I felt the gun waver, so I used my left hand to prop up my right elbow. "And then, joy of joys, Meg fell in love with you. But why not just divorce Renata and be with Meg?"

"You don't understand." Roy articulated each word carefully, as if taking to a child. "Meg wanted to be an actress too. But Renata would never give her the chance. She knew Meg would outclass her. Instead, she used her little sister as an unpaid maid." Roy shook his head in disgust.

I was getting the real picture now. Meg had no money of her own. And I expect Roy didn't have much either. Whereas Renata was making good money now, plus she had settlements from those previous husbands. They wanted the money as well as each other.

"And then Meg came up this plan."

So, this had been Meg's idea! The clever one. Oh, what fools we had been, taken in like we were. Meg had indeed inherited the acting gene, I thought bitterly.

"It was a good plan," Roy said. "This offer to go to Hollywood fell right into our hands. The timing was heaven-sent. Travelling to America seemed the perfect way to pull it off. Little sister could disappear off the ship en route. Meg could make a big splash in Hollywood masquerading as Renata and simply carry on."

Make use of her sister's name, acting reputation, and publicity. Oh, wasn't that a lovely plan by two unscrupulous people who would stoop to murder innocent people.

"We just never dreamed that anyone on this ship would know Renata. And then all these damned people from her past kept showing up," he said bitterly.

Stella Burke, George Eversleigh … and Tony! Dear shell-shocked Tony, who sat in the café chair to my right, trying not to show fear.

"Of all the rotten luck." Roy shook his head.

No remorse. No thought for poor Renata who lost her life, or Stella. Not to mention poor Polly, a lowly steward. I felt cold rage take hold of me and gripped the pistol harder.

"What happens now?" asked Meg. Her voice quivered. "Are you going to shoot me?"

I held my gun steady. Roy looked furious and frustrated, a dangerous combination in need of an outlet. "She won't do it. I don't even believe that gun is loaded."

It only took me a second. I tipped the handgun up at the barrel and shot into the dark leaves above his head. He ducked in shock, as I recovered my aim.

And that's when it happened. I only had a moment to catch the sight of bright green hanging down from the dark branch of the tree over Roy's head. It dangled for a precarious second, then landed on Roy's shoulder.

I tried to call out a warning. "Snake!" I hollered as Meg shrieked.

Roy screamed in pain as the snake struck. He dropped the gun, both hands reaching for his neck. I watched in horror as the long reptile slithered down and around his body, leaving a bloody trail, to land on the deck, kerplunk. I aimed and fired again. The snake shuddered a moment and then lay still.

Roy looked down at the four-foot reptile at his feet. "Boomslang," he muttered. "Christ Almighty. I'm a goner."

Meg shot up from her chair and stared at Roy for a long moment. Their eyes locked. Then she turned to me, mouth open, eyes wild. I will never forget the horror on her face. Saying no words at all, she moved away from us, then scrambled out of the café, knocking over a chair as she went, until she was out of sight. So much for true love.

Roy ignored the snake at his feet to watch Meg depart.

After a long moment, he turned his eyes to me and gave me a slow, deliberate nod. It was as if he were sending a secret message to me that I seemed to understand, without hearing. *We, who are about to die, salute you.* And that's why I watched, silently, with no fear, as he dropped to the floor, snatched up his own pistol, and without waiting, put the barrel in his mouth.

He pulled the trigger.

I sunk down into a café chair, still holding Bessie.

A few moments passed. Tony stood up and quietly walked over to look down at the body, both hands in pockets.

"Don't touch the handgun," I ordered weakly. "We need it as is."

Tony nodded. He understood the importance of leaving a crime scene untouched. We needed the authorities to conclude this had been a suicide.

"Anything we could have done?" he said, looking over at me.

I shook my head. "Nothing. And he knew it." I gulped. "He was the one who told me about boomslangs and the way they kill."

It's no fun to watch someone die of snakebite. Often it takes hours, and Roy knew very well the process with this species.

A gun to the head would be infinitely preferable. Quick. Although not pleasant for the rest of us to deal with after. I couldn't look at the floor.

Tony was remarkably cool in the circumstances. Detached, almost. He'd seen this and worse in the war, of course. Being detached was likely the only way to stay sane.

"Looks like you nicked it with that first shot. What was the bloody snake doing here?" Tony asked. He kicked it with his toe.

"Don't move it!" I warned again.

"Just checking it's dead," he said.

I took a deep breath. "It's dead." When I shoot, I don't miss. "Someone was smuggling them in from Africa. I thought it was Roy, but I guess not. One got loose from a cabin in second class, but Gray thought it would head for someplace warm, like the kitchens."

"There are cats in the kitchens," said Tony. He dropped down in a chair beside me. "They go after the rats. Snakes and cats don't like each other."

"Yes. It's been terrifically warm, this voyage. I guess it liked these potted trees outdoors here even more. Felt like home. They are tree snakes, after all. They glide through trees." My voice was even, and perhaps a bit dull. Funny how my brain works. To put off unsettling emotions, I seem to naturally focus on explaining things.

We kept a reluctant vigil over Roy. We'd both seen a lot of death in our short lives. *No one should have to be alone in death,* I thought. Not even the wicked.

Finally, Tony broke the silence. "Who's Gray?" he said.

CHAPTER 25

THE GUNSHOTS BROUGHT crew members before I had time to explain. Simon Leggatt, the captain, and others followed shortly after. I let Tony do most of the explaining, and when he got to the part where Meg bolted, Simon quietly slipped away.

I guess shock had set in. I heard the others talking but really wasn't able to convert the words to English. I sat there a long time, thinking of Meg. Meg who had no one now. No sister, no lover. No acting career. Just prison to look forward to.

It wasn't until I felt Elf's hand on my shoulder that I came to life.

She took the gun from my hand.

"I shot a snake," I said, limply.

"Damn fine shooting," she said. She turned to the captain. "I gotta take her back to the cabin. You can find us there." There wouldn't be any argument. No man is fool enough to argue with Elf.

Captain Miller nodded. Someone had put a jacket over Roy's head, I noticed. I allowed Elf to take my arm and guide me into the weather beyond the shadow of the smokestack. The rain was driving now, and the ship lurched heavily as waves hit, but that was no problem for Elf. She'd get me through any storm.

SOMETIME LATER, AFTER I'd had a deeply disturbing nap, I woke to find Elf had rounded up Gray and kept him captive. They were talking quietly in opposite chairs across the small table.

I sat up with a start. "I shot a snake!" I announced to Gray.

He smiled and rose to come over. "So I hear."

"That was a strange thing to say first," I admitted.

"All that training we got as kids paid off, it seems." He sat down on the bed.

"Did you find Meg?"

"Yes. Or rather, Leggatt did." Gray took my hand. He paused a beat. "She won't be going to prison."

Not going to prison? How could that be, after all she'd done? And then I got it.

I gulped. "How?"

"Pills. An easier way out."

Easier than poor Polly, bashed on the head and left for dead. Easier than Stella. I don't want to be the sort of person who wishes a hard death on anyone, but there are times …

"She'll get what she deserves in hell," Elf announced, as if reading my mind. I had to smile. Elf has a very literal version of hell in her head, right out of Dante's Inferno.

"You know everything now?" It was strange to realize he had been absent at the end. And goodness knows, Elf would be peeved at having missed out on all the fun. I'd hear about it tomorrow, for sure. The scolding, about doing dangerous things without her. I'd look forward to it, actually — the love behind her lectures. This is what I have learned: The only thing that truly matters in life are the people who care about you.

"Good thing your Tony was there to recount the whole story." Gray squeezed my hand.

"He's not my Tony," I said, squeezing back.

"Glad to hear it," said Gray. "But you might have to inform him of that."

"Lord Poncy-face is makin' like he's some kind of big shot hero," Elf said. "Expect he'll be giving interviews to the gutter press." She sniffed with her nose held high.

"Well, he does need the money," I admitted.

"Lord Poncy-face. I like that." Gray grinned. That lasted a moment and then it vanished abruptly. He looked down at the floor and kept his eyes there, as he said, "Now all I have to worry about is Leggatt."

Elf mirrored my gasp. Even she was surprised to hear Gray had genned to something between Simon and me.

"You don't have to worry about Leggatt," I said, patting his hand with my free one. Simon was a good man, and clever; a man I could have enjoyed spending time with. But he was being posted to Washington, and I ... well, Washington wasn't where I wanted to be.

I could see the next year ahead, with Gray. Gray and Elf. And Charlie, my dear son. Those were the people I wanted with me now. The future, well ... who knew? The future could take care of itself.

Elf popped up from the chair. "Leave you now. Got things to do."

I smiled at her back as she stomped out the door. Elf had her own beau, and yes, things to do.

Gray continued to look at the floor. He cleared his throat. "I should have discussed this with you in advance, but once we both return to England, I'm taking two weeks off work. There's a lot of time coming to me, as it turns out. I know it's terribly presumptuous of me. But I was hoping we could spend some of it together ..." His voice trailed off.

I reached for his other hand. "We can spend the first few days at my London townhouse. Then we'll go up to Eton to visit Charlie. Don't worry — he'll love you. Then we can drive down to the West Country in my roadster, and spend the rest of your leave at the castle —"

"The castle." Gray shook his head. "Always that damned castle."

"It's only a little one," I said.

He laughed, and it was joyous to hear.

ACKNOWLEDGEMENT

IT TAKES ME a year to write a historical mystery, from the endless research, the completion of the original first draft, to the edited finished work. And I have help along the way.

I can't say enough about my team at Cormorant. Marc Côté, Barry Jowett, Sarah Cooper, Sarah Jensen, Marijke Friesen, Fei Dong, and Gillian Rodgerson. They take my baby and make it better.

Brenna English-Loeb, my agent from Transatlantic Agency, is wonderful — professional, likeable, and a delight to work with.

My critique group and book-loving friends: Alison Bruce, Cheryl Freedman, Jeannette Harrison, Lynn McPherson, Chris Nielsen, Joan O'Callaghan, Nancy O'Neill, Des Ryan, Ang Tisiot — once again, thank you for holding my hand, and having my back as I plow through the various stages of writing (excitement, determination, doubt, despair, second wind, hope, triumph.)

My husband Mike: you have now experienced "the black hole of time" that sucks me up for hours and hours, spits me out, and leaves me bewildered about the real world. Thank you for being so very supportive.

It is always a thrill when a published book becomes a series. I will always be grateful to my dear friend and mentor, the late Don Graves, for insisting I write about Gina Gallo's great-grandmother, Lucy Revelstoke. (Gina Gallo is the heroine of the Goddaughter series, with Orca Books.) Don, I hope you can read this in heaven.

We acknowledge the sacred land on which Cormorant Books operates. It has been a site of human activity for 15,000 years. This land is the territory of the Huron-Wendat and Petun First Nations, the Seneca, and most recently, the Mississaugas of the Credit River. The territory was the subject of the Dish With One Spoon Wampum Belt Covenant, an agreement between the Iroquois Confederacy and Confederacy of the Ojibway and allied nations to peaceably share and steward the resources around the Great Lakes. Today, the meeting place of Toronto is still home to many Indigenous people from across Turtle Island. We are grateful to have the opportunity to work in the community, on this territory.

We are also mindful of broken covenants and the need to strive to make right with all our relations.